TROUBLE

GARY D. SCHMIDT

GRAPHIA

HOUGHTON MIFFLIN HARCOURT
Boston New York

For Marjorie Naughton,
with a grateful heart

www.hmhbooks.com

The text of this book is set in Horley Old Style.

The Library of Congress has cataloged the hardcover edition as follows:
Schmidt, Gary D.
Trouble / Gary D. Schmidt
p. cm.
Summary: Fourteen-year-old Henry, wishing to honor his brother Franklin's dying wish, sets out to hike Maine's Mount Katahdin with his best friend and dog, but fate adds another companion—the Cambodian refugee accused of fatally injuring Franklin—and reveals troubles that predate the accident.
[1. Automobile accidents—Fiction. 2. Death—Fiction. 3. Dogs—Fiction. 4. Family life—Massachusetts—Fiction. 5. Cambodian Americans—Fiction. 6. Prejudices—Fiction. 7. Refugees—Fiction. 8. Massachusetts—Fiction. 9. Katahdin, Mount (Me.)—Fiction.] I. Title.
PZ7.S3527Tro 2008
[Fic]—dc22
2007040104
ISBN 978-0-618-92766-1
ISBN 978-0-547-33133-1 pb

Manufactured in the United States of America
DOC 10 9 8 7
4500438529

1

HENRY SMITH'S FATHER told him that if you build your house far enough away from Trouble, then Trouble will never find you.

So the Smiths lived where their people had lived for exactly three hundred years, far away from Trouble, in Blythbury-by-the-Sea, where the currents of the Atlantic give up their last southern warmth to the coast of Massachusetts before they head to the cold granite shores of Maine. From the casement windows of his bedroom, Henry could look out over the feathery waves, and on sunny days—and it seemed as if all his life there had been only sunny days—he could open the leaded-glass doors and walk onto a stone balcony and the water would glitter all the way to the horizon. Henry's first word had been "blue." The first taste he could remember was saltwater. The first Christmas gift that meant anything to him was a kayak, which he had taken into the water that very morning, so calm had the sea been, because Trouble was so far away.

Henry Smith's house, begun in 1678 with the coinage of his seventeenth-century merchant ancestors, stood on stone ledges, braced against the storms and squalls and hurricanes and blizzards that blew out of the northeast. Its beams were still as straight as the day they had been hewn, and Henry could run his hands along the great oaks that dwelled beneath the flooring and feel the sharp edges left by the ancient maul strokes. The house had been changed and added to and changed again for a century and a half, so that now, under a roof of dark and heavy slate, three staircases wound to the second and third floors, and a fourth climbed up until it struck a wall whose ancient framing only suggested the doorway that had once been there. The house's eight fireplaces were each big enough to stand in, and one had a hidey-hole that huddled beside the hearth and was guarded by a secret panel in the wood closet. Henry and his brother, Franklin, and his sister, Louisa, would hide in it during the winter, because it was always warm. The floors of the house were wide pine downstairs, wider oak upstairs, quarried stone in the kitchen and the end-rooms behind it, and Italian ochre tile in the parlors.

The north parlor held lacquered Asian furniture brought back from Hong Kong and Singapore aboard nineteenth-century steamers. The south parlor showed the French Impressionist collection, including two Van Goghs and a small Renoir. The downstairs hall was an armory of Revolutionary War flintlocks that the Blythbury-by-the-Sea Historical Society borrowed for exhibitions on the Fourth of July because they still fired. The library held two shelves of medieval prayer books whose gold-and-red *ad usums* flashed as if they had just been scripted beneath the stern and glowing icons hanging on the dark paneling. Henry and his father would sometimes read them—"for the use of" this abbey, "for the use of" this monastery, "for the use of" this court—and then look out toward a gold-and-red sunset. "This house will stand until the Apocalypse," Henry's father would say reverently.

Henry believed him.

Blythbury-by-the-Sea had grown up slowly around the Smith

house. Now it was the kind of town where no one who lived there, worked there. Weekdays, the dark suits commuted in sleek foreign cars to downtown Boston—Henry's father drove to a prestigious and well-regarded accountancy firm where he was a partner—and then the suits came back at suppertime, glad to have escaped the noisy crowd of the city. On Sundays, Henry's family went to St. Anne's Episcopal Church—where their family had owned a pew since 1680—and in the afternoons, they took long walks beneath the broad maples of Townshend Park, or drove up to New Hampshire to buy maple syrup, or if the weather was warm, they climbed down into Salvage Cove, the long stretch of perfect white sand and huge black boulders below their house. Local guidebooks called it the finest private beach on the North Shore. Looking at the shore from the library windows, Henry agreed.

On Monday mornings, Franklin and Louisa drove early to Henry Wadsworth Longfellow Preparatory High School—where no one wore uniforms. Thirty minutes later, Henry's parents drove him to the John Greenleaf Whittier Academy—where all seventh- and eighth-grade students wore uniforms involving a white shirt, blue blazer, red-and-white tie (the school colors), khaki pants, black socks, black loafers, and—no kidding—red-and-white boxers. Longfellow Prep and Whittier Academy were both old schools, made of burnt brick and filled with kids whose names were so Anglo-Saxon that King Richard the Lion-Hearted would have recognized them all. In the fall, they played rugby; in the spring, they rowed crew.

No one was surprised that Henry, who was one of the smaller rugby players, liked spring a whole lot better than fall—especially since he could never hope to match the records that Franklin—Franklin Smith, O Franklin Smith, the great lord of us all,

Franklin Smith—had put up on the wooden Athletic Records panels for his rugby play.

Which Franklin reminded Henry of whenever he chose to notice him.

Blythbury-by-the-Sea was the kind of town where oaks and maples shaded quiet clapboard and brick and stone houses that had seen a whole lot of New England winters and were doing fine, thank you. Tight and prim, their windows presided over Main Street, whose two narrow lanes meandered into the town center, where tourists up from Boston and New York came to visit boutiques and rare-book shops and antique stores and fancy-jewelry artisans and gourmet delis. Occasionally, one of the town's two policemen would stroll past the boutiques and delis, sometimes stopping to pick up a bit of litter that someone from out of town had dropped.

Which is about the most they did in a day, because Blythbury-by-the-Sea was a town that Trouble could not find.

This is not to say that Trouble didn't try.

An autumn ago, Franklin had sprained his ankle so badly in rugby practice that he wasn't able to play in the Eastern Regionals. The entire student body of Longfellow Prep went into mourning. The sprain was so severe that Franklin couldn't even drive, so Mrs. Smith drove him and Louisa to school. Everyone at Longfellow Prep thought that Mrs. Smith drove because Louisa—who did have her driver's license, after all—was distraught about Franklin and the Eastern Regionals. But, really, it was because Louisa was a terrible, awful driver who panicked at stop signs, stoplights, and crosswalks. Mr. Smith said that she should never be allowed behind the wheel of the BMW—never mind the Fiat!

There had been four trips to Massachusetts General Hospital in Boston over Franklin's ankle, and the doctors had warned that the sprain meant that he might walk with a pronounced limp for quite some time. Still, Franklin rode the team bus down to Foxboro and crutched his way over to the course to watch Louisa run in her third State cross-country finals—and take first, even though she was still only a junior. And he drove in the Academy bus to Henry's rugby Districts in Deerfield, where Franklin was lauded as the star alumnus that he was, and where Whittier was whipped by Kenilworth with a score that Henry tried to forget but that Franklin wouldn't let him. By Thanksgiving, Franklin had decided to discard his crutches. By Christmas, no one who didn't know about the sprain would have noticed a limp. By the first January thaw, he was again running five miles a day, and people who lived in the clapboard and brick and stone houses clapped when he went by.

And Longfellow Prep won the Eastern Regionals, after all—which Franklin was mostly happy about.

Trouble.

Two summers ago, Henry had fallen while climbing the black boulders in Salvage Cove, just beneath his family's house. It was a long fall, ten or twelve feet. If he had fallen a bit to the right, he would have landed on sharp stone wedges that would have broken whatever hit them. If he had fallen a bit to the left, he would have landed on sharper mussel beds that would have cut him up. But he landed right between them, into calm water whose tidal current gently led him back into shore.

At dinner that night, Franklin said that he guessed he should teach Henry how to climb. He'd show him how to set his hands and balance his footing. He'd show him how to test rock holds

5

and how to use his fist as an anchor in a fissure. And maybe, if he got good enough, he'd take him up to Katahdin. Maybe they'd even climb through the Gateway and up to the Knife Edge. "That would be something to see, little brother," he'd said, and he'd reached over and rumpled Henry's hair.

Henry almost bowed down and did worship.

And Henry's father said again, "If you build your house far enough away from Trouble, then Trouble will never find you."

That was why Henry wasn't ready for it on the evening of his fourteenth birthday, while he adjusted the straps of the backpack his parents had given him so he could show Franklin how prepared he was for their hiking trip up Katahdin, because Franklin had finally, finally, *finally* agreed to take him, even though he told Henry that he'd never make it, that he'd have to quit halfway up the mountain, that they'd have to turn back, that he was only going because their father wanted him to take his little brother—who, Franklin said again, would never make it.

On that night, looking out the north parlor window, his parents standing beside him and holding back the curtains, Henry couldn't understand why the town's one patrol car was moving slowly down their drive, heading toward their house. It had been a spring colder than usual, and the trees were still unleafed, so they could see the patrol car's red light revolving and throwing fire onto the mostly bare oaks and maples. They walked out into the dark back gardens, dark because the moon was still not up and the sky was starless. The red light struck them full, so that when Henry looked up at his parents' faces, they were covered with blood.

Which is how he saw his brother's face when they reached the hospital.

The streaks of red were ghastly against his skin, which was stark white. The perfect tan that Franklin always carried had vanished and left behind this shocked pallor. Henry's mother stood at the foot of the bed, her hands tight on the aluminum rail, her eyes wide and unblinking. His father stood beside her, stiff, straight, his hands up to his face. Neither had taken their coats off. Neither spoke.

Henry sat down on his brother's bed. A clear plastic mask covered Franklin's face, and he breathed into a clear plastic tube that circled around behind him. Both of his eyes were bruised and swollen shut. His right arm lay white and still, tucked tightly beside him outside the sheet. Another clear plastic tube coiled out from the crook of his elbow. Dried blood edged his fingernails. At first, Henry thought that the other arm must lie beneath the sheet. But it wasn't beneath the sheet. It just wasn't there.

A dribble of saliva came from underneath the mask over Franklin's mouth. Henry reached to wipe it away.

"Don't touch that," said his father.

His mother began to moan quietly.

Henry sat on his brother's bed for a long time that night, as his parents came in and went out and came in and went out. There were the doctors to deal with and medical decisions to be made: "Another brain scan once he's stable," said Dr. Burton. "Relieve some of the pressure, and then assess the damage," said Dr. Giles. There were the two town policemen, who came to inform the Smiths officially that they had arrested the driver who had slammed into their jogging son.

Running, thought Henry. Not jogging. Running.

There was Father Brewood, who knew enough to say nothing but a prayer. And there was the reporter from the *Blythbury-by-*

the-Sea Chronicle, who sensed that he might have a story with more drama than a rugby score and sneaked into Franklin's room to get a quick picture of him before the two Blythbury-by-the-Sea policemen manhandled him onto an elevator.

Franklin's eyes had opened when the reporter's camera flash went off. But he didn't blink. He stared out straight, intent, still. What is he looking at? thought Henry. He reached his hand out in front of Franklin's eyes, but his brother looked right through Henry's fingers, focusing beyond them.

"Franklin," said Henry.

His brother's eyes closed.

Late, late at night, when there was no more to see, Henry's parents decided to go back to the house. Louisa hadn't been home when the policemen came; no one had told her yet. They tried to get Henry to come, too. "There's no more we can do here tonight," his mother said.

Henry ignored her.

He had never ignored his mother before.

After a very silent while, his parents left. Henry stayed on Franklin's bed.

Cold. The low hum of the overhead light, the clattering and clicking of elevator doors. The smell of antiseptic, of clean sheets, of bandages. The slight wrinkle of corruption in the air. Outside, a nurse patrolling the nearly empty hallways with the steps of someone who knows that all the world is asleep and it shouldn't be awakened.

Henry felt strangely peaceful . . . and guilty for feeling peaceful. But the lights in the room were dim and his brother was so still. He could hear Franklin's breathing, timed with the rhythms of the quiet machine behind him. The one window in the room was opaque with the reflection of the light over his brother's bed. Sometimes Henry crossed the room and leaned his forehead against the cold glass so he could see out. As the night went on, he did this more and more. He needed to remind himself that this one room wasn't the whole world.

Close to dawn, a nurse came in to change the dressing on the stump. "Do you want to wait outside?" she asked.

Henry shook his head. He wanted to watch. He wanted to see everything.

"I think that you had better wait outside," said the nurse.

She led him into the hall and then around the corner, and he sat down in a vinyl chair by the nurses' station. He let his head fall back against the wall.

He closed his eyes.

And he saw himself with his brother, hefting their packs up higher on their shoulders as they climbed through the Gateway and up, up to the Knife Edge, Franklin turning to him and saying, "I knew you'd make it. I knew it all along," and Henry nodding, not needing to say anything.

When Henry's parents came back to the hospital the next morning, they found him asleep in the vinyl chair. One of the nurses had put a striped cotton blanket over him, and he had curled up and fit as much of himself under it as he could.

They woke him, and together they went back to Franklin's room. Nothing had changed. Franklin still unmoving. Clear plastic mask and tubes. His eyes closed. His breathing still the same, in time to the rhythms of the quiet machine. The new bandage on the stump of his arm stained at the end. Henry thought he could smell whatever was doing the staining.

Perhaps the only thing that was different was that the sun was up and Henry could see out the window.

And his father hadn't shaved—which was, Henry thought, the first time that had ever happened.

Louisa had not taken the news well, his parents told him. She had been waiting for them when they got home, holding the quick note that Mrs. Smith had left for her in the kitchen. They told her about the accident. They told her that Franklin's arm was gone. That his brain had swollen and that the doctors were using drugs to relieve the pressure. That there would be tests as soon as the swelling went down. That everyone had to hope for the very, very best.

Then Louisa had dropped the note to the quarried-stone floor and run up to her bedroom.

They had heard her through the night, but she would not open her door to them.

She would not open the door in the morning before they left.

His mother reached out to Henry and drew him to her. He could not remember another time when she had held him so tightly. Or when his father—with his eyes closed and his hands up to his face again—had looked so . . . empty—as if the soul had left his body, and his body understood that it would never come back.

They stood that way, together at the foot of Franklin's quiet bed. That was how Father Brewood found them. They stayed that way during the psalm he read to them—"In the time of my trouble I sought the Lord: I stretched forth my hands unto him, and ceased not in the night season." But during his prayer— "Look down upon Franklin Smith, your servant"—Henry's stomach started to growl. Loudly. Then very loudly.

"I'm sorry," said Henry when Father Brewood had finished.

"No matter what happens, there is always the business of the world to attend to," said Father Brewood.

Henry went downstairs to the hospital cafeteria to find some breakfast. It was quiet and still there, too, and the mopped floor smelled slightly of disinfectant, as if someone had thrown up and the janitor had made a job of it. He found a waxed carton of orange juice and a pastry with no filling; they were both as tasteless as Henry expected them to be. He took small bites and ate slowly. He didn't need to hurry back to the room. Nothing would change, though he wanted more than he could say to have things go back to the way they had been before his birthday.

But Henry was wrong.

He knew it as soon as the elevator doors opened and he stepped onto his brother's floor. A white-coated doctor ran past him, and the nurses' station was empty. Henry sprinted toward Franklin, and when he turned the corner of the hall, he saw his parents standing outside the room, his mother holding his father, together looking inside. Father Brewood stood beside them, his hands on them both. The running doctor was pushing past them. The sounds that were coming from the room, the terrible sounds . . .

The smell of the cafeteria disinfectant came back into his throat, and Henry threw up.

The next time that Henry saw Franklin, his brother had a strap drawn tightly across his chest. His right arm was strapped down. The thought came into Henry's head: They don't need to strap down his left arm, because it isn't there anymore. I wonder where it is? He went to sit again on his brother's bed. He fingered the taut straps.

Dr. Giles was back in the room. There was a seizure, he said. Significant swelling of the brain still. Whatever damage there had been may now be more extensive. If the scan is positive, then surgery will be recommended to control the swelling. No visitors now. Stimulation to a minimum. Hope for the best.

Henry couldn't say whether the rest of that day went quickly or whether it dragged its wearisome self along. The brain scan came back with a report of "indeterminate brain activity." The decision was made, and Franklin was taken immediately into surgery to relieve the swelling. They waited for about forever. Finally, he came back, the top of his head wrapped in bright white bandages, his eyes closed. All the blood cleaned from his face and fingernails.

"With some patients, the scans are simply impossible to decipher accurately," said Dr. Giles. "But we'll be able to tell more in twenty-four hours. We'll have another scan then."

Sitting on his brother's bed, fingering again the taut straps.

Eating in the hospital cafeteria. Thick roast beef with thick brown gravy. Canned corn. Canned carrots, tasting like the canned corn.

And all of that seemed to take no time at all, because there was no time at all. There was only Now. In the hospital. Where they all sat in the middle of Trouble.

That night, Henry went home with his parents. He was astonished that the world was pretty much as it had been before he had gone to the hospital. He was astonished that he was sitting in a familiar car, riding along familiar streets, idling into the carriage house, walking through the back door of his home, climbing the stairs, coming into his own room. Is it possible for everything to change, and for nothing to change? He opened his casement window, and the clean salt smell of the sea rose to him. He could hear the waves cresting onto the black boulders along the cove, one after the other. The moon was coming up, throwing a startling silver light along the undersides of the clouds and setting them apart from the darkness.

Henry lay back on his bed and fell into sleep.

And dreamed again of the Gateway. His brother was ahead of him, always ahead of him, hefting his backpack up around his shoulders. He turned back to Henry. "I knew you'd make it," he was saying again.

And Henry desperately wanted to say something to him. Something to let him know how wonderful it was to be up on the mountain with him. Something so beautiful that they would both begin to cry.

But when he opened his mouth, all he could say was "Indeterminate brain activity." And still asleep, Henry did begin to cry, and the waves below him galled themselves on the dark stone ledges beneath the house.

2

IN THE MORNING—What day was it? Wednesday? Had he lost track?—in the morning, Henry came down and found yesterday's *Blythbury-by-the-Sea Chronicle* beside this morning's *Blythbury-by-the-Sea Chronicle* out in the back gardens, the first one damper than the second. The first had the reporter's hurried photograph of Franklin on the front page, and, thought Henry, you had to admire a guy who could focus and shoot that quickly. Part of his own back blocked the view of the machine behind the bed, and there was part of a hand—probably one of the policemen's—at the bottom. Otherwise, Henry's brother filled the image. No one could tell from this angle that Franklin's arm was missing, but the headline—"Longfellow Prep Student Loses Arm in Accident, Faces Brain Surgery"—helpfully added that detail.

Henry didn't read the article.

But he did read the article in the second newspaper, because there was a different picture. It was a yearbook picture, and a dark-haired, dark-eyed face looked formally out of it, as if it wasn't used to appearing over a suit and tie and didn't quite know how to hold itself.

"Chay Chouan of Merton Charged in Smith Accident," the headline announced.

Henry read through the article and found, when he reached

the end, that he couldn't remember a single thing—except for the dark-haired, dark-eyed face. So he read it again. Chay Chouan. Henry Wadsworth Longfellow Preparatory High School. Father and mother, Cambodian immigrants. Stone masonry business in Merton. One brother. Coming home alone after delivering a load of slate for a roof. Asleep at the wheel. Never saw the jogger.

"Runner," whispered Henry to himself; then he threw the two *Blythbury-by-the-Sea Chronicle*s into the garbage can in the carriage house before his father and mother could see them. In the kitchen, he fried up three eggs for himself. Toast. Fresh orange juice. And it all tasted like the canned corn from the hospital cafeteria.

He thought vaguely for a moment about Whittier and didn't decide not to go to school as much as he drifted away from deciding anything at all. And who would drive him? He hadn't seen Louisa since the accident and his parents were still not up. So he set his dishes in the sink and headed toward the cove, where the frothy tops of the small waves bending into the beach were white as milk, almost as white as the sky that backed the sea.

He untied his kayak from the high-water post and pulled out the paddle and life jacket from inside. He kicked off his shoes and rolled up his pants, drew on the life jacket, then carried the kayak into the first water until it floated bow up, stern up, bow up, stern up on the low waves. He got in, looped the paddle string around his wrist, and headed onto the milk-white sea.

He hadn't really decided where he was going. When he had first gotten the kayak, he had explored north along the coast, sneaking into every tiny inlet. Later, he had explored south near Manchester, paddling among the marina docks and the high-prowed boats, then along beaches stretched beneath the houses of Old Money—like his own.

But today, he headed straight out from Salvage Cove, paddling fast. It was still early in the morning, and who knew how far he could go? He let his mind turn as white as the waves, fading toward indeterminate brain activity, paddling, feeling the familiar, welcome strain on the muscles of his shoulders. He dug the paddle into the water and pulled. Dug and pulled. Dug and pulled. Soon he would be out of the cove's shelter and into the open sea. Already the swells were longer and deeper, and the white froth was turning a slight green. Stroking hard into an oncoming wave, he felt the spray dash to a mist around him.

And that was when he heard the frantic, panicked, cut-off yelp.

He turned toward the sound, somewhere off the north point of the cove, where the ledge dropped straight down into the breaking water.

And there—it came again. Desperate. Choked. Hard to hear above the ocean's heavings around his kayak, but still unmistakably there.

And there again.

Then Henry saw something struggling in the sea, thrashing the water around itself.

He turned the kayak and slanted it across the waves. Now he felt the force and muscle of the water, pushing him back directly into the cove. But he kept the kayak cutting across the swells even when he began to ship some water, and he paddled so that the spray from the bow flew back into his face. He knew that if he weren't paddling, he would be shivering, for the water was still spring cold, especially this far out from shore.

He kept on, faster now as the thrashing grew less, and he couldn't be sure if it was trying to float or getting too weak to struggle. Its head was low to the water, and now it was going under most of the oncoming waves. It wouldn't be long before it stayed under.

"Wait!" he cried. "Wait for me!"

The head went under.

Henry paddled desperately.

It came up again. And it turned toward him.

It was a dog. A black-faced dog, and as soon as it saw him, it began to swim out with sudden spurts of frantic energy, as if it could run through the water somehow, wrenching itself up and free from the waves, then falling back, then wrenching itself up again. Trying to yelp.

A dog.

Henry kept the kayak slanted, willing the waves to drive him by the stern. They did, and as Henry closed, the dog gave a choked bark, went under and came up again, tore itself toward him, went under, came up, and then, with an unbelievable final leap, careened from the water and threw its two front legs and as much of its chest as it could up over the kayak's bow.

And immediately dumped Henry over and into the sea.

Henry's mouth filled with water when he went under, and he tried to cough it out while he was still capsized—which only let more in. Quickly, he pushed himself down and away and came up to the surface, sputtering. The kayak was floating beside him, tipping bow to stern on the swells. He grabbed onto it, still sputtering.

The dog was gone.

"Here!" hollered Henry. He coughed up water. "I'm here."

And he was pushed under by two paws that had come up from behind him. His mouth filled again.

When he came up to the surface, he grabbed at the dog's neck. "Stop . . ."—more choking and coughing and sputtering— "stop doing that," he said.

So the dog stopped, and instead it began to rake its back legs along Henry's chest as if it could somehow use Henry as a ladder and climb right out of the water. Henry felt the laces of his life jacket start to give way.

"Stop doing . . ."—cough, sputter—"that, too," he said.

So the dog went back to throwing its front legs over his shoulders and holding him down under the water. Henry let go of the kayak, which floated away from him.

He decided he would have to do something differently. So he coughed up as much of the water as he could, took a breath, swam under the next wave—which is not easy with a life jacket on— and came beneath the frantic dog. Then he reached up from under the water, grabbed whatever he could grab, and pulled the dog beneath the surface. When they both came up, the dog's eyes were round and shocked, and it coughed up more seawater than Henry could believe.

"Now stay still," said Henry. He put one hand under the dog's chest to hold it up; with the other he began to stroke toward the kayak. If it had been any rougher, he thought, they would have been in . . . trouble.

He was glad it wasn't rougher.

When they reached the kayak, Henry grabbed hold with one arm, held the dog with the other, and began to kick. It took a while to make progress, so by the time Henry, the dog, and the kayak all reached the point where the waves began to break in to shore, Henry was starting to shiver. The dog was already shivering so badly, it could hardly swim at all. Its eyes looked at him with more trust than he felt he deserved.

"Almost there," he said.

And they were. Two breaking waves knocked him under, and the dog as well. Coughing, sputtering. Then a third wave almost flipped him over, and the dog as well. Coughing, sputtering. But that was the wave that finally brought them to where Henry could touch bottom, and he held the dog and kayak against the ocean's tow, pushed toward the shore with the next wave, held on against the tow again, came in more on the following wave, and so stumbled up onto the beach of Salvage Cove, and collapsed.

He looked up toward his house. His parents were probably still asleep. Maybe Louisa, too.

During all that trouble.

The dog stood uncertainly, spreading out its back legs to keep itself from falling over sideways. Its back was arched against the coughing spasms that spewed out white water from its guts— which was also true of Henry. He finished before the dog, and figured that he shouldn't do anything until it had cleared its lungs. So wiping his mouth and still coughing, he got up and went out into the water to grab the kayak and drag it from the waves and onto dry sand. Then he sprawled on his back beside the kayak and looked into a sky that was starting to blue.

It had never looked so blue before.

Until the dog came and stood over him, its face panting and looking down into his own. It licked him once and then drooped down beside him on its back, still heaving.

They lay together, dog and boy breathing heavily and to the

same rhythm, the salt strong in their mouths. Overhead, seagulls flew randomly, and their shrieks pushed the sun higher. A cool breeze came off the sea, ruffling the hair of both, but neither noticed. The sand warmed beneath them.

Henry was the first to open his eyes. The sky was full blue now. He propped himself on one elbow and looked down at the dog, who instantly opened her eyes, too, and watched him. She was, Henry figured, the ugliest dog since Genesis. Her snout was all beat up and scabby—and some of the scabs had torn away during their frantic swim and were bleeding. She was missing a good chunk of her left ear—which gave her head a lopsided look—and a little of her right. As her black hair—her short black hair—was drying in the sun, it was getting duller and duller, and the bald parts near her hindquarters and down her legs showed yellow skin. Every rib stood out from her sides to be counted, and where the rib cage stopped, her body cascaded inward like a deflated bag. When Henry ran his fingers down her spine, he could feel the ridge of each vertebra, as sharp and distinct as the mauled beams beneath his house.

This dog hadn't moved far enough away from Trouble.

"What were you doing in the water?" Henry said.

The dog watched his eyes.

Henry wondered if she had been looking for something to eat on the ledge and then slid in. "Are you hungry?" he said.

The dog was still. She watched his eyes.

Henry wiped the sand from the dog's face. He thought he should try to clean away the blood from her snout, too, but she pulled away when he reached for it. When he stood, she jumped up, almost on her toes, but she kept her head low and she curled her tail between her back legs. "C'mon," said Henry, but he hadn't taken three steps down to the water before the dog had run ahead of him, lain down on the beach, and rolled over to show her belly.

Henry reached down and scratched her behind the ears. "Stop fooling around," he said, and walked past her.

Another three steps and she was in front of him again, her belly up. She did not move. She watched his eyes.

"C'mon," Henry said, but this time he took only two steps before she was in front of him again, lying on her back but still able to wag her tail.

It was a slow walk down to the water, and when they finally got there, Henry had to struggle to make the dog stand and not flop down and turn up her belly. He didn't think she would get back into the waves—and she didn't—but he cupped some water in his hands and dribbled it over the bleeding wounds. The dog did not move—except for her tail, which she tightened beneath her. Henry cupped water onto her snout until all the blood was washed away and the exposed flesh beneath was pink and white.

But she wouldn't let him touch the broken scabs.

"You are a mess," Henry said.

The dog watched his eyes.

Henry walked back up the beach to secure the kayak—this took a long time, since he couldn't go three steps without having the dog flop down in front of his feet, and he had to reach down every time to keep her bleeding snout out of the sand. She lay beside him, belly up, while he knotted the kayak ropes; and when he climbed the black boulders up to the house, she clambered on ahead and was waiting for him, belly up, when he reached the top.

"You look like you haven't eaten since the day you were born," said Henry. He walked around to the back service door and the dog followed him, her head down, her tail still tucked tightly between her legs and up against her body, looking like a mongrel that nobody loved, the kind of dog that hangs around the edges of a dump and tears open garbage bags.

When Henry reached for the door latch, the dog stopped her flopping. She stood rigidly beside him, watching the latch, up on her toes, waiting for the door to open. But Henry knew that his parents would never, ever, *ever* let a dog into the house. Never. Especially an ugly, bleeding dog that was starting to smell as if she really did hang around the edges of a dump.

She watched his eyes.

"Stay here," Henry said. "I'll bring you out something to eat."

But once the door opened, the dog would have none of that. She slid in like smoke as soon as a crack appeared, sticking her nose through and letting the rest of her follow. "No!" Henry called in a kind of whispered shout, but the dog went in, the nails on her paws clicking loudly on the pine boards, and her tail—up for the first time—striking against the wall and leaving wet strokes as she went.

"You sorry dog," said Henry

But she was ignoring him now, and Henry watched her follow her tingling nose, which led her past the mud room, down the hall—her nails click, click, clicking on the floors so loudly that everyone in the house must be hearing it—and so on into the spotless kitchen, where she immediately found the garbage pail beneath the sink and stood waiting politely for Henry to open the door so that she could explore it. Henry opened the refrigerator instead and looked around. It was pretty much empty, since no one had been doing any shopping for the last couple of days.

One shelf was taken up by the whipped-cream cake for Henry's birthday celebration, now with most of its whipped cream turning yellow and sliding off. There was some milk and butter and a drawer of carrots and broccoli and lettuce heads. Nothing that a dog would want. But in the cupboard Henry found some beef stew, and while the dog watched eagerly, he opened a can, dumped it all into a mixing bowl, and set it down. The dog's bleeding snout was in it before it hit the floor.

Her tail was still curled low between her legs.

When she finished, Henry dumped in another can of beef stew, and she went to it, slobbering her jowls and throwing gobbets of the stew against the light maple cabinets.

The kitchen was beginning to smell like cold beef stew and wet dog, so Henry was hardly surprised when his father came in—wearing an untied bathrobe, unshaved, uncombed!—and began to sniff. He looked over the kitchen island to see what the snuffling sounds were on the other side. He sniffed again.

"It smells like you have a dog in here," he said. "A wet dog." His voice was tight.

It did not seem useful to Henry to lie about this.

Especially since the dog came around the corner of the island and sat down, her head cocked off to the side so that the ear with the large missing piece stuck out.

Now Henry's father's face grew tight, too.

"Get the dog out of here," he said.

"I just saved her from drowning out in the cove."

"That was a mistake. You don't go looking for Trouble, Henry. . . . Get away."

The last part was directed not at Henry but at the dog, who had come to sniff Henry's father to see if he might be at all interesting.

"Get away," he said again. "Black dog, get away."

The dog lifted up a paw.

And Henry's father kicked her about as hard as a slippered foot can kick. Enough to skid her across the quarried-stone floor.

She did not cry out. When she stopped skidding, she turned on her back, put her feet up in the air, and showed her belly.

"Why did you ever bring that dog in here?" said Henry's father. "Look at her. Who would want a black dog like that? Lying there, all beat up. Bleeding. Pieces of her missing." He stopped. He leaned against the kitchen island and put his hands across his eyes. "Pieces of her missing," he said again. His body trembled, slowly, and then a little bit more, and a little more, like a building that is beginning to feel the earthquake starting under its foundations.

Then his mouth opened, and though no sound came out, his silent howls filled the kitchen.

Henry held his father. Tight. Very tight. He felt the black dog come back to them. He felt his father reach down to scratch her behind her chipped ear. He saw the dog roll her face with pleasure against his father's untied robe—and hoped that his father would not see the pus and blood that she left there.

They stood, the three of them, together in the kitchen, and two things happened.

First, Black Dog had a home and a name.

Second, the telephone rang. It was the hospital.

Henry changed while his parents dressed. They were already waiting for him in the BMW that his father had pulled around. "Leave the dog out in the carriage house," he said.

"Dog?" said his mother.

They raced through Blythbury-by-the-Sea, so fast that if it hadn't been a car they recognized, the town's policemen would have stopped the Smiths by the end of Main Street. They reached the hospital, bounced across the parking ramp, half-walked and half-ran through the hospital lobby, smacked at the elevator button until the doors opened, and ran through the corridor to Franklin's room, where three nurses—two of them big enough to be impressive rugby players—were holding Henry's brother down.

"Another seizure," one of the nurses said. "He almost tore the straps off."

Henry's mother sat down on the bed.

"He's sedated now, but there were signs that another one was about to start."

Henry's mother laid her hand over her son's heart.

"Franklin," she said softly.

He opened his eyes. They were bright and fierce. The nurses tightened their grip on him and spread their legs, ready for the next monumental struggle.

But Franklin did not struggle. He looked around from face to face, wildly, quickly. It was as if he was in a room full of strangers and he was desperately trying to find the one face that he knew, the one face that meant something to him.

And then he found it.

He looked at Henry. His eyes fixed on him, so bright that Henry thought they were about to burst into flame.

He spoke, his voice as urgent as a prophet's. One word to Henry. One word.

He turned to the window and looked far out.

And he said the word again, softly.

Then the fire died, his bright eyes dulled and closed, and the strength of his body deflated into the bed. But the word echoed in the room and in Henry's brain.

"Katahdin."

He first saw her from high up, while standing on the scaffolding, the slate pieces stacked around him. It was late in the day, and she came out of the house with a bowl of cereal in her hand and walked toward the ledges over the sea. And just before she got there, she turned and waved to him. Just waved. Only for a moment.

He waved back.

And his father, tied carefully to the roof, told him to keep his eyes where they were supposed to be kept.

But that was the beginning.

3

IN THE THREE CENTURIES that the Smith house had stood on the ledges over the sea, no dog had ever tramped through its rooms. Not a one. The stout oaken timbers had held all the forces of nature at bay. Earthquakes, hurricanes, solar eclipses, meteorite strikes (there had been two), lightning (four times)—none had shaken it. Powers, principalities, and dominions had sometimes warred against its frame: British regulars had almost burned it, General Stonewall Jackson had boasted that he would use it as his campaign headquarters someday, and a German U-boat commander off the coast during World War II had wondered whether a torpedo against the ledges would collapse the house into the sea.

But nothing had shaken it—until Black Dog.

When Henry and his parents got back from the hospital late in the afternoon, Black Dog was not in the carriage house, where Henry had left her. Somehow she had figured out how to pull down the latch and open the doors. But that wasn't the height of her miracles. After she escaped from the carriage house, she had gone back around to the service door—which was unlocked, because the house was so far from Trouble—and pulled down the latch on that door as well. It was still open, and the Smiths walked into the hallway and slowly followed her trail with impressed horror.

Black Dog had gone into the kitchen first, probably since she was familiar with it. She had nosed open the cupboards until she found the pantry, and she had pulled all of the soup cans and sacks of onions and jars of canned vegetables and applesauce and bottles of New Hampshire maple syrup out into the kitchen before she found what she wanted: a jar of peanut butter with a loose lid. She had licked it clean, eating what she wanted and then smearing the rest all over the quarried stone floors and the light maple cupboards.

Then Black Dog had gone into the library and climbed up onto Henry's father's desk—a desk older than the house and once used by Oliver Cromwell's secretary—and left peanut-butter paw prints there. Then she had jumped down onto the couch and sunk her toenails deep into the red leather—which apparently she enjoyed, since she had walked all over it until settling down to taste the left armrest.

From there, Black Dog had gone to the south parlor and wiped what must have been the rest of the peanut butter from her snout onto the linen tapestry from Bayeux. Then she climbed up into the window seat to enjoy the view of the Atlantic. Finding the cushions a bit lumpy, she had torn most of their stuffing out. Afterward, she had jumped down and chased her tail—at least that's what Henry figured, since the scratch marks on the Italian tile went in circles.

Then she had gone upstairs, and at the top—oh, there had been some peanut butter left, after all, and she had wiped it off on the Oriental runner—at the top, she had inspected the antique blue chinaware collection that had been settled on those shelves when Massachusetts Bay was still a colony, tottering the pieces on the lowest shelf toward the edge. The notion of a dog's snout in the Smith porcelain shivered Henry's parents.

"Find that dog and put it out," said Henry's mother, turning to the shelves. "Then start cleaning up. You're the one who brought her into the house, Henry. You're responsible."

Henry had to acknowledge that this was fair, and he went to find Black Dog.

This turned out not to be too difficult; all he had to do was to follow the peanut-butter smears along the hallway walls. He tried to imagine the cataclysm of peanut butter that must have engulfed the dog in the kitchen—a cataclysm still in evidence when he finally found her, wrapped up in the down quilt that covered his bed, her peanut-buttery nose tucked under her peanut-buttery tail, asleep, breathing quietly, absolutely and completely content.

His room reeked of peanut butter.

He cranked open the windows, and the moment he made a sound, Black Dog's head was up and her ears were forward and her eyes bright. She jumped down off the bed, dragging the quilt with her—"Now listen, Black Dog!"—and she circled around him, almost prancing—"You've got to"—until she finally flopped down at his feet and turned her belly up to him—"cut all this out." She pawed the air and waited for Henry to scratch her and tell her what a good dog she was.

Which, of course, he did.

Then he took her back down to the carriage house and secured the latch with a chain so that she wouldn't get out again.

He spent the rest of the afternoon cleaning up the peanut butter, while his mother washed the chinaware and called the furniture shop.

Henry and his parents tried not to listen to Black Dog whine and beg and cry and bark pathetically during their otherwise very quiet and very still supper. But during their quiet and still dessert, they couldn't help but hear the latch opening on the back service door, and the click, click, click of toenails across the quarried-stone floor, and the great bark of joy and delight when Black Dog found Henry in the dining room.

Beside his chair, she turned over and showed her belly. Am I not amazingly smart? she asked.

Henry's mother sat back. "You're going to have to get rid of that dog," she said.

"Maybe she'd quiet down if I took her for long walks," said Henry.

"You'd have to take her for marathons. And besides, Henry, she's awful. She smells."

"Just because of the peanut butter. I'll give her a bath."

"And she's destructive."

"I can keep her tied up."

"And I don't think those scars will . . ."

Silence.

Long silence.

"No, they won't," said Henry's father, finally.

They all watched Black Dog on her back, panting happily and waiting to be scratched.

Then Henry stood, stepped over Black Dog, whistled, and together they headed down to Salvage Cove, where Black Dog sprinted up and down the beach in her floppy run, staying far away from the water, and coming back over and over again to show Henry her belly.

That night, Henry tied Black Dog to a budding maple below his window, and after she had whined and begged and cried and barked pathetically for a couple of hours, Henry sneaked down through the house and brought her inside. He had to carry her across the floors so she wouldn't wake his parents—if they had gotten to sleep at all—and she squirmed as if she were being carried above the Abyss. But once he got her up to his room—which still smelled slightly of peanut butter—and put her down, she was up on her toes and prancing around him happily.

"Cut it out," Henry whispered, maybe too fiercely, since Black Dog lowered her ears and dragged her tail beneath her belly.

"Lie down, right there," said Henry.

Black Dog followed the circle patterns on Henry's rug and lay down among them. She squirmed a bit into the warm and soft thickness, then put her head down. Her eyes—her lovely brown eyes—followed Henry's every move.

"Stay," said Henry, and he turned off the light.

The moon glowed. It was full and bright, so bright that everything in Henry's room turned silver. Beneath him far below, lazy waves sashayed onto the rocky ledges.

"Good dog," said Henry.

Which was enough of an invitation for Black Dog to raise her head and, in one fling of her body, jump onto Henry's bed.

"Black Dog!" he said.

But Black Dog was already digging at the down quilt and organizing it around herself. She looked at Henry, grinned, and collapsed. She was asleep in a moment. With soft hands, the moonlight buffed what fur she had and made it glow.

Henry lay back.

But he did not go to sleep.

He listened to the loud and slow rhythm of Black Dog's breathing, and over it he could hear his brother's voice.

"Katahdin." He could see his brother's open eyes, searching for the one face he wanted. Henry's.

"Katahdin."

In the dark, Henry could see the mountain. Its long peaks rising out of the flat green land. The circle of the mountain, as if it had risen to guard the blue lake in which it dangled its feet. The sheer stone of its sides. The way the heated, rough granite would smell. The sound of the wind streaking across the craggy trails along the peaks. He lay there, listening to Black Dog's snorting dreams, and listening, too, to his brother's urgent voice.

"Katahdin."

"Why Katahdin?" Henry had asked a month ago.

"Because it's there, little brother," Franklin had said. "You scared?"

"No."

"You *should* be scared. You don't call a trail 'the Knife Edge' for nothing. People die there all the time."

Henry had listened with round and wide eyes.

"You do that climb, you have guts. You can handle anything."

"Handle what?"

"Handle Trouble. Like, suppose you hear at school that someone who doesn't deserve to be at Longfellow Prep is talking with Louisa. And maybe he wants to do more than talk. You have to handle that. You have to find this guy so it's just the two of you, and you put your finger in the middle of his chest and you tell him to stay away from her, and to show him you mean it, you shove him up on the wall and hold your forearm across his neck—like this." Franklin had shoved Henry against the wall and pressed his forearm against his throat. "You let him know that you're ready for Trouble. You let him know that you're not going to let other people think you'll put up with someone like him touching your sister. . . . See what I mean?"

"Yes," said Henry. He didn't.

Franklin took his arm away from Henry's neck. "That's what climbing Katahdin means," Franklin said. "It shows you've got guts, and that you're ready to stand by yourself and handle Trouble. Except there's one problem, Henry."

Henry had stared at him.

"I saw you play Kenilworth, and you don't have any guts." Franklin punched his arm. Too hard. Then he laughed and walked away.

Henry lay in the darkness. Black Dog dreamed dreams.

The next morning, Henry got up for Whittier for the first time since Trouble had come to find him. He got up early so he could secretly carry the squirming Black Dog out of his room and out of the house. And he almost succeeded—until Louisa appeared in the kitchen at the last second, ready for Longfellow Prep. She didn't say anything. So Henry let Black Dog down and she ran over to Louisa, showed her belly, and panted happily. Louisa crouched and patted her lightly. "She smells like peanut butter," she said.

"I still have to give her a bath," said Henry.

"That's not all she needs," she said quietly.

Then their mother came in. Louisa stood. Black Dog grinned up at her and whined. Louisa looked down at the scarred and battered dog. Then, suddenly, as if the moment had broken in two and let everything fall out of it, she ran across the kitchen and into her mother's arms and began to sob, but with no sound, and with no words. Her mother stroked her dark hair. But it all lasted only for a few seconds. The moment jarred back together, and Louisa pulled away. She ran out of the kitchen. The sound of her footsteps on the stairs came back to them.

Henry's mother put out a hand to the kitchen island to prop herself up. "Take the dog outside," she said.

Henry led Black Dog out of the house and down to Salvage Cove. The tide was high, and the waves came in, and came in, and came in, battering on the shore, sounding like *Katahdin, Katahdin, Katahdin*. Henry's heart beat wildly within him, thinking of how Louisa would love to run with Black Dog. How Franklin might have loved to run with Black Dog, and now he might never. . . . And then he squashed down the traitorous thought.

Of course Franklin would run again. He was Franklin Smith, O Franklin Smith, the great lord of us all, Franklin Smith.

But Henry had to admit, deep down, that he hoped that Black Dog would rather run with him than with his brother or sister.

Then his mother called him back from above the black boulders.

Mr. Smith, who had planned to drive Henry into school, had decided to stay home that day—he hadn't been to his Boston office since the accident. So Henry's mother drove him instead. Black Dog rode in the back seat, because she jumped in before they could do a thing about it. Except for Black Dog's panting, they drove in silence. Silence, Henry figured, was Trouble's good friend.

Henry was surprised that Whittier was so unchanged, since he had been gone for something like half a lifetime and the whole world had changed for him. But Whittier—and maybe even the whole world, too—had gone on as if what had happened to Franklin Smith didn't much matter. The clipped grass was sotted with the morning dew, as it had been every spring morning. The ivy that ran up the burnt brick walls had not faltered but was greening up in the spring sun. The paths across the quadrangle were perfectly swept—as they always were. The bright flags of country, state, and academy flew briskly—as they always would. The cars were arriving one by one to let off students, their books shiny with red-and-white Whittier Academy book covers. Inside, the slightly sweaty smell of the halls mixed with the wax of Bates Gymnasium and the meat loaf aroma of Thwaite Cafeteria. It was all the same.

Henry stopped at his locker, and his fingers told the combination. His books still in the same place. The red-and-white crew sweats he kept meaning to bring home to wash but kept forgetting to. Notebooks leaking frayed paper. Very, very important school announcements to bring home scrunched up in balls.

It was all the same.

He went in to his first class, American History, which hadn't made much progress since they began Lewis and Clark.

When Sanborn Brigham sat down behind him, Henry pointed this out. "You're still on Lewis and Clark? How can you still be on Lewis and Clark?"

"Because Lewis and Clark are Great American Heroes, True Adventurers who Helped Found Our Country. Because we need to read Every Single Page of their journals Out Loud."

"I guess that explains it," said Henry.

"That explains it."

Sanborn, as it turned out, wasn't kidding. Mr. DiSalva came into the room, nodded at Henry to show that he knew he was back, and cleared his throat while he adjusted his red-and-white

Whittier tie and extracted from a briefcase a pair of leather-bound books that held—really—every page of every journal that Lewis and Clark ever wrote.

Mr. DiSalva began to read aloud, pointing out Significant Places on the map of the western United States behind him as he read.

Henry tried not to fall asleep.

During the rest of the day, a few of his teachers—and even Dr. Sheringham, Whittier's principal—did more than nod at him. Their voices got low and quiet, and they tilted their heads, and they asked him politely and sadly how his brother, Franklin, was doing. Was it true that he had lost his right arm? What a shame for such a fine athlete. Was he in much pain? Undoubtedly, he was being drugged to relieve the discomfort. How was the family holding up under the strain?

Franklin was in an induced coma, you jerks, thought Henry. Was there any pain? He'd had his arm ripped off! Was it a shame? Are you kidding? *A shame?* Of course he was on drugs now, idiots. Either that or he'd be screaming in agony all the time. And no, they weren't holding up under the strain. The strain? His father hadn't gone into work for days. He never left the house. He didn't answer phone calls, or shave, or wear shoes. His mother went around so tight that she was about to snap in two. Louisa had come out of her bedroom once, and then run back in. They were all about to break apart.

"Franklin is fine," said Henry. It was his left arm. He didn't think there was much pain now. He supposed there were drugs to relieve the discomfort. And his family was doing fine. Just fine. They were all fine. They were all so fine they could be America's Fine Family. Fine.

That's what he said.

And then there was silence, because no one knew what to say after they had figured out that everything was fine. Not even Sanborn, who was the only one at Whittier to ask, "How are you?" But he asked too late in the day.

"Fine, Sanborn. Just fine. How else would I be doing? I mean, I've just got a brother lying in a coma in the hospital with indeterminate brain activity—whatever that means—and missing most of his left arm. I should be fine, right? Every time I go to bed I try not to sleep because I think I'm going to dream about this bloody stump where an arm should be, but everyone has dreams, right? I'm fine, Sanborn, fine. *So stop asking.*"

Sanborn stopped asking.

It was a relief to get to Physical Education, where he could run and work his head off and where Coach Santori never said anything except threats against all health and happiness and future success.

"Three weight sets, and do them well or you'll do them all over again," he announced. And after they were all done lifting, "Two paced miles, and I mean paced, or you'll run them again—barefoot." Henry ran them very fast.

That afternoon after school, he rowed hard at crew practice—and not just because he had missed a few days, and not just because he was afraid of any new Coach Santori threats. He rowed so hard that it was impossible for him to keep the rhythm, and more than a few times Brandon Sheringham, the perfect and unerring coxswain, barked at him for upsetting everyone else's stroke. "Stay together," he yelled, mostly at Henry. "Together."

That's what I'm trying to do, thought Henry. Stay together.

Afterward, in the varsity locker room, Brandon Sheringham

wondered kindly if Henry might think about taking this season off, since it must be hard to keep his mind on rowing. Henry wondered less kindly if Brandon Sheringham might think about keeping his nose out of his business, even though it must be hard to keep a beak that size out of anything.

He ignored Brandon Sheringham's glares, dressed, and went to Thwaite—Why did it always smell of meat loaf?—where he watched Sanborn and the rest of the debate team finish haggling over the future of nuclear power. Then he and Sanborn waited outside for Henry's mother to come pick them up.

"I've got a dog," said Henry.

Sanborn looked up from his note cards on nuclear power's danger. "Your parents let you have a dog?"

"Yes, my parents let me have a dog. Sort of, anyway. I guess it depends on what she does to the house in the next few days."

"What kind?"

Henry shrugged. "Black."

"Does your dog have a name?"

"Of course she has a name. Black Dog."

Sanborn raised a single eyebrow crookedly. "Black Dog? So she's a pirate, right? Billy Bones. Long John. Black Dog. Like that."

"If you're going to make fun of someone's name," said Henry, "shouldn't you be pretty sure you have a decent one yourself?"

"If you're going to name a dog," said Sanborn, "shouldn't you use a little more imagination than 'Black Dog'?"

"She likes 'Black Dog,'" said Henry.

"Oh, she came up to you and said, 'I really like this stupid name you gave me, and it doesn't matter that it sounds like something out of a first-grade reader.'"

"It doesn't sound like something out of a first-grade reader."

Sanborn looked at him sadly. "Here comes a dog. It is black. It is a black dog. 'Let's call it Black Dog,' says Sally. 'Oh, yes,' says Jane. 'Here, Black Dog. Good, Black Dog.'"

"You know, I think I'm going to beat you up right now," said Henry.

Sanborn laid his still unorganized nuclear power's danger note cards on the ground. He reached into his pocket and pulled out two dimes. "You better make some calls to get help."

Henry and Sanborn were testing to see if any calls were necessary when Henry's mother came to pick them up. They brushed themselves off, found their scattered books, picked up the now very unorganized nuclear power's danger note cards, and nodded when they got in. She nodded back—like Mr. DiSalva—and they didn't say a single word while they drove home. Henry figured she had been in the hospital all day, and what was there to say after that? He wished she would turn the radio on.

When they got to Sanborn's house, he punched Henry lightly on the arm and got out. "Thanks, Mrs. Smith," he said. She nodded and put the car in gear. But before they could pull away, Sanborn's mother was out of the house. Henry heard his own mother sigh as she rolled down the window.

"How are you, Mary?" said Sanborn's mother. She held her cigarette away from the car window.

"Fine," said Henry's mother. "We're all doing fine."

"I've heard that they're thinking of charging that Cambodian boy with attempted murder. Is that true?"

"I don't know," said Henry's mother. "I suppose it could be true. It was an accident."

"Well," said Sanborn's mother, "that's not what some say.

Those people." She shook her head. "Someone has to do something. And how is Franklin? Is there any more news?"

"Franklin is doing fine," Henry's mother said. "All the doctors have high hopes."

"Isn't that fine," said Sanborn's mother.

"Yes, fine," said Henry's mother.

Henry thought he might start laughing out loud.

They pulled away. Silence, except for the sounds of the road.

"Fine?" said Henry.

"Well, what should I tell her?" his mother said quickly. "That I sat in my son's hospital room for six hours and he didn't move once? That when Dr. Giles opened his eyelids and flashed a light into his eye, the pupils didn't dilate enough to measure? That the sounds my son makes . . . are like none that any boy should ever make? You want me to tell her that the bloody stump is still oozing? You want me to tell her that the nurses come in every two hours to change him because he can't even use a bedpan? What do you want me to tell her, Henry?"

"That he woke up and said, 'Katahdin.'"

His mother shook her head. She was trying not to cry. "It didn't mean anything," she whispered.

But as they rode home, and as Henry laid his head heavily against the window, his heart would not believe that "Katahdin" didn't mean anything. The heart knows what it knows.

When he first saw her at Longfellow Prep, her eyes swept past him as if he were nothing, another student, someone she didn't know or care to know. But then her eyes had come back, and she put her hand up to her mouth, and she walked over to him.

"Aren't you . . ."

He nodded.

"This is the first time I've seen you on the ground."

He wasn't sure that he still was.

"Welcome to Longfellow Prep. Ignore all the jerks. Just because this is Longfellow Prep doesn't mean we don't have our share of idiots."

He felt as if he had come to shore after a long voyage.

4

THE TOWN OF MERTON was only half as old as Blythbury-by-the-Sea, but those dwelling in Blythbury now had called Merton a ghost town all their lives. And they were almost right.

It wasn't always that way. Merton had been blessed with two fast-flowing rivers, and so was about as fine a town in which to build a water wheel as Massachusetts could offer. Huge brick mills went up, and canals between the rivers, and then more mills, and boarding houses to support the mill workers, and homes for the mill managers, and stores for the boarding-house managers, and libraries for the girls who worked in the mills, an athenaeum, and churches. For the two generations that spanned the Civil War, the textile looms clanked and clattered and shook the iron frames of the brick mills.

But the day came when waterpower was no longer needed, and the sounds of the mills became little . . . less . . . nothing. And then the dim ghosts came, living quietly in the mills and in the boarding houses, moving slowly past windows at night, sounding their whispers into the lonely winds that drifted over the canals and up into the abandoned shafts of the mills.

The stores and mills and libraries and churches all went quiet, and only the occasional horse and cart rode the streets past the empty buildings; and then the occasional Lizzie; and then the occasional finned car. Governors and senators swore for a hundred years to resurrect Merton. But the houses that held on outside the mill district fell into lonely decay, and the schools that the state built with noble design grew gray and sullen.

And the dim ghosts laughed their breathless laughs.

Until a people who knew something about ghosts began to come. They came from places with names strange in a New England mouth: Phnom Penh, Kompong Cham, Battambang, Siem Reap. They came with almost nothing and were amazed to find in Merton what they thought they had lost in the whirlwind of war: Hope. And with hope, they began to build. First the streets were cleaned and the broken store windows began to gleam with new glass. Markets sprang up in the shadows of the old boarding houses, offering vegetables never before grown in New England soil. Restaurants served foods that Massachusetts had not tasted, and their scents filled the evening air, while from the houses a music with new harmonics twisted with the scents, and children played by the cool stoops, speaking a tongue with new words.

The dim ghosts fled and the newcomers came out at night and walked the streets, and they looked at the strange stars and felt that, though they had come far and though they would always remember Cambodia as home, this new place was good.

The old mills were opened and dusty rooms cleaned and remade, and businesses moved in: camera shops, food markets, restaurants and delis and clothing stores and hardware stores. New carpenters found work in the rebuilding, and plumbers and electricians and plasterers joined them. The Chouan family founded Merton Masonry and Stonework on the first floor of one of the old boarding houses, and father and sons began to build stone walls and hearths and luxurious patios for homes all the way east to Marblehead and west to Amherst. One summer, they spent two weeks repairing the slate roof of the Smith house in Blythbury-by-the-Sea, hardly able to stop watching the waves of the strange sea they had never seen before.

People in Blythbury-by-the-Sea said that you could drive down some of the streets in Merton and you'd never know you were in Massachusetts. Why, every sign was in Cambodian! And maybe that was all right for people in Merton. Probably they weren't complaining, because the town needed the tax revenue. But can you imagine all of your neighbors speaking that indecipherable language! And their food! And those gaudy temples!

Sometimes, members of the rugby team from Longfellow Prep would drive over to Merton late on a Saturday night. They would drive slowly down the streets, their windows wide open, the bass of their music loud. They would holler and hoot at the scents and the clothes and chiming music—at the people who walked the streets beneath the resurrected mills. And the words they used to holler and hoot were as Anglo-Saxon as their names. It was great, Franklin told Louisa and Henry. You should see them scatter.

When Louisa's eyes told Franklin that his sister couldn't see why that was great, Franklin reminded her that those people didn't belong in Merton, anyway.

When Henry's eyes told Franklin that his brother couldn't see why that was great, Franklin told Henry what he already knew: He had no guts.

The sky changed as Henry and his mother drove home from Sanborn's house after Henry's first day back at Whittier—which he might have pointed out to his mother, except that she was so full of Franklin that she wouldn't have heard him. The clouds had been thick all day long, but now high winds came out of a single quarter and pulled at their fleecy undersides. They began to move quickly inland, though when Henry got out of the car to watch, he felt no wind at all.

He wondered whether Franklin could see this out his window.

Black Dog was not in the carriage house. She had shoved aside three boxes of Funk & Wagnalls encyclopedias in order to get at the door latch, which she had apparently opened without any difficulty at all. And she hadn't had any difficulty with the back service door to the house, either; it was open again, too. They did not find Black Dog in the kitchen—and neither did they find the four chicken breasts that Henry's mother had left out to thaw. They followed the trail of shredded chicken packaging upstairs and into Henry's room. Black Dog was nested in his down quilt. Asleep.

But she bounded up as soon as she saw them, leaping in one not graceful movement from the bed, through the air, and into Henry's arms, and since it is no easy thing to catch a leaping all-kinds-of-a-dog dog, Henry staggered back against his mother, so that in the end, they both caught her and she began right away to lick their faces.

"She certainly is a friendly dog," said Henry's mother.

Black Dog nodded and grinned. She certainly was. She licked Henry's mother's face again.

". . . even if she did eat our dinner."

Black Dog lowered her ears to show her sorrow.

Who could not like a dog like this? Which is what they told Henry's father when he came out from the library for supper.

"Hmm . . ." he said, considering whether he could not like a dog like this. But when a dog is up on her toes and gamboling around your feet and doing her very best to show that she is good and loyal and true and blue—and fun, besides—you can't not like her.

"We'll see," he said.

They ate a salad for dinner that night.

"Don't you usually make this with grilled chicken?" Henry's father asked.

"It's much healthier as a vegetarian dish," said his mother.

And it all seemed so normal, so absolutely normal, so absolutely right. It was suddenly as if Trouble had never come, after all, and as if Franklin's missing Haviland plate and his empty chair meant nothing at all. And as if Louisa's unfilled Haviland plate and her empty chair meant nothing at all.

But in the fork-clinking-against-plate silence that followed, Henry remembered that Trouble *had* come. How could he have forgotten it, even for a moment? And then he thought, How sweet it is to have forgotten it for a moment. And then he was so mixed up that he just ate the crescents of yellow bell peppers and tried not to think at all.

That night, Black Dog went up with Henry and slept on his bed, since she was so used to the down quilt. Henry figured that this was all right; the wounds on Black Dog's snout were scabbing over again, so there wasn't any more blood to wash up. Still, it wasn't easy to sleep with Black Dog on the bed. She kicked and panted and breathed and sometimes even barked in her dreams. Four times she woke up to rearrange the quilt, which meant a lot of digging and pawing. Twice she fell off the bed, and both times she jumped up and licked Henry's face to let him know that he didn't have to worry. She was fine.

Fine.

Through all of this, Henry watched the dim suffusion of the moon illuminate the clouds from behind. He couldn't see a single star, but the pale spread of light caressed his window until the clouds thickened so deeply that they hid the moon completely.

In the morning, the sea was wild and rough and green. The clouds were still running fast, but the wind had slanted down and was snatching the froth from the whitecaps and throwing it up high onto the shore. Henry and Black Dog climbed down into the cove to tie the kayak farther up, and the wind was so strong that the salt spray spat into their faces.

Henry's father decided to stay home again that day, so Henry's mother drove Henry, again, to Whittier.

They stopped at the hospital before school. Franklin was very quiet. Henry's mother took his hand and held it, but it was limp. Indeterminate activity.

Everything is so white, thought Henry. The sheets. The bandage around Franklin's stump, folded in triangles like a linen napkin. Even Franklin's skin—white. It was as if he had never been out in the sun, as if he had never scrambled on a rugby field.

Henry's mother dropped him off at Whittier Academy.

American History, still studying the explorations of those True American Adventurers, Lewis and Clark.

Language Arts, reading the "Prologue" to *The Canterbury Tales*, trying to remember the distinguishing characteristics of every pilgrim—and there were a bunch.

Life Science, a black-and-white film on the migration patterns of sea turtles.

Sea turtles!

Government, on how congressional districts are drawn up within states.

"You know, Sanborn," Henry said at lunch, "do you ever have the feeling that nothing we do here really matters?"

Sanborn took a bite out of his sandwich. It was grilled chicken. Henry watched it hungrily. "You just figured this out?" said Sanborn.

"No, I mean really, *really* doesn't matter."

Sanborn took another bite of his grilled-chicken sandwich. Henry fingered his lettuce-and-bologna sandwich.

"Don't get all cosmic, Henry. That gets really weird really quick. Besides, it does matter. Did you know that grilled chicken tastes a whole lot better than bologna?"

"So you're a better person because you know about the migration patterns of sea turtles."

"If Lewis and Clark hadn't discovered whatever it was they discovered . . . I don't know, we'd all be living on the East Coast or something. And if *The Canterbury Tales* hadn't been written, there would be one less good story in the world—and don't make that face. You know it was good—even if it is Delderfield reading it. And if sea turtles didn't migrate . . ."

"Yeah, what if the sea turtles didn't migrate?"

"Then the world would be a less beautiful place, and that *would* matter. Especially to the sea turtles." Sanborn finished his grilled-chicken sandwich and licked the mayonnaise off his fingers.

"Especially to the sea turtles?"

Sanborn nodded. "Especially to the sea turtles."

"You are a piece of work, you know that, Sanborn?"

Sanborn stood and held his arms wide open. "The finest craftsmanship around," he said.

Henry chucked the rest of his bologna sandwich at him, and

got hollered at first by Sanborn and then by cranky Coach Santori—who was the cafeteria monitor that day (which explained why he was cranky)—and then by Sanborn again.

When he got home that afternoon after crew practice—and after only one holler from perfect coxswain Brandon Sheringham, and after running the eight barefoot laps ordered by Coach Santori because he threw food in the cafeteria—the green sea was wild. Henry went down to tie up his kayak even higher—Black Dog took one look at the waves and wouldn't come down to the cove with him. Henry was amazed to see how greedy the sea was, pulling at the sand as if it would suck out the whole of Cape Ann.

All the late afternoon, the wind grew stronger, wailing around the cornices of the house, gusting so fiercely that the great oak beams shuddered, remembering what a storm could do. Black Dog, curled up tightly in her quilt, watched the casement window with wide eyes, whining when the wind shrieked high, and then raising her head when the first bands of rain blew down, so thick and solid that Henry could not tell if the darkening day was the coming night or the coming storm.

At supper—Black Dog huddled beneath the dining room table—Henry's mother decided not to go in to the hospital to visit Franklin. Instead, she and Henry went to watch the storm come in. But it was hailing now, and the ice beat at their faces, so it was hard to see. When Henry's mother shone a flashlight past the black boulders, it seemed as if the entire cove had collapsed and the waves were rolling across what had once been sand. But with the dark and the hail and the shrieking wind, it was hard to be sure.

They did not stay out long.

Black Dog was waiting for them in the kitchen, her tail below her belly and her ears looking as if someone had pulled them down and tied them beneath her chin. She yelped when the power flickered, and yelped again when it went off entirely.

Never before had Henry seen the house absolutely darkened.

He and his parents found candles and lit them. They called up to Louisa, who called back that she was fine and they could leave her alone. So they went and sat in the north parlor. The rain flooded the windows, falling like drapes. The wind was loud enough that they had to shout at each other, and the water dashed so hard against the house that Henry began to wonder if it was the waves, and not just the rain, that were reaching up the ledges.

They tried to play Scrabble, which is hard to do by candlelight, and which no one except Henry's mother and Franklin liked to play—his mother because she was so good at it, Franklin because he could be aggressive at anything.

"D-I-S-A-S-T-E-R," she spelled out for them, setting down each tile precisely. "And on a triple word score."

Henry's father sighed.

Black Dog whined.

Henry held one of his tiles up to the candlelight and stared at it.

A sudden silence; then the wind whipped around the eaves of the house and rushed down through the chimneys, moaning and howling as if it had lost its way.

"That's enough for tonight," said Henry's mother. She took the tile from Henry's hand.

Henry went upstairs with a candle to do his homework. Black Dog followed, flopping belly-up in front of him as they went down the hall—and even up the stairs—until finally Henry set the candle on the chinaware shelves and picked her up just so he could make some headway. He laid her down in her quilt—her legs got all scrambled in her eagerness to get covered—and he retrieved the candle. But when he sat down at his desk, Black Dog leaped from the bed and curled beside his feet—which he gladly snuggled beneath her warm body.

He started in. But all the new shadows that the flickering candle called out from the corners of his room began to spook him, and it is hard to do pre-algebraic equations when you are spooked, even just a little. It's especially hard to do pre-algebraic equations when you are pretty sure that they matter even less than the "Prologue" to *The Canterbury Tales*—which he was supposed to be prepared to translate up to the lines "Now have I toold you shortly, in a clause,/ Th'estaat, th'array, the nombre, and eek the cause/ Why that assembled was this compaignye"— which, Henry told Black Dog, took a lot of guts to write, since Chaucer had written seven hundred lines before this one and there was nothing "shortly" about it.

So Henry tried calling Sanborn—at least they could do the problems together—but the phones were out, too.

Lightning, flashing full and fast across the sky. Thunder over the sea, louder than all the waves on the stones.

Henry put his pencil down. He looked outside into the flooded darkness. "I guess we may as well get ready for bed," he said.

Black Dog leaped from beneath the desk and jumped back onto her quilt. She pawed at it, then sprawled down into a heap.

Henry changed into shorts and blew out the candle. But before he got into bed, he looked out the window again, and then went over to the glass doors and peered through. The rain was crashing onto the stone balcony, and past that there was nothing but rock and water for uncounted miles.

He reached out his hand for the doorknob.

Lightning again, turning all the glass white for a second. Black Dog whining in her quilt. Thunder, bellowing and licking its chops so loudly that Henry felt the vibrations in his bare feet.

He let his hand drop. He shivered, then got into bed and pulled as much of the quilt as Black Dog would let him have over himself. He shivered again.

Lying there, Henry wondered what would have happened to Chaucer's pilgrims heading to Canterbury in a storm like this one. And what would have happened to Lewis and Clark in the thunder and lightning? Would they have turned back and headed for shelter in St. Louis?

And where do sea turtles go in a storm, so that they can keep their beautiful selves safe and away from Trouble?

Lightning, and then thunder again. Very close.

Henry got up. Black Dog raised her head and perked her ears high. Henry crossed the room, and with a jerk he opened both glass doors and stepped out onto the stone balcony.

It was even wilder than he had imagined, but warmer, too. The hail had stopped, but the rain beat against him so that in less than a moment he was completely wet. He held out his arms—which was not easy, so strong was the wind—and felt the entire planetary atmosphere pushing against the house, against him. He staggered. But even so, he stepped to the edge of the balcony and looked down. The waves, freighted with crashing tops, threw themselves against the rocks like suicides.

And in the darkness and noise and space, Henry was all

alone—until Black Dog came and gently stood beside him, leaning against his dripping legs.

She whined only a little bit.

Henry reached down and scratched her behind her immediately wet ears. Together, they watched the storm torment the night, and even when the hail came again with its piercing cold pricks, they watched, until finally Black Dog wasn't whining just a little bit. So they went back into Henry's room and closed the glass doors. Henry fetched a towel from his bathroom and dried off Black Dog—though not before she shook herself to spread most of the rain around the room—and then Henry dried himself off, too, even though he hadn't realized that he was down to his last towel and now it was sort of soggy and doggy.

Henry and Black Dog slept well that night, lying close together, while the storm ground its teeth, and threw its tantrums, and snatched at anything that could move—including Henry's kayak, which it grabbed from its tie-up by the high rocks and sucked away from shore, thrashing it along the tops of the waves until it sank into a silence deep and still.

By morning, the storm had passed and the sky had hued to an opal lavender. Black Dog, who had slept in a pretty damp quilt, was ready for the new day, and so was Henry—after he found a new towel and showered. He dried his hair out on the stone balcony, Black Dog sitting beside him. It seemed as if they were on a different planet. The sea was a spring blue, and the high rocks were drying in the morning sun. Seagulls flew everywhere, squawking and screeching over what the storm had dragged up from the ocean bed. The horizon curved with geometric purpose.

Henry's mother was not in the kitchen when Henry and Black

Dog got down. In fact, she didn't seem to be anywhere in the house. Henry went outside and looked in the carriage house— the BMW and Fiat were still parked there.

He finally found her in the back gardens, on the path that led down to Salvage Cove. She stood, just looking, and when Henry and Black Dog came up, he could see why.

Most of the beach within the cove was gone. Close in, the black boulders had been torn down into a jumble. Between them and the far end of the cove, only a small strip of sand remained.

And at the far end lay uncovered the framing and decking of an old and ruined ship.

The waves were still high, so Black Dog would not go down, but Henry and his mother clambered into the new landscape and across to the wreckage. Silt covered much of the ship's backbone and rib cage, but there was no mistaking the beams that jutted up out of the sand, warped and twisted around the collapsed deck planks. The prow had come loose and lay flat, and the stern work lay in ruin. But most of the ship was still pretty much in place. Inside the rib cage, barrel staves, strewn planks, and the stumps of two thick masts emerged from the sand, all covered by clumps of dark seaweed.

Henry reached out to touch the end of one of the curved ribs. It was charred with fire. In fact, all of the ribs were charred. The decking was licked black along its edges.

"Who knows how long this has been buried here," said Henry's mother, "and we never knew it."

Henry stepped inside the rib cage—"Careful," said his mother, "there may be something sharp"—and he kicked at the sand as if to release the ship. But most of the sand was hard and solid, like sediment. It would take a whole lot more than kicking at it.

So he decided to pull away some of the clinging seaweed from a board pegged along the ribs. But even this was slow work, since the wind had thrown the seaweed in armloads and tied it in knots. He pulled at it anyway, and when one big knot finally came loose, Henry glimpsed a metallic black beneath, and heard an iron clunk.

"I think I've found something," he called, and his mother—and Black Dog, who couldn't stand being left alone above the cove—came over. Black Dog stuck her snout into the seaweed and sniffed cautiously, her back legs tense and ready to bolt if anything should turn up.

Henry pulled off the remaining seaweed, and more and more of the metal began to show, rounding into curves, and then a ring of circles, and then a mostly decayed clasp that, at one time, must have opened and closed. Henry looked up and down the stout board. Clumps of seaweed had knotted themselves along its length, all at the same height, all clinging to the chains and clasps fastened deep into the plank.

"Chains," said Henry. "This must have been the cargo hold. They would have tied up animals here, probably. Maybe cows to transport. Or sheep."

His mother reached for the clasp and hefted it up; probably it was heavier than she had expected. "No," she said, "sheep would have been in pens. And for the cows, they would have used ropes, not these." Some of the iron flaked away in her fingers.

Then, suddenly, she dropped the clasp she had been holding.

Henry looked at the chain again. He looked at the size of the clasp, and thought about what it might go around, what it might hold in the dark and sunless hold of that ship.

Black Dog backed away.

Henry felt a tightening at his throat.

He looked back up at his house. His father was standing at the library window, looking down at them. His hands were up to his face.

She gave him a collection of Keats. In the autumn, you have to read Keats, she told him. And so he did, late at night, after his brother had gone to sleep. He hid Keats deep in his heart. "It sure must be almost the highest bliss of human-kind, when to thy haunts two kindred spirits flee," he whispered into the dark.

But his father looked at him as if he knew. "Remember, you were Cambodian before you were American," he told him. His eyes were hard. And now, when they worked after school, his father turned to work with his brother—even on those jobs where he was too young.

He worked alone. With Keats hidden in his heart. And her there as well.

5

MR. CHARLES EDWARD CHURCHILL, who was the Smiths' lawyer, recommended that the family not do anything about the ship until he had investigated the legal rights of ownership. Though the wreck was clearly within the boundaries of the Smiths' property, the Commonwealth of Massachusetts might have jurisdiction over finds of a historical nature that might render null the rights of individual ownership. (Mr. Churchill always talked like this.) There would most likely be local ordinances that would need to be consulted, and assuredly federal codes as well. So the Smiths, he insisted, should not advertise in any way information about the find until he had finished his research—though by the time that Mrs. Smith gave Henry this cautionary news, he had talked about it all over Whittier Academy, and Mr. DiSalva was so excited that he was already planning a Whittier field trip to Salvage Cove. The find, he pointed out, might even explain the cove's name.

"We'll need some experts on early American shipping to help us," he said, and so it was probably his phone call to the Blythbury-by-the-Sea Historical Society that brought the society's president, Dr. Cavendish, and the society's corresponding secretary, Mrs. Lodge, and the society's librarian, Mrs. Templeton, out to the cove the very afternoon after the storm.

Henry and Black Dog led them down—Henry held Black Dog's collar because Mrs. Templeton did not like dogs and could not understand why this particularly ugly and rambunctious one should not be in a cage—and though the members of the historical society were all unhappy about the steep angle of the descent, they gasped in awe and delight when they saw the ship's stark ribs. They pronounced themselves excited.

Probably it was Mrs. Lodge who, as the society's corresponding secretary, called the *Blythbury-by-the-Sea Chronicle* after their visit. The next morning, the reporter from the paper drove up just as Mrs. Smith was driving out of the carriage house to take Henry to Whittier. The reporter pulled up beside them, but Henry's mother was firm. No, he could not have an interview. No, he could not go down to the cove to take pictures. No, she had no comment to make, and would he please leave now, as he could see that they were very busy.

"This wreck is a hugely important historical find," said the reporter. "Don't you think that you owe it to—"

"No, I don't," said Mrs. Smith. "Haven't you intruded enough?" She rolled up her window, waited for the reporter to back out, and then she and Henry drove to school.

But the picture of the ship that appeared on the front page of the *Blythbury-by-the-Sea Chronicle* the next day showed that the reporter didn't believe that he had intruded enough. "He obviously waited until we left, then came back and went down into the cove," said Henry's mother at dinner.

"I suppose so," said Henry's father.

"You didn't see anyone?"

"Not a soul," said Henry's father.

His mother sighed.

Henry quietly ate his two fresh scrod fillets—which were fresh because the fish they came from had been swimming off Cape Ann while Henry had been in Language Arts that morning, trying to figure out why stupid Chaucer gave the stupid Squire some cruel locks. He usually ate four and sometimes five scrod fillets, but Henry's mother had left them out for just a minute, and Black Dog had smelled them, and so they were all on half-rations.

"Wouldn't you have seen someone prowling around the property?" Henry's mother said.

Henry's father did not answer.

Henry's mother wondered aloud why Black Dog hadn't said anything, and what good was a dog if she couldn't chase Trouble away?

Black Dog, happily filled with fresh scrod fillets, lay under the dining room table and did not answer.

Mr. Charles Edward Churchill was not pleased when he saw the picture of the ship in the *Blythbury-by-the-Sea Chronicle,* and he drove over that night to express his disappointment that they had not heeded his advice and had even encouraged publicity— "We never encouraged publicity," said Henry's mother—and allowed a field trip! Mr. Churchill hoped that they would be more circumspect in the other matter that he had taken up on their behalf.

"The other matter?" said Henry's father.

Henry's mother coughed quietly.

"The matter of the pretrial hearing for Chay Chouan," said Mr. Churchill.

"Oh," said Mr. Smith. "Of course."

"You understand that you all absolutely must attend the pretrial hearing," he said.

"Is it absolutely necessary that *all* of us attend?" said Mr. Smith.

Mr. Churchill nodded like God. "I would go so far as to call it mandatory," he said.

"Louisa will never come," said Henry.

"Then Louisa must prepare herself, because she must come," said Mr. Churchill.

"Louisa hardly comes downstairs anymore," said Henry. He didn't say that his father never went outside the house anymore, either.

Mr. Churchill shook his head. "The judge needs to see a family that has been forever changed by an egregious incident," he said. "Everyone must be there."

"Not 'forever,'" said Henry's mother. "Franklin is going to get well."

Mr. Churchill inclined his head to acknowledge this, but Henry could see that he didn't believe at all that Franklin was going to get well.

Henry wanted to smack his jowled face.

"Nevertheless," Mr. Churchill repeated, "you all must be at the hearing. Louisa as well."

So a week and a half later, Henry's parents and Louisa got into the BMW. Inside the carriage house, a yowling Black Dog was tied to the tool shelves. Henry figured the rope would keep her busy long enough for him to lug three bags of dry cement against the carriage house doors, then for him to scramble into the car, and then for the car to get out to the road. By that time, Black Dog would be at the carriage house doors, planning her escape. They left the service door to the house unlocked, since if Black Dog didn't get in that way, she would try to find another, more expensive, way in—maybe through the armorial windows, for example.

They drove out beyond the back gardens—*yowl, yowl, yowl* behind them—and along the driveway and past the cove, and Henry looked down on the bones of the ship, streaky with salt as they dried in the new sunlight. Members of the Blythbury-by-the-Sea Historical Society had been at work on it, and now most of the backbone of the ship was naked and exposed, along with half a dozen orange barrel hoops, five cutlasses (whose placements were marked but which Dr. Cavendish had taken with him because Mr. Smith had let him—which was not Henry's recommendation), the long barrels of two small cannon, and the stout board along the backbone, whose chains and clasps were now cleaned of their seaweed coverings.

Henry put his hand up to his neck, and shivered.

He missed his kayak. He wished he were heading out in it now, on this green late-April morning, the waves swishing gently against the shore, each one bringing back a few grains of the sand that had been sucked away. He wished he could feel the waves rolling beneath him—the waves and the kayak and his body, one thing.

But instead, he was in the silent car, dressed as if for a Father Brewood sermon, driving in midday traffic, heading for the Manchester courthouse and Chay Chouan's pretrial hearing. His father, in the front passenger seat, was staring blankly out the window. Louisa, next to Henry, was pressed against the seat and already crying silently.

He wished he was in his kayak.

Mr. Churchill met them in the courthouse lobby and escorted them to a paneled waiting room that had only a single high window in it. He led Henry's parents in, and asked Henry and Louisa to wait outside for just a few minutes. He closed the door.

Louisa sat down on a bench in the hall, and Henry sat next to her. She was still silently crying—Henry figured that Mr. Churchill would be pleased at the effect. He reached over to take her hand, but she moved abruptly away from him and wrapped her arms around herself.

Henry looked at her huddled and tight shape. His heart almost stopped. He almost began to weep himself. But instead, he leaned over to her. "Do you remember watching *The Wizard of Oz?*" he said.

Louisa turned and looked at him.

"Whenever the Wicked Witch came, I'd hold your hand, and we'd duck under the blankets we'd rigged up between two couches. Remember? And we'd wait until the music changed. And when it did, that meant Dorothy and Toto were back on the Yellow Brick Road again. And we'd come out from the blanket fort."

Louisa nodded, even almost smiled. "And then we'd say—"

"Oz," Henry finished.

"Oz," Louisa said. "Because everything was okay for now."

"Even though we knew we'd go under the blanket when the Wicked Witch showed up again."

"But we could breathe until that happened," Louisa said.

Henry held his hand out. Louisa looked down and took it. "Tell me when we can say 'Oz,'" she said.

"I'll let you know." And they leaned in toward each other.

This was how Mr. Churchill found them, and he was clearly disappointed—Louisa was not crying. He led them both into the small waiting room, and they sat down across from their parents at a smooth table. "Now," said Mr. Churchill, "to what all of you are required to do." He folded his hands together. "This is a pretrial hearing. That means the judge will be deciding whether there is sufficient evidence to recommend that Chay Chouan be bound over for trial on charges of aggravated assault and leaving the scene of an accident resulting in serious bodily injury. The hearing will probably be brief, since neither party is contesting the facts. It is still important, however, that you as a family present yourselves to the judge in a way that will incline him toward the prosecutor's position. So . . ."

Mr. Churchill described how the Smiths ought to present themselves in a way that would incline the judge toward the prosecutor's position. They would be, he said, the Grieving Family.

By the end, Henry wanted to hit his jowled face again.

Mr. Churchill looked at his watch. "Questions? No? Then I suggest we all go in."

And so they did.

The courtroom smelled a little like St. Anne's Episcopal Church without the scent of the beeswax candles. The oiled wood, the slightly worn cushions, the smell of reverence and formality everywhere. Henry settled into his seat as if it were a Sunday morning. Except for one of the Blythbury-by-the-Sea policemen, the reporter from the *Blythbury-by-the-Sea Chronicle*, Dr. Giles— who nodded at them—and Dr. Sheringham—principal of Longfellow Prep and father of Brandon Sheringham, perfect coxswain, and clearly the genetic source of his nose—the courtroom was mostly empty. Again, like St. Anne's.

Then the Chouans came in, walking behind their lawyer.

They sat down on the opposite side of the courtroom. Mrs. Chouan was a tiny woman, and she walked like a wary bird, a short bit at a time, looking down at the floor as if she could pretend that nothing else was around. Mr. Chouan was small, too, but with forearms like posts—which anyone could see because they stuck far out of a jacket that didn't fit him. He walked behind Mrs. Chouan; as he came in, the sight of the policeman made him take his wife's arm.

The Chouans did not look at the Smiths. Henry could not take his eyes away from them.

The Chouans sat—still warily—and then one of the doors at the front of the courtroom opened, and Mrs. Chouan gave a short cry that she stifled into her husband's shoulder. Chay Chouan came into the room with the bailiff and a policeman behind him. He was dressed in an awful orange jumpsuit that was too big for him. His head was down. His hands were manacled.

Henry looked at Louisa, who was about to start bawling out loud. Mr. Churchill will be so pleased, he thought.

Chay Chouan's lawyer left his parents and went to Chay. He walked with him to the defendant's table and they sat down together. Chay held out his hands, and the policeman unlocked the manacles and then went back to the door and stood at attention, one hand on a hefty revolver at his side, ready, Henry figured, for anything desperate. The prosecutor came in, nodded to the Smiths, and spoke briefly with Mr. Churchill. Then he sat and arranged papers around his table.

Chay Chouan rubbed at his wrists.

It looked, Henry thought, like the "Prologue"! People introducing themselves around the court, like Chaucer announcing that he's going to tell the condition of each one of the pilgrims "er that I ferther in this tale pace"—and not giving away that he's going to take a few hundred lines to do it. Except here, Henry was himself one of the pilgrims.

And everything mattered.

When the prosecutor finished arranging his papers, everyone was still. For the next five minutes—a little longer than it once would have taken Franklin to run a mile—no one moved. No one seemed to breathe. Even Louisa was still. It was as if they were in a cruel lock, Henry thought.

So when the judge finally came in—"All rise," called the bailiff—Henry was relieved. The Prologue was over. He could be the Grieving Brother pilgrim—and then get out of there.

"This is the pretrial hearing for the People versus Chay Chouan, on the charges of aggravated assault and leaving the scene of an accident," announced the judge. "Mr. Quincy, please call your first witness."

And he did. The Blythbury-by-the-Sea policeman walked to the witness stand, raised his hand, took his oath, sat, and told what everyone in the courtroom already knew. How he had come upon Chay Chouan running down the road and waving his arms to get his attention. How Chay Chouan appeared very excited. How he had said that there had been an accident, that he had fallen asleep at the wheel of his pickup, that he had hit someone running on the side of the road. How he had taken Chay Chouan into his patrol car and how they had driven back to the scene of the accident and found Franklin Smith alone and unconscious. How he had called an ambulance and, while they were waiting, worked with the defendant to put pressure on the bleeding. How the ambulance arrived within six minutes, and following its departure, how he had read Chay Chouan his rights and then placed him under arrest based upon his admission that he had struck the victim. How he had taken the defendant to the Blythbury-by-the-Sea police station, where he had called his family. How the next morning, in the presence of his lawyer, Chay Chouan had made a formal statement, acknowledging the fact that he had struck the victim when he fell asleep while driving alone, back to his family's home in Merton.

"Do you have a transcript of the statement made by Mr. Chouan?" asked the judge.

The policeman took the transcript out of a manila folder.

"Give it to the bailiff, please. Mr. Chouan, I'd like you to look at this transcript to be sure that it is faithful to the statements that you gave that morning. If it is, then I would ask that both you and Mr. Giaconda sign and date it."

The bailiff handed the statement to Chay, who set it down on the table. He and his lawyer read it over slowly. Chay nodded. He took the pen that Mr. Giaconda handed him and signed the transcript. Mr. Giaconda signed as well. The bailiff took the statement and handed it to the judge.

"Is there anything else from this witness?" asked the judge.

"No, your honor."

"Then, Mr. Giaconda, your witness."

Mr. Giaconda rose—a little. He was short, but he walked as though he dared anyone to tell him so. He stood next to the policeman on the witness stand, facing Chay.

"Are you aware of any other police record for Chay Chouan?"

"No."

"Any tickets?"

"No."

"Speeding tickets? Parking tickets?"

"No."

"Tickets for broken taillights?"

"No."

"So, before this accident, Chay Chouan had no encounters with any law enforcement officers of the Commonwealth."

"None that I am aware of."

"In your police report, you wrote that when you arrived on the accident scene, there was a bandage on Franklin Smith's arm. What was that bandage made from?"

"It was a shirt."

"Was Chay Chouan wearing a shirt on the night he found you?"

"No."

"May we assume that Chay Chouan tried to bandage the wound at the scene?"

"That is what I stated in my report."

"Yes, you did. So Chay Chouan bandaged the wound and then went to find help, finally flagging you down and driving back to the scene with you. Officer, would you say that the charge of fleeing the scene of an accident is an appropriate charge for these actions?"

"Objection," said Mr. Quincy. "Calls for legal opinion."

"I'll restate. In general, is it the case that a person charged with fleeing the scene of an accident is trying to avoid complicity in that accident?"

"Yes, in general."

"Were the actions of Mr. Chouan on that night consistent with the actions of someone trying to avoid complicity in an accident?"

"Not to my mind, no."

"You testified that Chay Chouan was arrested after he admitted that he had struck the victim. Let us be clear on this point: Did that admission come before or after you had read him his Miranda rights?"

"He blurted it out when he first came up."

"So the answer to my question is, *Before* you read him his Miranda rights."

"Objection," said Mr. Quincy. "The witness is capable of answering the questions without Mr. Giaconda's helpful editing."

"I'll repeat the question without editing. *Before* or *after*?"

"Before."

"Thank you." Mr. Giaconda sat down.

The prosecutor called Dr. Giles next, but Henry could tell by looking at the judge that things had already been decided. All he needed was enough to go to trial, and the policeman had already given enough. But it seemed as if the court wanted to "ferther in this tale pace."

Dr. Giles spoke about the amputation of the mangled left arm below the shoulder, the damage to the rib cage, the collapse of one lung, and the trauma to Franklin Smith's brain, its indeterminate activity. When Mr. Quincy asked if the brain had been permanently impaired, the doctor said that it was his medical opinion that it might be irreversibly impaired, but he reminded the court that, as yet, the scans were still indeterminate. When the prosecutor asked if Franklin Smith's life was in danger, the doctor nodded.

"Can you give the court a percentage, Doctor, on his chances for a full recovery?"

Henry felt the Grieving Mother pilgrim stiffen beside him.

"Typically, patients who have experienced the kind of trauma that Franklin Smith has experienced do not survive twenty-four hours. That already makes this case remarkable. And I understand that Mr. Smith was an exceptional athlete. That, too, works in his favor. I would say that the chances for a full recovery are very guarded."

"Thank you," said the prosecutor.

"Are there any questions for the defense?" asked the judge.

Mr. Giaconda rose again.

"Doctor, you said that the chances for a full recovery are very guarded. What does 'very guarded' mean?"

"It means that we cannot be sure that a full recovery is likely."

"Is 'possible' a word you could use?"

Dr. Giles considered this. "Under certain circumstances, it might be a word I could use. I have seen the unlikely happen."

"Thank you, Doctor," said Mr. Giaconda.

Dr. Giles walked back to his seat.

Unlikely, thought Henry. Seen the unlikely happen. He doesn't think that Franklin is going to make it. He thinks Franklin is going to die but he doesn't want to say so.

And for the first time—for the first time *really*—Henry wondered if it might be so.

It was as sweet as he had imagined. Just riding together. Just talking. Laughing, even. It was so easy, with the sky dark. No moon. No stars. Just talking.

He had never believed this would happen. She was from Blythbury. It couldn't happen.

But it had. And he was telling her things about himself he had never told anyone. That he loved Keats. That he wrote poetry him-self. He told her that he wrote poetry.

And when he had told her, she touched his arm, and he knew that she was smiling.

Maybe this is what she had hoped for, too. Hope rose in him like a singing, fluting bird.

And then, the runner on the side of the road. Eyes locking and eyes turning and eyes coming back again. Hard.

A scream, another, and blood. How could there be so much blood? And the arm! Where had it gone? The arm!

Go home! Go home now! Go! Now!

Don't see this.

And then, alone, the smell of the blood.

The smell brought it all back. How had he forgotten that smell? How it rose up to him from the sunlit fields—from what was lying in the fields. His tiny mother trying to hide his eyes. But she could do nothing about the smell, or the heated buzzing of the gathering flies.

Desperately wrapping the stump, and then, and then, the other sound he remembered—or was it the sound he was hearing now? Moans.

6

DR. SHERINGHAM TOOK THE STAND. He sat like a principal, crossing his legs and perching his folded hands on his upper knee. He reached down to adjust his pant cuffs over his black socks. He reached up to adjust his yellow-and-blue tie. Then he waited for Mr. Quincy.

"Dr. Sheringham, you are the principal of the Henry Wadsworth Longfellow Preparatory High School in Blythbury-by-the-Sea."

"Yes, I am," said Dr. Sheringham.

"You are familiar with both Franklin Smith and Chay Chouan?"

"The administration and faculty of Longfellow Preparatory make it a point to be familiar with all of our students."

"Dr. Sheringham, please tell the court the circumstances of Chay Chouan's enrollment."

"Chay Chouan and his parents met with me. They explained that they were hoping for an education superior to what they were finding in their local public school. I described our curriculum to them, as well as the many college and university connections that Longfellow could offer. They seemed very pleased. Chay Chouan matriculated the following fall term as a sophomore."

"Were there any difficulties when he came to your school?"

"At that time of his matriculation, he was two years older than most sophomore students, due to his background. There were the expected academic difficulties coming out of a public school education. We anticipated some language issues, but none of his teachers felt that these were significant enough to warrant special help."

"How about social difficulties, Dr. Sheringham? Chay Chouan is from a very different background than most of your students."

"He is, and we anticipated some problems there as well. There were some reports of incidents"—Mrs. Chouan leaned over the railing to Chay's lawyer—"but nothing more than the high spirits of boys welcoming a new student into their school. They quickly quieted down, and Chay became part of the Longfellow community."

"There was a more serious problem last January, however."

Dr. Sheringham nodded. "There was. Last January there was an altercation in the North Gym locker room in which Chay Chouan and another boy had to be separated."

"The other boy was Franklin Smith."

"Yes."

"What was that altercation about?"

"Students at Longfellow do not tattle on each other."

"Did you investigate further?"

"There was no need. The boys shook hands in my office. I considered the affair closed."

"Do you consider the affair closed now?"

"Objection," said Chay Chouan's lawyer. "Calls for opinion."

"Sustained," said the judge.

"Do you believe that the two boys parted as friends?"

"It would be naive to think that," said Dr. Sheringham. "But they certainly understood what was expected of them in terms of their behavior at Longfellow."

"Thank you," said the prosecutor to Dr. Sheringham. "Your witness."

Mr. Giaconda walked across to Dr. Sheringham.

"Dr. Sheringham, you are very proud of your school and its students."

"I am."

"Do you not find it remarkable that Chay Chouan, after spending most of his childhood in a refugee camp in a war-torn country and after traveling for thousands of miles to escape such camps, was able to enter a school as prestigious as yours and do well in his classes?"

"I find all the students at Longfellow to be remarkable."

"But don't you find it even more remarkable when one who has had none of the advantages of the others still succeeds there?"

"Not particularly, no. Many of our students overcome handicaps to improve themselves and to succeed at Longfellow."

"So, many of your students have had their sisters shot in front of them?"

"No, but . . ."

"Or their brothers taken by force?"

"No."

"Or been forced to flee their homes with nothing and arrive in a foreign country without the ability to speak a single word of that country's language?"

"No."

"Dr. Sheringham, on the first day of Chay's matriculation, a group of students met him in the lobby of the school and bab-bled at him, pretending to speak an Asian language. Would you call this the high spirits of boys welcoming a new student into their school?"

"I realize that Mr. Chouan, who was not familiar with our traditions, may have interpreted this to be more hostile than it was meant to be."

"Dr. Sheringham, were you aware that a week later, on September fifteenth of last year, Chay Chouan's locker was broken into?"

"Yes, I was made aware of the incident."

"Can you tell the court what was done to all of Chay's books?"

"They were spray-painted."

"They were spray-painted red, to be precise. Why do you suppose that particular color was used?"

"I don't know."

"Do you know the cost of replacing those books?"

"Textbooks are expensive. I would imagine over one hundred dollars."

"One hundred and sixty-five dollars. Did the school pay to replace these books?"

"The expense of textbooks is assumed by each of our families."

"This is quite an expense to pay twice, wouldn't you say? Are we still in 'high spirits'?"

Mr. Quincy rose. "Objection, your honor. In addition to moving toward badgering this witness, Mr. Giaconda has shown no relevance."

"Your honor, Mr. Quincy opened the issue of the relation-ship between my client and Mr. Smith by implying that Mr.

Chouan's altercation with Mr. Smith may have had something to do with the accident we are investigating today. It is only fair for the defense to explore the atmosphere in the school that may have led to that altercation."

"Mr. Quincy, this is a line of questioning that you have opened. Proceed, Mr. Giaconda."

"Dr. Sheringham, do you call the destruction of one hundred and sixty-five dollars' worth of textbooks 'high spirits'?"

"All schools are marked by pranks, Mr. Giaconda. It is a sign of an imaginative and energetic school body."

"In October, the *Longfellow Prep Ledger* ran an editorial against Cambodian immigration into the United States." Mr. Giaconda walked back to his table and pulled out a copy of the newspaper from a manila folder. He turned to Dr. Sheringham. "The cartoon depicts a Cambodian refugee stepping off a boat and into the halls of Henry Wadsworth Longfellow Preparatory High School. Have you seen this cartoon or shall I show it to you now?"

"I have seen it."

"Would you like to comment on the depiction of the Cambodian immigrant?"

"At Longfellow Prep we teach the values of responsibility and integrity to all of our students. We also teach the value of freedom of expression and freedom of the press. We stand by that union of responsibility and freedom."

"You are suggesting that the cartoon in question represents responsibility and integrity?"

"Balanced with freedom, yes."

"How many students from Cambodia are currently enrolled at your school?"

"The figure in the cartoon is meant to be representative, not an individual. It is a political argument, not a personal one."

"And clearly this is one more way that an imaginative and energetic school body is bringing Chay Chouan into the group."

"Objection," said Mr. Quincy.

"I'll withdraw the statement. Dr. Sheringham, I have cited cases of what you call 'high spirits.' This is not how the Chouan family saw them. They saw them as deliberate harassment. I have records here of eight more such incidents. How many of these did you investigate at their request?"

Dr. Sheringham unclasped his perched hands, uncrossed his legs. "Excuse me?"

"How many of these incidents in which Chay Chouan was the recipient of harassment did you investigate?"

"I read the reports on all of them and spoke with Mrs. Chouan three times. Language issues prevented any kind of resolution. But I dispute vigorously your description of these events as 'harassment.'"

"What followed your reading of the reports?"

"I filed the reports as I normally do."

"Well, not as you normally do. Last February, you investigated a reported harassment of another student, did you not?"

Dr. Sheringham crossed his legs again.

"Louisa Smith," said Mr. Giaconda. "She, too, had a locker that was broken into."

Dr. Sheringham nodded.

"She had a shirt that was damaged. Correct? I would like a verbal confirmation, please."

"Yes."

"How was the shirt damaged?"

"Red paint was sprayed on it."

"I'm sorry, Dr. Sheringham. What was the color of the paint?"

"Red."

"The cost of replacement for that shirt was fifty-six dollars. Longfellow paid for that replacement, did it not?"

"Yes."

"After you investigated, you found that two girls had been involved in the incident. What was your response?"

"Vandalism is extremely rare, and we look upon it as a serious breach of school ethics. Each was suspended for five days, and their families were asked to reimburse the school for the cost of the replacement."

"Do you see this response on your part as being consistent with your response to the damage done to Chay Chouan's textbooks in September?"

"Different students and circumstances require different responses. The administration of a school is not a cookie-cutter business. It demands understanding and flexibility."

"Dr. Sheringham, how much money did the Smith family donate to the Henry Wadsworth Longfellow Preparatory High School last year?"

"Excuse me?"

"It's a perfectly simple question. How much money did the Smith family donate to the Henry Wadsworth Longfellow Preparatory High School last year?"

"I don't carry those figures with me."

"I do," said Mr. Giaconda. He walked back to the defense table and opened his notebook. He ran his finger down a pad and then whistled. Without turning around, he asked, "Would you say that the Smith family is one of your most important benefactors?"

"They have been exceedingly generous for a very long time, and Longfellow values their presence in our community more than I can say."

He turned around. "Does Longfellow Prep value their presence more than that of Chay Chouan?"

Dr. Sheringham did not answer.

"You can't say. Dr. Sheringham, do you find it remarkable that a student continually harassed since his matriculation would do everything he could to save another Longfellow student who was hurt?"

"I do not find that remarkable," said Dr. Sheringham. "The sense of communal responsibility is very strong at our school."

"Really?" said Mr. Giaconda. "I would say that statement is the most remarkable one we've heard yet."

"Objection," said Mr. Quincy.

"I'll withdraw," said Mr. Giaconda. "Dr. Sheringham, did you ever discover the cause of the altercation between Franklin Smith and Chay Chouan?"

"No."

"Never tried?"

"Never tried."

"So you do not know that Franklin Smith, in the company of four of the players on the Longfellow rugby team, attacked Chay Chouan in the North Gym locker room?"

"I do not respond to rumors."

"So you do not know that while the four rugby players pinned Chay Chouan against a bank of lockers, Franklin Smith punched him in the stomach to knock the air out of him, and then pressed his forearm against Chay Chouan's throat until he fell unconscious."

"As I told you, I do not respond to rumors."

"Or that they left him unconscious and alone on the locker room floor, not knowing whether he was severely injured. You must define 'communal responsibility' in very broad terms, Dr. Sheringham. Most people would call that 'an act of cowardice.'" Mr. Giaconda looked for a long time at the principal. Finally, he said, "Thank you, Dr. Sheringham," and turned back to his table.

But Henry did not look away. He stared at Dr. Sheringham. He felt Franklin's forearm against his neck, pressing. He heard his voice. "*You* have to handle that. *You're* ready to stand by yourself. *You* have to find the guy so it's *just the two of you*."

"*You* don't have any guts."

"An act of cowardice."

Henry tried to breathe again. He looked at Louisa. Her face was in her hands. He thought he could almost hear her moaning.

"Are there any witnesses for the defense?" asked the judge.

Mr. Giaconda looked back at the Chouans. Mr. Chouan shook his head, and Mr. Giaconda turned back to the judge. "None at this time," he said.

The judge arranged papers on his desk. He has even more than the prosecutor, thought Henry. Then he signed two, then three of the papers, looked at his watch, and signed another.

Henry heard the clock ticking on the back wall of the courtroom. He wondered why he hadn't heard it before. Louisa was quiet now beside him, but she reached over and took his hand. If only they had a blanket fort to climb under. If only the music changed. If only he didn't feel a terrible tightness against his neck.

Four rugby players held Chay Chouan down while Franklin . . .

The judge finished with his papers and looked up.

"It is the opinion of this court," he said, "that in the case of the People versus Chay Chouan, the charge of Assault Seven, leaving the scene of an accident, has no bearing and is dismissed. It is the further opinion of this court that the charge of Assault Six, aggravated assault, should stand. Chay Chouan is hereby bound over for trial on that charge, that trial commencing no less than eight weeks from this date. Bail is set at $300,000."

Mr. Giaconda jumped up. "Your honor, there is no danger that Chay Chouan will flee the jurisdiction of the court. I ask the court to set a bail in line with the family's financial circumstances."

"Mr. Quincy?" the judge asked.

The prosecutor rose. "Your honor, I would remind the court that this case might well involve a charge of homicide, depending upon future circumstances. I would also remind the court that the Chouan family has numerous connections remaining in Cambodia. Given this possibility, the court is bound to take reasonable steps to insure that Chay Chouan remains in its jurisdiction."

The judge nodded. "Bail is set at $300,000," he said. "This pretrial hearing is closed," and he banged his gavel.

"All rise," hollered the bailiff, and they all did. Slowly, without looking at anyone, the judge stood and left, followed by the bailiff. Then the policeman came back and stood beside Chay, who, Henry realized, had never raised his head through the entire hearing. He reached down, pulled at Chay's hands, and manacled them again. Then, finally, Chay did look up, and he turned to his mother. She reached over the rail, gently put her arms around his neck, and drew him to her. Her shoulders shook with the weight. His father stood stiffly, unmoving. Mr. Giaconda waited, and when Mr. Chouan finally drew his wife away, she whispered something to Chay, and Chay nodded. Then his head lowered. The policeman took his arm, and they headed for the door.

But just before they were gone, Chay looked back again. He looked across the courtroom—past the policeman, past the bailiff, past his parents, past his lawyer. And as Henry watched, Chay looked straight at Louisa—who had also looked up and who was staring at him, her arms so tight around herself that she looked as if she was trying to crush her own heart.

Then Chay turned his head, and he was gone.

The Smiths left the courtroom before the Chouans, careful not to look at them. In the courthouse lobby Mr. Churchill told them about the likely possibility of a plea bargain in the next day or so, especially since Chay Chouan had no past offenses.

"Do you mean," said Mrs. Smith, "that he could simply be freed?"

"No, no," said Mr. Churchill. "I mean that since no one is disputing the facts, it might be that the defense will want to avoid a trial and offer a plea of guilty in exchange for a reduction in the charges or in the sentence. On our part, it would avoid the complicating problem of the Miranda rights."

"Who would approve of the reduction?" Henry's mother asked.

"The prosecutor and the judge would both need to approve."

"Does our opinion matter?"

"It most certainly matters," said Mr. Churchill.

"And would anything change if . . . if Franklin's condition changed?"

"That would be negotiated as a part of the plea bargain."

It was, Henry thought, unfortunate that this was the moment that the Chouans walked into the courthouse lobby with Mr. Giaconda, and that Mrs. Chouan, seeing the Smiths, left her husband and walked over on her tiny steps to put her arm on Mrs. Smith's shoulder. "I am so sorry about your Franklin," she said. "Every day we pray for him."

"Thank you," said Mrs. Smith, cold as one of the marble pillars holding up the courthouse ceiling. "We do, too."

"My son, too," Mrs. Chouan said softly. She began to cry.

Louisa fled the courthouse lobby.

Henry watched his mother. He watched as she almost yielded. As she almost leaned down into Mrs. Chouan. As she almost began to weep herself.

Two mothers.

But his mother hardened, and she moved away from Mrs. Chouan's hand. She turned and left the lobby. And what could the rest of them do? They followed her out and found her behind the steering wheel in the car, stiff and cold, as if she might shatter with a touch. And Louisa was hunched as far against the side of the car as she could be, her arms over her head.

They drove to the hospital in silence. In silence, they gathered around the quiet, indeterminate Franklin—except for Louisa, who refused to come up. Franklin had been shaved and his hair was combed—parted on the wrong side. His hand and fingernails were clean—unnaturally clean, as if they belonged to a newborn. The machine behind him pumped rhythmically, and they watched Franklin's chest rise and fall.

Henry wanted Franklin to open his eyes. He willed Franklin to look at him, to remember the mountain.

To explain his forearm against the throat.

But Franklin was still. His chest rose and fell as his mother sat on the bed and told him what had happened in the courtroom. Henry and his father watched.

On the way out of the hospital, Henry told his parents that it was too late in the day to take him and Louisa to school, so they all went home instead. There, the carriage house doors were open and the bags of dry cement scattered. They parked the BMW and walked over to the house, where Black Dog met them happily at the open service door, wagging her entire rear end. The remnant of the rope was still tied to her collar, and she danced around and around, swirling it until Henry could grab hold and untie her.

They all went into the kitchen, which Black Dog had left untouched!

Louisa went up to her bedroom.

For lunch, Henry and his parents ate peanut-butter-and-honey sandwiches with tomato soup while Black Dog watched hopefully on her toes. And afterward, Henry climbed down into Salvage Cove—what was left of it—with Black Dog. Together they clambered between the ribs and into the belly of the ship and stood where the cargo must have been centuries ago, before she had been beached. All the chains and clasps were gone, taken by the Blythbury-by-the-Sea Historical Society so they might be preserved without further loss. Little yellow tabs marked where they had been. Henry ran his hands along the stout board, and then along the smooth, soft grain of the beams, reaching up to their charred tips.

Then, high on the wind, he heard his brother's word still

echoing, as though it had finally escaped the hospital room and was echoing up and down the New England coast: "Katahdin."

And suddenly, immediately and surely, Henry knew what he was going to do.

He was going to climb Katahdin. He was going to do what Franklin thought he could never do. Then he would come back and tell him, and Franklin would do the unlikely thing: He would get well.

He would climb Katahdin. Alone. Well, with Black Dog. And afterward, everything would be what it used to be before Trouble came.

A deep heat filled his guts. He would climb Katahdin.

In the dark, in the light, always imagining her face, remembering her face in the moments before the accident. Her laugh. Her easy wave. How her wave had been the first thing about her that told him all he needed to know.

How had his father guessed? "Remember, you were Cambodian before you were American." And so his father had taken his dog to teach him what he had to learn. He beat her. He made him watch. He starved her. He made him watch. "Learn how to be strong," he said. Then he took her away. "The dog is drowned," he said when he returned. "Learn to be cold inside."

But this was not what he learned, as his heart ached, and a drowsy numbness took hold.

He had not realized how much he had missed her face.

7

THE NEXT DAY, they waited for the plea bargain that Mr. Churchill expected.

Henry's mother said nothing about it when she picked up Henry and Sanborn at Whittier that afternoon, or when they dropped Sanborn off at his home. She said nothing about it to Sanborn's mother—who just about came out and asked but didn't quite dare. She said nothing about it when they drove home with the radio playing a ten-minute commercial for Terrian Green Dietary Drink with Turtle Egg White Supplement. She said nothing about it when they stopped outside the carriage house and Henry dragged the six new bags of dry cement away from the doors while Black Dog barked and romped inside.

But when they all got into the kitchen—even Black Dog— Henry's mother stood with her hands on the edge of the sink and began to cry. She would not be comforted. Not even when Louisa came downstairs—Henry could hardly believe it!—not even when Louisa came downstairs to cry beside her. And not even when Henry's father came out from the library as well— unshaven, hair uncombed, clothes the same as yesterday.

He took his wife up to their bedroom, but they walked as though they were behind a bailiff and heading toward prison.

When Louisa started to leave after them, Henry stopped her.

"At least help me figure out what we're going to put together for supper," he said.

"Supper?" said Louisa, as if she had forgotten that there ever had been such a thing. "There's not going to be any supper."

This was not a happy word for Black Dog, who whined and then flopped down with her belly up beside Louisa's feet and made herself look as pathetic as possible.

"If you don't want to help," said Henry, "at least keep me company. And—"

"All right," said Louisa. She sat down on a stool by the kitchen counter. "Happy?"

"Ecstatic."

"Good."

"Fine," said Henry. He opened the refrigerator door and looked in.

Louisa said nothing as he brought out several packages of celery, assorted peppers, a dozen eggs, a package of bologna—whose green edges could be trimmed off—a hunk of provolone—whose blue edges could be trimmed off—a package of bacon—whose gray edges could be . . . well, nothing could be done with it and Henry threw the thing out—cups of yogurt with suspicious expiration dates, a bag of baby carrots, and something wrapped in plastic that didn't need to be identified, just discarded.

"You could try an omelet," said Louisa.

"Good idea," said Henry.

He got out a bowl, put eight eggs into it, and handed it to Louisa, who looked at him. He waited, and finally she took the bowl, removed the eggs, and began to break them into it, one by one. He handed her a whisk, and she beat them. He poured some milk in, and she beat that as well. Then he cut up the peppers and the baby carrots, added an onion that had begun to sprout in the pantry, and grated the provolone—the parts that weren't blue. He looked into the garbage at the package of gray bacon again, and decided against it. Reluctantly. He looked in the freezer and found some frozen spicy sausages; he took out eight and put them into a skillet to fry.

The whisking stopped.

"Henry," said Louisa.

He looked at her.

"Do you think Frank will be all right?"

He closed the bag of spicy sausages. "Yes, I do," he said. He put the bag back in the freezer.

"We don't know that for sure."

Henry turned the burner on under the skillet. "He'll be all right. He's Franklin, remember. Destined to be the next Great American Hero."

Was that a smile? If it was, it was quickly gone.

"Great American Heroes don't go around choking—"

"I know," said Henry quickly. The spicy sausages in the skillet began to sizzle.

Louisa whisked the eggs again. "Do you think . . . Henry, do you think Frank will remember what happened that night?" she said.

"You mean the accident?"

Louisa nodded.

"Probably not."

Louisa whisked the eggs up a bit more.

"But I guess we'll never forget," said Henry.

Louisa reached for two more eggs, cracked them, and dropped them in. Whisking again.

"You're not supposed to put the shells in, too," said Henry.

"*We'll* never forget what it was like," said Louisa.

Henry took the bowl and scooped most of the shells out. He added a little more milk and whisked it again. Then he added the chopped vegetables and sprinkled the provolone on top.

"You heard Dr. Giles," Henry said. "He's seen the unlikely happen. Why shouldn't it happen with Franklin? Anything is possible."

"Not anymore," said Louisa quietly.

The eight spicy sausages started to spurt up their hot oils. Henry found the largest frying pan in the cupboard and poured in the whisked eggs and vegetables and cheese. He put it on the stove beside the spurting sausages.

Henry set the table while their supper was cooking, and when he was finished, he went upstairs to get his parents—he was afraid to send Louisa up, since he was pretty sure that she might not come back down again.

Which would have made for a lonely meal, since his father didn't come down, anyway.

But his mother did, walking carefully, holding her hands carefully, holding her face carefully. She sat down as if she had been beaten up. She smiled—the kind of smile that everyone in the room knows is put on deliberately—and ate a forkful of omelet. And another. Then she put her fork down.

"It's good," she said. "And filling." She reached into her plate with a fingernail. "You're not supposed to put the shells in, too, unless you want to add fiber."

"Look," said Henry, "I never said I could cook. But no one else was here to—"

"You're right," said his mother. "And I'm not complaining,

Henry. Really, I'm not." She picked up her fork and ate another piece. Henry heard a distinct crunch. She put her fork down. Then she let the deliberate smile fall away.

And so the phone rang. It rang three times before Henry's mother stood to answer.

She was gone long enough for the omelet to turn cold.

When she came back in, she did not even try to put on the deliberate smile. She sat and left her hands on the table because she didn't know what to do with them. Her shoulders sloped as if the weight of the slate roof was upon them, and there were no great oaks to support her. "A plea bargain was offered this afternoon. Mr. Churchill thinks that we should accept it," she said.

Henry and Louisa waited.

"The Chouan family agrees to plead guilty to reckless injury. In return, Chay Chouan would be sentenced to two years of probation, the loss of his license until he is twenty-one, and two hundred hours of community service. When he turns twenty-one, he will get his license back, and the incident—that's what they call it, 'the incident'—will be wiped from his police record." She took a deep breath. "If we accept, it will be binding, and it will not matter if Franklin's condition changes."

Silence in the kitchen. Even Black Dog was quiet, though she smelled the omelet and knew that it was turning cold and was hopeful.

"That's it?" Henry said finally. "Franklin's missing an arm for the rest of his life, and the guy who did it to him drives around in a few years like nothing ever happened?"

"That's it."

"No jail time?"

She shook her head.

"After trying to kill Franklin?"

"He didn't try to kill Franklin," said Louisa quickly. "It was an accident."

"Mr. Churchill says it's the best we can hope for," said their mother.

Henry threw his fork into his omelet.

"He says that a jury will see it as an accident. And that he did all he could to help Franklin. And he has no previous record."

"And he's Cambodian," said Henry.

"That's not fair," said Louisa.

"Of course it's not fair. Poor refugees, let them get away with anything because they've had such a hard life."

"No one is saying that," said Louisa.

"Franklin would say that, but Franklin isn't talking. He's in a hospital room with his brain smacked around, and Chay Chouan is sitting at the dinner table eating egg rolls. 'Everything is going to be fine, after all.' That's what they're saying. 'Pass the ginseng.'"

Louisa stood. "Don't think you know everything, Henry. It isn't like that at all."

But Henry stood, too. "And how would you know what I think, Louisa? You have no idea, because you've been hiding up in your room since Franklin got hit, and you don't know a single thing about what we've been going through while you mope around by yourself. So don't tell me what I think. Don't you dare tell me what I think."

"I do know what you think. You think that Frank is the next Great American Hero, but it doesn't help anyone to live a lie. Because he isn't. No, he isn't. Just say it, Henry, because you already know he isn't."

Henry put his hand up to his neck.

"That's right," Louisa said. And then she went upstairs.

Neither Henry nor his mother ate much of the omelet. And it wasn't because of the eggshells. Or because it was cold.

They didn't talk while they did the dishes.

Black Dog flopped at their feet with her belly up.

But she did eat the rest of the omelet that they scraped into her bowl. Even the shells.

It was still light out after supper—the days were getting longer now—so Henry and Black Dog went down to what was left of Salvage Cove again. Henry brought a Frisbee—though Black Dog didn't understand the point of the game. Henry would throw it, and Black Dog would sit beside him and watch to see what happened next. So Henry would fetch the Frisbee and come back with it, show it to Black Dog, and throw it again. And then Black Dog waited until Henry went to fetch it again. Henry tried six times and finally gave up after Black Dog yawned and stretched out on the strip of sand, bored. He lay down beside her, and together they watched the waves turn black-purple before they broke and their white insides erupted.

Before they left, Henry threw the Frisbee down the beach once more—in case Black Dog had finally gotten the hang of it. Black Dog watched it sail, and then she yawned.

"Good dog." Henry sighed and went to fetch the Frisbee, stopping to rub his hand along the clean ribs of the ship.

He didn't expect the jagged splinter of wood that pierced his palm. When he jerked his hand back, he pulled the wound open farther and left a streak of blood along the wooden beam. The blood caught the very last light and glistened darkly. Henry pressed his two hands together, and then went down to the water to rinse off in the stinging salt. But the wound was deep, and the blood did not stop. When Black Dog came to investigate and smelled the scent of it, she howled and howled like Disaster.

And "Disaster" was the word Blythbury-by-the-Sea used when word got out about the plea bargain.

It was reported in the *Blythbury-by-the-Sea Chronicle*. Mr. Horkesley, on his way to make his deposit at the Blythbury-by-the-Sea Bank of New England, told Mrs. Ramsey, on her way to the Blythbury-by-the-Sea Delicatessen, that it was a scandal, a perfect scandal, and that the Smiths must certainly refuse it. Mrs. Taunton, checking books back into the Blythbury-by-the-Sea Free Public Library, assured each new patron that of course the Smiths would refuse it. Wasn't their son still lying in a coma in the hospital with both arms gone? Of course they would refuse it. Mrs. Syon, who ran the Blythbury-by-the-Sea Antiques and Collectibles Shoppe, mentioned more than a dozen times that she knew Mrs. Smith quite well—she'd furnished her with an Oriental rug and two Phoenix glass lamps—and she knew for a fact that the Smiths would never, ever accept such a ridiculous plea bargain with those foreign people.

But they did.

Henry hid the next *Blythbury-by-the-Sea Chronicle*, since he read the "Letters to the Editor" first and he didn't think his parents needed to.

Because the letters were right. Chay Chouan had crashed into his brother. Franklin's left arm was gone. He might not ever open his eyes again. And Chay Chouan was going to have his driver's license suspended? His *driver's license*?

Henry did what he could to not think about it. He rowed so hard in crew practice that Coach Santori said that if everyone only worked as hard as Smith here, then maybe they'd make it to State. As it was, Coach Santori wondered if they'd even make a respectable showing at Regionals—if they even got that far, because no one was working as hard as Smith, and they should all do what he was doing if they wanted to represent Whittier with anything approaching pride. And if they didn't want to represent Whittier with anything approaching pride, then they should get out of his shells before he took them out of his shells, and they had better move to someplace else—like Little Cambodia in Merton—because they wouldn't want to stay here and find out what he was going to do to them.

Which speech, of course, made everyone—especially Brandon Sheringham—hate Henry's guts for the rest of the afternoon and probably accounted for his shampoo falling off the shelf and emptying into the shower drains and his missing red-and-white boxers—which he discovered with an identifying note hanging beneath the red-and-white Whittier Academy flag when his mother dropped him off the next morning and he went to see what everyone was looking at.

Meanwhile, Blythbury-by-the-Sea seethed. The unfairness of it. The injustice. The judge must, *must* be going after the immigrant vote. Probably he was looking toward a political career. If these people wanted to come to America, why wouldn't they agree to abide by American laws? When was this country going to wake up? Everyone in Blythbury-by-the-Sea believed that something should be done. Something had to be done.

Everyone except Sanborn.

"There wasn't anything else your parents could have done,"

he said while they waited together after Debate—still on the future of nuclear power.

"Wasn't it just a few days ago that I beat you up?" said Henry.

"You must have been dreaming that, little man. Chay Chouan has no police record. He tried to help. He bandaged Franklin's arm. And he went to find the policeman."

"And he's Cambodian. And no one is supposed to say anything mean about Cambodians, because America is big enough for everyone and we should try to understand people who are different from ourselves. Do you want me to keep going, Sanborn, or should I just go ahead and throw up now?"

Sanborn shook his head. "I think you did just throw up," he said.

"And since when did we become everyone's business?"

Sanborn shrugged. "People like to see other people in trouble, as long as it isn't their own."

Silence.

"I really can take you, you know," said Henry.

"I think I could probably pin you in under a minute," said Sanborn.

"Maybe, Sanborn. Maybe you could pin me in under a minute—if I had triple pneumonia and five broken bones and a really, really runny nose."

But Sanborn was pretty close when Henry's mother drove up to bring them home.

The last week of April and then the first week of May came in soon afterward. There were sweet showers, and the forsythia burst into yellow blossoms, and the purple and white lilacs began to swell, and the tender daffodils bobbed back and forth in the warm breath of the wind. The gardens along the back side of the house came out with their solid greens and shy yellows and blues—as they did every year, to show that some things do not change.

And still Blythbury-by-the-Sea seethed, and there were more letters in the *Blythbury-by-the-Sea Chronicle* that Henry had to hide.

And Henry grew more and more eager to climb Katahdin.

He did not tell his parents about his plans. He didn't tell anyone except Sanborn, who looked at him with his eyebrow crooked as they jogged laps during PE under the baleful eye of Coach Santori. The new May sun was warm on their bare backs.

"You're going to climb Katahdin alone?"

Henry nodded.

"How are you going to get there?"

"I don't know. Thumb, I guess."

"And you're going to climb it alone?"

Henry smacked him on the arm. "Gee, Sanborn, you catch on real quick."

Sanborn smacked him back. "Gee, Henry, it's been nice knowing you. People die when they climb mountains alone."

"Like in Tibet, they do."

"You know that Katahdin has a ridge called the Knife Edge?"

"Yes, Sanborn. Are you my mother?"

"And you know that you're not even allowed up there most of the year?"

"You know, I'm really glad I told you about this. I've got this new surge of confidence."

"I'm going with you."

"You've never climbed a mountain, Sanborn."

"So?"

"You've never even camped out overnight."

"I repeat: So?"

"And you couldn't even stay up with me around this track if I was half trying."

"Okay. So can you press your own weight?"

"Yes."

Sanborn didn't answer.

"Can you press your own weight?" asked Henry.

"With you on top of it."

"Liar."

"Fool."

"Big butt."

"Skinny runt."

And that was the way the rest of the laps went, until the last one, when Henry did sprint ahead and did come in way before Sanborn and didn't begin with the intention of locking Sanborn out of the locker room but did it anyway, so that Sanborn had to go way around the school and in through the front doors and fuss with Dr. Sheringham about not having a pass and coming into Whittier without a shirt on.

Henry dressed before Sanborn could find him, figuring that nuclear power's dangers would give him a chance to cool down from any desire to murder his best friend.

That afternoon at home, Henry and Black Dog went into Franklin's room. Black Dog had never been in there before, so she set to sniffing around. Henry opened Franklin's closet and found his backpack. He took out Franklin's compass, his propane stove, and a length of rope. In the front flap of the backpack he found the maps of Katahdin's trails, and he opened one to look at the Knife Edge—which did look steep as all get-out. He wondered if he would need to have Black Dog tied close to him when he crossed it. Then he took out the tube saw, and the steel hatchet, and the match canister, and even a couple of flares that Franklin had kept for a long time—just in case—and which his mother would have hollered about if she knew he had kept them in the house. Henry took it all back to his room and stored it in his own new pack, which he slid carefully under his bed when he was finished.

He would wait for the right time to go. And he wouldn't tell Sanborn about it anymore.

After supper, he went down again to the cove. The Blythbury-by-the-Sea Historical Society had finished digging all around the ship, and her entire backbone was being held up by wood and steel supports and cables. They had found three more swords (which they had also taken away), more than a few cannonballs, shards of broken bottles, and more round barrel hoops, mostly melted out of form. There had been four muskets (they had taken these, too), and more broken brown pottery than anyone could ever hope to piece together—which had not stopped the Blythbury-by-the-Sea Historical Society from resolving to try.

Black Dog sniffed around at all the new smells they had left behind. Henry checked to see that the stain of his blood was still along the ship's rib.

It was. He could see it plainly in the long light of the lengthening day.

And that was when he smelled the smoke.

It came from the west. It wasn't strong, but even so, it sent the seagulls scattering and shouting into the air, and Black Dog turned and lifted her snout toward it. They watched as far away smoke columned upward, and after the sky darkened, Henry could make out a dim glow diffusing against the clouds. He thought he could hear sirens.

Henry and Black Dog watched the opening story on the late local news that night. It reported that one of the old boarding houses had been burned to the ground, representing a huge historical loss to the town. The only business destroyed was Merton Masonry and Stonework, which occupied the boarding house's first floor. It was owned by Mr. Chouan of Merton, whose son had been involved in the recent hit-and-run incident in Blythbury-by-the-Sea. No one had been injured. The police had not ruled out the possibility of arson.

Black Dog, who was curled up in front of the television, her nose in her tail, never moved at the news. But the palm of Henry's hand began to throb.

8

BY THE NEXT MORNING, arson had been confirmed.

No one in Blythbury-by-the-Sea got that news sooner than Henry, who got it around seven from two Merton policemen who came over to ask a few questions. They were large, really huge men whose presence filled the kitchen. When Black Dog put her ears down and lowered her head to be scratched—which the bigger of the two policemen did—Henry couldn't help but feel that she was being a traitor.

Maybe Henry's mother felt this, too. She didn't offer the policemen any of the coffee percolating happily on the counter.

They sat down at the kitchen table. The less big policeman wiped away some muffin crumbs left over from breakfast. "That coffee sure smells good," he said.

Silence for a minute. The bigger policeman coughed lightly. Then he opened a notebook and turned to Henry. "Yesterday, did you come home right after school?" he asked.

"After crew practice."

"And what time was that?"

"Around four thirty," said Henry's mother.

"And, ma'am, were you here when he arrived home?"

"I drove him home."

The policeman turned back to Henry. "And your school

is"—he checked his notes—"John Greenleaf Whittier Academy."

"Yes," said Henry. He tapped his knee so that Black Dog would come over to him, which she did—good dog.

"Here in Blythbury?"

"Yes."

"Pretty snooty," the less big policeman commented.

Henry's mother stiffened.

"Did you know anyone in the Chouan family, Henry?"

"Not personally."

"I'm guessing that you're pretty angry at that family."

Henry didn't answer.

"Are you angry enough to burn down a business they own?"

"I didn't burn down any business," said Henry.

"Henry has already told you where he was yesterday afternoon," said his mother.

The bigger policeman looked hard at Henry. "Do you know anyone who might want to burn down the Chouans' business because they were angry enough?"

"Maybe everyone in Blythbury-by-the-Sea."

"Anyone in particular?"

"No."

"Any guesses?"

"No."

"Huh," said the bigger policeman. He scratched the back of his head, sort of the way Black Dog did. "Henry," he said, "this is serious business. I mean, really serious business. If somebody had been in that building, then the charge would be murder—and who knows if whoever did this won't do something like it again. So I'm asking you again, Henry, do you know anyone who might have burned down the Chouans' business?"

100

"No," said Henry.

"Have you ever heard someone threaten to—"

"How many times does Henry need to answer the same question?" his mother snapped.

"I'm hoping to hear something that's helpful, ma'am. Maybe something that could save a life," the bigger policeman explained. He was being officially polite.

Henry's mother stood up and Black Dog went under the kitchen table. "We're done here," she said. "Henry has to get ready for school."

Neither policeman moved. They heard Black Dog's nails clicking on the quarried-stone kitchen floor as she circled and circled, tramping down whatever it was she was tramping down before she could collapse.

"We could take the kid in for questioning," said the less bigger policeman.

"If you had a warrant. And Henry won't be saying anything to anyone without our lawyer present."

"Well, Mrs. Smith, technically we don't need a warrant to . . ."

The bigger policeman stood—and when he stood, he stood a whole lot higher than Henry's mother. "Why so uncooperative, Mrs. Smith? We're investigating an arson case and you're—"

"And I'm about to drop my son off at school and then head to the hospital, where my other son is lying in an induced coma to control the swelling in his brain, while you want to harass Henry after he's already told you what he knows about an arson case involving a family that almost killed my boy. Who's being uncooperative?"

"Then maybe we should speak to your daughter." The bigger policeman looked down at his notes again. "Louisa Smith."

Henry's mother shook her head. "I don't think so. No."

"Why not?"

"Because the justice system has been so kind to us."

"Mrs. Smith, you really don't think that these two cases are unrelated."

Henry saw his mother stiffen even more. She leaned over and put her hands on the kitchen table. They were trembling. "I hope that they're not," she said quietly.

"Mrs. Smith—"

"But if they are, we had nothing to do with it. And I don't like you coming into my house thinking you could have your case all nice and solved if you could prove that this was a case of revenge, because the family who has to live with a maimed son for the rest of their lives are angry because the one who did it to him got off with a slapped wrist. I don't like that at all, and I wish you would leave now."

The bigger policeman closed his notebook. He looked at Henry and his mother and smiled. "I understand," he said. "But these are questions that have got to get answered. We could have done it here. Maybe now it'll be under a court order. But I want you to know, Mrs. Smith, I do understand." He nodded to the less bigger policeman, who rose. They all stood together—even Black Dog, who jumped up to have her head scratched again.

"Come here, Black Dog," said Henry's mother. She reached down, grabbed Black Dog's collar, and held her close to her side.

"I'm sorry for what's happened to you," said the bigger policeman. "Nobody deserves that kind of trouble."

"Thank you," said Henry's mother.

"That coffee sure does smell good," said the less bigger policeman.

Henry's mother nodded.

"Since we're here," said the bigger policeman, "do you mind if we go down to see the ship? I've been reading about it in the papers and I'm something of a history buff."

Henry's mother hesitated, then nodded again. Slowly.

"You want to show it to us, kid?"

Henry's mother started to speak.

"I promise, no questions about arson cases."

She looked at him, then at Henry. "Only for a minute or so," she said. She let go of Black Dog.

So Henry took them both down to Salvage Cove, along with Black Dog, and the bigger policeman whistled low and rubbed his hands along the boat's ribs. He paced off the length and width of the wreck and wrote down the figures in his notebook. He stepped inside and stood on the ship's exposed backbone, and Henry could see him imagining the ship as a living thing, twisting to let cold currents slide beneath her chin.

"Quite a sight," said the bigger policeman.

"I'd rather have the whole beach back," said Henry.

"I guess I would have, too, when I was your age. But now I look at this, and it reminds me that some things are made to last—like this boat. Look at that keel. You could imagine her still sailing after three hundred years."

"Not after it's been burned."

The policeman shook his head. "No, not after it's been burned. This shore has had trouble before, Henry. Lots of it. A boat that catches fire doesn't get washed up. It comes apart and sinks. This boat was beached and then set on fire. It probably started up by the bow." He pointed. "You can see how the damage is more extensive there than down to the stern." He looked up and down the ship again. "Someone wanted it destroyed."

"Maybe it was an accident," said Henry.

"Or maybe it was someone who was angry."

"Maybe," Henry said, "but you weren't going to ask any questions about arson."

The bigger policeman put his hands in his pockets and studied Henry. "No," he finally said, "I guess I wasn't." He looked at the wreck again. "It's quite a ship, Henry. I wonder if you'll ever find out what really happened to her." He studied Henry again. "She deserves to have someone find out what really happened to her." He held his hand out, and Henry shook it. The less bigger policeman nodded. Then they climbed back out of Salvage Cove, and the policemen got in their car and drove away.

Henry and his mother left for Whittier not long after—but long enough for Mrs. Smith to call Mr. Churchill, and for Mr. Churchill to issue stern warnings against saying anything to any policeman—any policeman at all—about the Merton arson case without him being present.

But the news of the arson had already reached Whittier, so when Henry got there, it was all anyone wanted to talk about.

Even his teachers.

There was Mr. DiSalva in American History.

"You've all heard about the fire in Merton?" he asked Henry's class.

Nods.

"Burned the place down like it was made of cheap matchsticks. That's what comes of not having strict building codes. Sometimes fires have changed the face of an entire city and affected the course of human events. So today we're going to take a break from Lewis and Clark and look at the burning of Chicago. Who can tell me under what president that occurred?"

And there was Mrs. Delderfield in Language Arts.

"Have you heard about the fire?" she asked.

Nods.

"Have you heard that the policemen in Merton are saying that it might well be a case of deliberate arson?"

Nods.

"What an awful thing," said Mrs. Delderfield. "Do you all know the poem by François Villon?"

Henry looked at Sanborn, who was rolling his eyes.

> *"Prince, n'enquerrez de semaine*
> *Où elles sont, ni de cet an,*
> *Qu'à ce refrain ne vous ramène:*
> *Mais où sont les neiges d'antan?"*

The class was pretty much silent.

"Isn't that a pretty poem?" said Mrs. Delderfield. "'Where are the snows of yesteryear?' Doesn't your heart thrill to Villon?"

"*Oui,*" said Sanborn.

And there was even Coach Santori in PE.

"If you don't pick up the pace on these laps, I'm going to light a fire under you hotter than anything they had to put out in Merton. Hear that, Brigham?"

"I think he's asking you a question," said Henry.

"PE teachers don't ask questions," said Sanford. "They holler out whatever comes into their pea-sized brains inside their thick-boned heads."

"Did you hear what I said, Brigham?"

Sanford picked up the pace. Henry stayed with him to urge him along, until Coach Santori yelled at him, too, wondering if he'd like to do sprints up and down the bleachers when he'd finished.

But by the end of the day, no one at Whittier—at least, no one that Henry heard—had said what everyone was thinking, and what everyone knew everyone else was thinking: That someone from Blythbury-by-the-Sea had burned down Merton Masonry and Stonework, that it was probably someone from Longfellow Prep, and that whoever did it should somehow, in secret, be declared a Blythbury-by-the-Sea hero, since he—or they—had done what the courts wouldn't do with a Cambodian immigrant. Justice had been served, after all.

But when Henry thought about the fire, or heard someone talk about the fire, the wound in his palm began to throb, and the deep heat that hid down in his guts—the heat to get to Katahdin—began to roil, so that he could hardly sit still through the burning of Chicago, or even François Villon.

The only place where Henry could ease the burning was at crew practice, and there he rowed as if it were Katahdin itself he was rowing to, stretching his legs and pulling back with all his might—even if it did make his palm scream for mercy. He passed his heat on to everyone else in the boat—even Brandon Sheringham—and they, too, rowed beyond what they had ever rowed before, so that Coach Santori began to smile—really—and he started to make grand predictions in the Whittier Academy newsletter about the great success that he was anticipating in the Cape Ann Coastal Invitational, where they would host crews from up and down Cape Ann, including, for the first time, a crew from Merton. After that, there were Regionals, and then maybe State. And who knew? Perhaps even Nationals!

"A crew from Merton?" said Henry's mother, when she read the newsletter in the afternoon.

"A crew from Merton?" said Henry's father, when he read the newsletter that night.

"A crew from Merton?" said Henry to Sanborn the next day. "They've never had a crew before. How can they have a crew?"

"Oh, I don't know, Henry. You get a boat, you put it in the water, you get eight guys into the boat, they row, you've got a crew. What's so impressive about that?"

"First off, it's a shell, not a boat. And second, that's not all a crew is, you jerk. There's coaching, and all the training, and learning how to row together as a squad. Crew isn't something you just start up. You have to have a long tradition behind you."

Sanborn looked behind Henry.

"I don't see anything behind you."

Henry looked behind Sanborn.

"I see a big butt behind you."

Which was why Sanborn was crushing Henry's face into the grass out in front of Whittier when Henry's mother came to pick them up that afternoon.

After they dropped Sanborn off, Henry's mother asked if he wanted to go to the hospital. But he didn't. In fact, Henry was going to see Franklin less and less, even though his mother asked him every afternoon if he wanted her to take him over. But what was there to go for? Franklin didn't even know that they were there. And every time Henry saw him, Franklin was whiter and stiller. And he would think of his brother, the great Franklin, of his rugby records, his powerful legs, his powerful arms. He would remember him laughing after a match, easy, strong, his hands bloody, maybe, his face gritty with sweat and dirt, but still laughing, like a champion who had condescended to play hard at a game he knew he could not lose.

But now he was white and still. And now, when Henry looked at his own legs, his own arms, his own face after a crew practice, he knew that he was the stronger one. And something deep and tiny within him was . . . glad. It took all of his strength to crush the thought.

But it didn't matter, because Franklin didn't even know they were there.

Except maybe once.

It was late afternoon, on a day that God couldn't have made any better if He had set out to try. The sun was yellow, the skies blue, the new leaves gold and green. His mother had driven to the hospital after school without asking Henry if he wanted to come. While she went to the nurses' station to see if there was anything at all to report—there never was—Henry went to his brother's clean room and looked out the window. Bright green everywhere, the canvas on which all the other colors showed off. The grass was growing full and every tree had begun to dress itself. He could see pink and white blossoms in nearby orchards, and farther away, the brief yellow of the daffodils, so bright, they looked as if Van Gogh had just come from them with his paintbrush still wet in his hand. And everywhere, the branches, supple with their new juices, bowed and dipped and thrust upward with the sea breeze that had come far enough inland to whisper up the red brick sides of the hospital.

Henry reached up, unlocked the window, and opened it to let the breeze in—probably breaking all sorts of rules about germ infiltration and hygiene that the hospital had ever conceived. But he didn't care. The breeze came in immediately and filled the room with its cool breath. Henry pulled it down into his lungs. Deep. Then he thought he heard the sheets on his brother's bed rustle, and he turned.

The light over Franklin's bed was off and the long curtain that hung beside him shadowed his pale face. But Franklin's eyes were open. He was looking past Henry, out the window. His eyes were open. Henry was as sure, as certain as the tide. He watched.

Then Franklin's eyes closed. It was as if a ghost had flickered into Franklin's body and, with all the elusive ways of ghosts, had chosen to ignore him.

"Franklin," Henry whispered. He walked to the bed on his strong legs. "Franklin." He lifted his brother's right arm with his strong hand.

Nothing. His brother's skin was baggy and wrinkled and dry to the touch.

Henry did not tell his mother that Franklin had opened his eyes when she came back in. He wasn't sure why he didn't. Maybe because she wouldn't have believed him. Maybe because he might have been wrong. (He wasn't.) Maybe because he wanted to hold this one piece of his brother to himself. But for whatever reason, he insisted that they keep the window open that afternoon, even when the nurse on duty came in to fuss.

His brother had opened his eyes.

But it was the only time, and as the days—then weeks—went by, and May started to think about letting June have her way, Henry grew less sure, after all.

What he *was* sure of was that the Whittier Academy crew team was going to dominate the Cape Ann Coastal Invitational.

The thought of the Merton shell stoked their practices. And every dual meet on every Saturday morning brought them a new victory—by three, sometimes four, boat lengths. Each meet led to another *Blythbury-by-the-Sea Chronicle* front-page article about how this crew was the finest that Whittier Academy had seen in decades, how it didn't look as if any regional crew could hope to touch it, how when these rowers had graduated and moved up to Longfellow Prep, state high school records would fall. Quickly.

Henry knew they were right. He knew they'd see the unlikely happen.

How could anyone have ever guessed that the cost would be knowing? Once and for all, knowing. Knowing finally why there were tears and laughter for the younger brother. And knowing finally why there were no tears and no laughter for him.

Knowing finally why he was never touched, why he was never held. Why there was disgust and blame. And when he knew the terrible story for the first time, it was as if mountains had slammed shut forever.

Knowing meant there was nothing for him. Not the past he had believed, which was a lie. Not the future he had hoped for, which he had hoped for in those moments when hope can stir against all reality.

In the cold morning of the nothing, there was first shame, and then loneliness.

And in the loneliness, another terrible knowledge grew: He had to leave home, because it was no longer home. Maybe it had never been home.

He would leave home, fade far away, dissolve.

9

WHEN THE DAY for the Cape Ann Coastal Invitational finally came—the last Saturday in May—most of Blythbury-by-the-Sea turned out. Its cheerful citizens arranged themselves along the banks of the Charles River, where the invitational was being held since so many teams were competing. They stood dressed in red and white, holding traditional Whittier Academy banners—a lion and unicorn rampant—and singing the school song while the Whittier Pep Band played loudly.

> *Whittier, Whittier,*
> *All hail to thee!*
> *In thee our past is bright,*
> *Forever red and white.*
> *Whittier, Whittier,*
> *Hail, Victory!*

They clapped and cheered loudly at the end of each rendition—and started up again whenever the pep band blared its brassy tones into the blue sky, over the blue river, and onto the blue-clothed crowd from Merton, who stood together, sort of quiet and huddled, watching events on the river that they really didn't understand. But nevertheless, every so often they shouted encouragement in words Henry did not recognize, calls that were answered by flashing smiles and waves from the Merton crew manhandling their shell into the Charles.

The Whittier team slid their shell in and watched it bob merrily on the water before climbing into their places. The wind cutting in from Boston Harbor made the river a little choppy—there were even some whitecaps—but Henry settled down into the shell and felt his body sway easily to meet the low waves. They pulled out into the river for warm-ups, and Henry felt the good familiar pull of muscle against water; still, when they got out onto the water, the wind struck his back, and he knew that this was going to be a hard row.

But he figured that it was going to be a harder row for the Merton team, who were struggling with the choppy waves and their uncooperative shell, and whose coxswain had already been dunked once and was probably shivering in the cool wind. The invitational's referees would have to give them a little more time—a lot more time, Henry thought—to get themselves together—which they very patiently did.

Meanwhile, the Whittier Academy crew team moored for Coach Santori's last-minute encouragement, giving the Whittier parents and students and everyone else from Blythbury-by-the-Sea another chance to cheer and holler and sing the school song— "Hail, Victory!"—and wave the school banners bravely in the breeze. It was Coach Santori's usual encouragement: "Bring home the trophy today or you'll be holding this shell over your heads and running laps on Monday." So motivated, Henry went up on the dock to take one last gulp of water.

Sanborn was waiting for him. "You ready?"

Henry swallowed and nodded. "Not even a challenge," he said.

Sanborn nodded to the Merton crew heading toward the starting line. "They're eager."

Henry looked around.

"The boat from Merton," said Sanford.

"It's not a boat, Sanford. It's a shell."

"Yeah, well, can you make out the first rower?"

"So?"

"It's a Chouan."

Henry turned around and stared at the first rower. "How do you know?"

"Everyone knows." Sanborn waved back at the Blythbury-by-the-Sea parents. "That's all they're talking about back there— at least, between songs."

Henry did not look at the Blythbury-by-the-Sea parents; he looked at the Merton parents, and he found them—the Chouans—the tiny Mrs. Chouan, the post-thick arms of Mr. Chouan around her. Henry wondered if Chay was there, too, cheering on his younger brother.

He turned back to Sanborn. "We'll give them something else to talk about," he said. "When we cross the line, Merton won't even be in sight."

Which is what he told Coach Santori when he climbed into the shell. Which is what he told the other rowers while they waited at the line, tipping up and down in the unruly Charles. Which is what he told himself as he watched the Blythbury-by-the-Sea parents prepare to run to their cars to reach the finish line in time. You'd better hurry, Henry thought. Then he felt his body grow tight, tighter, *tighter* as he waited for the shot from the starting gun and the first powerful pull of his powerful arms and powerful legs.

Then the shot came, clear and sharp.

And eleven shells plowed into the water, the spray of the Charles thrown up and dashed back across the rowers.

But that was not how it was for the twelfth shell—the Blythbury-by-the-Sea shell. At the very first stroke, the shell leaped clear of the river, as if it would take to the air, and its rowers were almost into their second stroke before their bow came back into the Charles, cleaving through the water cleanly and purely, as if the river were parting before them. They had not gone four strokes before Henry could glimpse the other crews already falling behind. They had not gone ten strokes when he could see that they had already pulled a full length ahead of Merton.

He could almost have laughed.

Henry felt the wind against his back, cold and hard, as if it had a mind to push him sternward. But the thrust of his legs and the pull of his arms were strong, and he fell easily into the rhythm of his crew, as if every thrust and every pull was not his own but belonged to the shell itself, slicing through air and water and current. With every pull, Henry felt stronger. With every thrust, he felt the other rowers perfectly in the rhythm that Brandon Sheringham called out. We must be a joy to see from the shore, he thought.

By the half-mile mark, the Blythbury-by-the-Sea boat was four lengths ahead of the other eleven teams, and Henry was strong; he figured they could row down the Charles, out into Boston Harbor, and on to Portugal without much trouble. Two of the other boats had drifted too close to each other in the lanes and were clashing oars. Another had a coxswain who was wallowing them from side to side—probably because they hadn't worked up enough speed to keep them going straight in this choppy water. The others looked game enough, but it was pretty clear that whoever was left was competing for second and third place—or, at least, some sort of showing in which they would not be completely humiliated. Of these, the crew from Merton looked slightly ahead, though it was hard to tell. If they hadn't been splashing their blades so much, maybe they would definitely be ahead. As it was, they were throwing up more white water from their sides than any other boat, and sometimes their oars would smack against each other loudly, and sometimes their rowers wouldn't go deep enough and just skim the surface—a wasted stroke—or they would go too deep and not come up soon enough for the rhythm of the next rower— so the oars would smack together again.

Henry smiled and pulled cleanly, feathering his blade and sliding it above the water, then catching it down and slicing into the river, and then drawing it back, sending the boat forward. Propelling the boat forward!

The banks of the Charles River fled past as the John Greenleaf Whittier Academy crew team rowed by young forests, bright green still in their late spring attire. They rowed past corporate offices wealthy enough to situate their glass-fronted selves alongside a river view. They rowed past crew teams from Harvard and MIT and Boston University, warming up for their Saturday morning practice, who clapped as Whittier flew by. Henry watched it all, and his pulls stayed strong and even.

The crew from Merton was definitely in second place now— even with all of its splashing and missed rhythms. The Blythbury-by-the-Sea boat was seven or eight lengths ahead, and Brandon Sheringham had already slowed their pace down, preparing for the sprint of the last five hundred yards. Henry felt his body relax, but he could see that there was no relaxing in the Merton shell. If they couldn't get the rhythm right, and if they didn't have a shell nearly as sleek and clean in its lines as the Blythbury-by-the-Sea shell, and if they had a coxswain who hadn't any idea about what to do in choppy water like today's— well, they would simply muscle their way through it all. Or maybe it was simply guts powering the Merton shell.

Which was now six lengths back. The wind was catching the splashes they put up and soaking the coxswain and stern rower.

Henry watched as Brandon Sheringham turned around at the sound. He seemed surprised when he looked back at his squad, and immediately he picked up the rhythm of the strokes.

In the Merton shell, the bow rower turned around to see how far ahead Henry's boat was, and when he turned, Chay Chouan's brother looked full into Henry's face.

He knew who Henry was. Henry could tell. And Henry knew who he was.

Henry held his blade suspended for a second—less than a second. And it was slapped out of his hand by the pull from ahead.

"What are you doing?" cried Brandon Sheringham.

Henry grasped wildly for the handle of his oar, but the blade was still in the churning water, and it danced away from him. He felt the shell sheering.

"Smith!" shouted Brandon Sheringham.

Henry grabbed the dancing handle. He tried to fall immediately into the crew's rhythm, but he struck first the oar ahead, then behind, then ahead again. He feathered his oar up out of the water until he could get the timing right, and missed it the first time, and the second. He felt the coxswain shift the rudder, but the shell tilted away from the center of the lane.

Finally, on the third try, Henry got his oar aligned with his crew's. He heard Brandon Sheringham hollering and probably swearing, and he felt the shell tip back sharply and briskly toward the center of the lane, go too far, and then start to come back. He pulled hard with the new and strong rhythm, and the shell straightened.

But when Henry looked out to the river again, the Merton shell was only a single length behind them. Their coxswain was screaming as if Trouble itself was riding on their stern.

Henry thought he was going to be sick.

The whole world contracted: two shells desperately rowing their last four hundred yards, the shell from Blythbury-by-the-Sea pulling in perfect and beautiful rhythm, the shell from Merton tearing through the choppy Charles with brute force. Henry could see nothing else—not the fleeing banks of the river, not the oars feathered outside the boats, not the water itself. He could see only the length of his own shell, and just past it, the length of the Merton shell and the rounded back of Chouan in the bow, pulling, pulling, pulling.

Probably the Blythbury-by-the-Sea parents and the Merton parents were screaming and hollering from the riverside, but if they were, the sound did not reach Henry. The only sounds he heard were Merton's splashes in the river, the stretch of the oars against the oarlocks, the harsh breathing of his crew, the shrieks of Brandon Sheringham and the Merton coxswain. And the beating of his own heart. It all came to him in a rush of noise; he couldn't have sorted it out if he tried.

"Eyes on me!" hollered his coxswain, and Henry focused, pulling, pulling, pulling, but his eyes could not help but glance over at Merton. At Chouan.

Two hundred yards to go.

The Merton shell drew up to within half a length.

One hundred yards to go.

Less than half a length.

And Chay Chouan's brother, in the bow of his boat, and Henry, midships, were pulling side by side.

They did not look across at each other.

Henry wondered wildly if Chouan was as aware of him as he was of Chouan. But he couldn't figure this out, because his own brain was so tied to the rhythm of the blade, the strokes, the pressure and release of the water.

Then he did look over.

At the same time that Chouan looked at him.

"Smith, eyes in the shell!" yelled Brandon Sheringham. And Henry turned back and closed his eyes and rowed. He felt the muscles in his arms and legs grow thick and slow and tight. He felt his back bend almost to breaking, as if his spine had brittled like that of the wrecked ship in the cove. He felt a darkness in the center of his chest, a place where all the air had been sucked and had turned solid, so that nothing else could get in.

And so, when they crossed the finish line less than a quarter length ahead of the Merton boat, the rower behind Henry had to grab his arms to tell him that he could stop rowing. No one in the shell was cheering except for Brandon Sheringham, and even he could barely croak out, "Whittier! Whittier! Whittier!"

Henry sank into himself, and sweat suddenly drenched him.

They drifted.

One by one, the rest of the crews crossed the line, and Henry watched them as if he were far away and not connected at all with what had just happened. From the shore he could hear the

Whittier parents chanting "Whittier! Red and White! Whittier! Red and White!" as their parents had chanted before them, and their parents before them. But as they half-rowed, half-drifted back to the landing dock, all Henry could think of was the glance from Chouan.

The flushed, strained, . . . and indeterminate glance.

But Brandon Sheringham was not indeterminate. He was jubilant. He leaped out at the landing and held the bow of the shell up as, one by one, Henry's crew climbed out. Slowly. Henry's legs felt as if the bones in them had dissolved and he was quivering on jelly. But the Whittier crowd was singing their song again, and their cheers snapped like flags in the brisk breeze. Coach Santori had their team jackets ready—their red and white shining like royalty—and Henry quickly put his on, since already he was feeling the chill of his cooling sweat. But "cool" might also describe Coach Santori's face as he handed his jacket to him. Definitely cool. Maybe even cold.

He was not a happy Coach Santori, and Henry wondered if they would be running laps while holding their shell over their heads, after all—even though they had won.

Or if he might be running the laps by himself.

As the parents organized the Whittier crew for the group victory pictures—"All hail to thee!"—Henry looked over at the Merton team—who had no team jackets, no sweats—and he watched Disappointment cloak them. They had beaten the other Cape Ann teams. And the Merton parents were cheering and clapping, too. But no one from the Merton crew was celebrating.

After the pictures, all the crews lined up—the south side of Cape Ann in one line, the north in another—to shake hands. "Good race," "Good race," "Good race," Henry said again and again to the Beverly team, and the Ipswich team, and the Gloucester team, and the Rockport team. "Good race," "Good race." But all the time, he was aware of Merton's crew behind his own, shaking the hands that he shook first. And when they had finished and the two lines turned to shake each other's hands, Henry stayed only until his crew came to the first Merton rower, and then he turned back to the landing dock.

The rest of the John Greenleaf Whittier Academy crew team followed.

Even Coach Santori, who gathered his crew in a tight group and congratulated them, looking every one of them in the eye and nodding—at everyone except for Henry, who thought once again that he might be running laps on Monday. Not even the sight of the elegant glass-and-silver trophy raised above Brandon Sheringham's head cheered him.

He left before anyone else on his crew, and he drove back home with his mother and Sanborn.

"Congratulations," she said. "That was your closest race yet."

Henry said nothing.

"It looked like you missed a stroke out there."

"I did," said Henry. "More than one."

"You seemed to take a while to get back into the rhythm."

"Yup."

"You still won," said Sanborn.

No one is saying what we are all thinking, thought Henry. That I almost let a team of Cambodians beat us because I blew a stroke.

"Even though you almost let a team of Cambodians beat you," whispered Sanborn.

But Henry did not even answer. They rode the rest of the way home silently.

Which was not how Black Dog greeted them.

And which was not how she was after supper when she got up on her toes and pranced around the beach while Henry skipped rocks down in Salvage Cove and watched the low breakers roughing up the water and tossing the red buoys back and forth, sounding their low *clong, clong, clong.*

Henry stretched his arms back and tensed his legs. The sweet ache from this morning's race had set in. If he had his kayak, he would have been able to work out the soreness by paddling up and down the cove. Maybe he would have been able to work out the memory of his missed stroke.

But he didn't have his kayak, and the soreness hung on him.

And then, suddenly, he felt the whole world stop. Even Black Dog quieted and looked up into the sky. It was as if everything near to him, and everything far from him, had decided to hold its breath, and the immensity of that holding fell down on him like slate weight.

He tried to shrug it off. He threw a few more stones along the troughs left by the smaller waves. But the weight would not go away. When Black Dog came and lay down by his feet, she gave a little whine and poked her snout into the palm of Henry's hand, which suddenly burned with the wound from the ship. He drew his hand quickly back—so fast that Black Dog dropped her head as if she expected him to hit her—and Henry shook his hand to ward off the pain that he thought was coming.

The telephone in the house rang. Henry could hear it clearly. It rang nine times, as if it would not surrender until someone finally picked it up.

Then someone did. Or it stopped. Henry couldn't tell.

Henry walked back to the wrecked ship—to the same rib that he had wounded himself on earlier. And he put his palm there again and felt the same spiky splinter of wood. He could almost feel the blood on his palm surging.

Then, suddenly, there was his mother at the top of Salvage Cove, calling down to him.

Henry did not want to hear her.

"Henry," she called.

He kept his hand on the rib.

"Hen. . ." She could not say his whole name.

Black Dog started up the stones toward her. Henry watched her, her tail wrapped below her belly. She climbed up the rocks slowly, her head low, her ears limp, while the wind swirled strongly into the cove.

Black Dog stopped by Henry's mother and sat at her feet. His mother reached down and touched Black Dog on the head.

"Henry," she called again. "The hospital."

And then the waiting Immensity gave up and let go its breath.

Henry pressed his hand against the rib of the ship. The wound broke open again. He walked up the cove toward his mother, carrying with him the stigmata of Sorrow that would never, ever leave him.

His mother knew he would leave. He saw that she knew in the way that she touched him. In the way that she would moan softly when she thought he did not hear. In the way she looked at him as if she wanted to memorize everything about him.

His father—the man who had been his father—would not look at him at all.

122

He had to leave home, because it was no longer home. He would leave at night and drive out into darkness where there were no tears and no laughter. He had to leave home, where but to think is to be full of sorrow and leaden-eyed despairs.

He packed the volume of Keats.

10

"WE JUST DON'T KNOW," the doctors said. Perhaps a seizure in the night. The brain scans had always been indeterminate, so it was impossible to tell exactly what had happened. It might have been another stroke. Perhaps a clot caused by inanition that entered the brain. Sometimes the patient may simply lose all will to live. "We just don't know," they said.

But Henry knew what had happened.

His brother, Franklin—Franklin Smith, O Franklin Smith—had been dying that early morning while Henry was rowing on the Charles River and his mother was cheering him on and the Cambodian team was trying to muscle their shell past the Whittier shell.

And then, sometime that afternoon, when the world had held its breath, Franklin Smith had let his own breath go out forever.

He had been all by himself.

No one would be seeing the unlikely happen.

And Trouble had found Henry's home and settled in.

The house grew very, very quiet.

If they hadn't had Black Dog, Henry didn't know what they would have done, because to Black Dog, all seasons, all hours, all moments were now. If she wanted to run down to the cove with Henry, it was now. If she wanted to roll over on her back and be scratched by Henry, it was now. If she wanted to untie Henry's shoelaces, it was now. If she wanted to wrestle wildly with Henry, it was now. And for Black Dog, if Henry was nearby, then Trouble was far away. And it is hard to weep when you are running with a dog by the shore of a blue cove.

But at night, when Black Dog curled down deeply in her quilt at the end of Henry's bed, and the sky turned dark, and the sea was dark, and the cold weight of the darkness pressed against his throat, Henry thought about his brother.

Then he would lean down and wake Black Dog, and she would put her wet snout into the palm of his hand without opening her eyes.

But the night was still dark.

The funeral for Franklin Waldo Smith was on the very last day of May. It rained, a dismal rain that kept everyone indoors. The funeral was private, in any case; Blythbury-by-the-Sea's two policemen were stationed outside the church doors to see that the reporter from the *Blythbury-by-the-Sea Chronicle* and the local-news cameramen gathered across the street from St. Anne's Episcopal did not disturb the mourners.

Henry sat with his parents. Louisa did not come.

The organ music was low; the solemn notes came out of the pipes and fell toward Franklin's casket, which lay under the white-and-gold tapestry that St. Anne's reserved for this ceremony.

From the mahogany pulpit, Father Brewood spoke the old words: "I know that my Redeemer liveth, and that he shall stand at the latter day upon the earth: and though this body be destroyed, yet shall I see God: whom I shall see for myself, and mine eyes shall behold, and not as a stranger."

Henry was surprised, even amazed, to find himself thinking about Black Dog during the service. About how much Black Dog loved to run. About how Black Dog would never, never go near the waves. About how much Franklin would have wanted her.

He saw his mother and father, sitting beside each other. Separate. Apart. Tight.

He thought of Louisa, who would not get in the car for the funeral, who fled back to her room and would not be comforted—who would not see her brother Frank put in the ground.

"We brought nothing into this world, and it is certain we can carry nothing out. The Lord gave, and the Lord hath taken away; blessed be the name of the Lord."

"Blessed be the name of the Lord," whispered Henry's mother.

Blessed be the name of the Lord? wondered Henry.

And when the service was over, Henry and his parents followed the casket quietly down the aisle, their steps not sounding at all on the thick carpet. The eyes of the mostly unknown but respectful cousins and uncles and aunts who had come fixed upon them. At the door, helpful men in black suits held umbrellas over their heads as they all went out into the rain.

The Smith plot was large, one of the largest in the graveyard behind St. Anne's, and it was surrounded by a low wrought-iron fence. A white obelisk stood in one corner, erected for the two Smith boys killed at Antietam. But the graves went back to the 1680s—dark, thin slates with urns and weeping willow emblems. In the dead center of the plot, a large double-sized and double-arched stone—SMITH—unfolded over the graves, its winged skull brooding toothlessly and blindly over the silent, sodden spot. Someday, it said to Henry, you will be here. Another dead Smith. I will brood over you, too.

Until today, Henry had never really believed it. Now he did.

Beneath a black canopy and behind the center stone there was a terrible gash in the ground. It was covered with a bright green tarp. They gathered under the canopy, and the helpful men in black suits—now with black raincoats—pulled the tarp back; it came away with dark mud and grass on its underside. The rain sounded hard over Henry, over his parents, and over Father Brewood.

"Unto Almighty God we commend the soul of our brother Franklin Waldo Smith departed, and we commit his body to the ground; earth to earth, ashes to ashes, dust to dust; in sure and certain hope of the Resurrection unto eternal life."

Then the helpful men laid ropes across the terrible gash, laid the casket on the ropes, and so laid Franklin into the earth.

"Most merciful Father, who hast been pleased to take unto thyself the soul of this thy servant; Grant to us who are still in our pilgrimage, and who walk as yet by faith, that having served thee with constancy on earth, we may be joined hereafter with thy blessed saints in glory everlasting."

Henry tried not to taste the earth and ashes and dust in his mouth.

"Amen," said Father Brewood.

So the helpful men removed the ropes from the earth, and Henry's parents turned to leave.

But Henry did not go with them.

"Henry?" said his mother.

Henry left the black canopy and went over to the pile of earth and sand and stones beyond the terrible gash. He reached down and pulled away the wet tarp that was over it, and then pulled out the shovel that stood beside it. He heard the *chang* of steel against stone as he jerked it out.

"Henry," said Father Brewood, his arm across Henry's already wet shoulder, "we have people to do that. You had better get inside with your parents."

Henry thrust the shovel deep into the pile of earth, and pulled it back, and walked over to his brother's grave, and threw the first earth onto the casket.

The thud of it. Earth to earth, ashes to ashes, dust to dust. The loud, reverberating thud.

Then he walked back to the pile and did it all again. His parents watched him.

He shoveled enough earth into the grave so that he could no longer hear the hollow sound as it struck the casket. But he kept on, digging the shovel into the pile, and carrying the earth to the grave, and dropping it into the terrible gash, and so covering his brother, Franklin Waldo Smith, settling him beside the brooding stone.

He carried the earth until it became mud in the rain, and still he carried it, himself wet and muddy, and then sore, and his face wet with the rain or with something else. Slowly he filled in the gash with the earth and sand and stones, until it seemed a low swelling of the ground. Earth to earth, ashes to ashes, dust to dust.

And when he was finished, Henry's mother took him by the hand—his palm was bleeding from the work of the shovel—and they walked together to the car where Henry's father was waiting. They did not go back to the unknown and respectful relatives gathered in the church parlor, sipping coffee in the cool spring morning, eating carefully prepared sandwiches. They went to their house by the sea. And though Trouble had made its home there, when they went in, Black Dog was waiting, too. And though Henry's father went in to the library and closed the door, and though Henry's mother went to the north parlor and closed the door, and though Louisa would not open her door, Henry at least had Black Dog, who thrust her almost completely healed snout into Henry's hand. And she did not whine at all, though the wound on Henry's palm had been torn open again and she could smell the blood.

That night, she lay beside Henry, and he stroked her sharp shoulder blades and scratched behind her ears. He did this late into the night as he listened to the low and terrible moans that swept through the hallways of the house and that were not from the lonely wind but from his lonely mother, who had lost her oldest child and would never have him back again.

Trouble, Henry learned, is not content to stay put—no more than Black Dog would stay put on a clear and bright June morning. Trouble is of a mind to spread, as it did in the days following Franklin's funeral, seeping out from behind the quiet doors of the Smiths' house and traveling down the long drive, following Main Street and so on into Blythbury-by-the-Sea, slithering into the fancy shops and gourmet delis, and from there down to the clapboard and brick and stone houses, and from there to Whittier Academy and Longfellow Prep, and even down to the little police station, where the town's two policemen shook their heads and wondered at the injustice of it all, and what are we coming to when a boy from Blythbury-by-the-Sea can be run down and killed and nothing happens to the killer from Little Cambodia but losing his license?

What are we coming to?

In the *Blythbury-by-the-Sea Chronicle*, the letters to the editor raged in a torrent of righteousness, first about the inappropriateness of the punishment to the crime, then about the failure of our justice system, then about the bleeding-heart liberals who were more sympathetic to new immigrants than to those who had settled America in the first place, and how those immigrants didn't come to America to become Americans but to take advantage of true American generosity, and about how something ought to be done—must be done.

Henry watched his father—who always seemed to be up so late now. He watched him read these letters, and saw his face grow gray and set.

He watched his mother grow angry.

Finally, Mrs. Smith wrote a letter herself, and it appeared on the front page of the *Blythbury-by-the-Sea Chronicle*. Her son's death was an accident, Henry's mother wrote. A terrible accident. It was tragic but still an accident. Nothing that anyone could say or do now would bring Franklin back to them. The Smith family was trying to accept this and to move on. Mrs. Smith asked that Blythbury-by-the-Sea do the same.

Henry hated her letter.

He wanted to hate Little Cambodia the way Franklin would have wanted him to hate it. Franklin wasn't there any longer to handle Trouble. Henry was responsible now—like Franklin had said. So he would hate Chay Chouan, and he would climb Katahdin and hike the Knife Edge because it would show that he had the guts to do it. Even without Franklin. And after that, he'd be ready to handle anything. By himself.

So Henry hated his mother's letter. And so did most of Blythbury-by-the-Sea.

The very next issue of the *Blythbury-by-the-Sea Chronicle*

brought the worst letters yet. It is all very well, they said, to play the forgiving Christian and to turn the other cheek. But with all respect to the grieving Smiths, this trouble had been coming on Blythbury-by-the-Sea for some time, and the community needed to understand that those who have come late to this country do not have the same regard for human life that the founders of this nation built into the very fabric and experience of American life.

Henry stopped bringing in the paper each morning. He left it on the stoop when he went to run Black Dog down to the cove. Afterward, he would pick it up and take it to the garbage can inside the carriage house.

But Trouble is not easily quieted.

This seemed especially true at Whittier, where no one—not even Coach Santori—had given Henry grief over his missed strokes during the Cape Ann Coastal Invitational. He wished that Coach would make him do laps until he dropped, or make him sprint up and down the bleachers. Something. But everyone believed Henry was filled with Outrage, and they wanted to share it.

The only one at Whittier who understood what was burning in Henry's guts was Sanborn.

"You know that Katahdin is five thousand two hundred and sixty-seven feet high, right?" he said.

Henry looked at him. "Monday we start final exams," he said, "and you're reading about how high Katahdin is?"

"It is sort of miraculous, isn't it? And what's even more miraculous is that I can read about how high Katahdin is and still do better than you on every final."

"You are a wonder, Sanborn. How is it that the United States government hasn't picked you up yet?"

"They're too ignorant. Do you think we can do it?"

"Do what?"

"Speaking of ignorant . . . climb Katahdin."

"Of course I can climb Katahdin. I'm a big boy."

"I'm going with you."

"You'd never make it, Sanborn. You're not coming with me."

"I'll end up having to carry you."

"You'd never make it."

"Why don't you say that a third time, Henry, because after you say something three times out loud and tap the heels of your shoes, then it becomes true."

"You'd never make it."

Henry was surprised at both the strength and fierceness of Sanborn's initial assault, and how, despite a couple of pretty good blows to Sanborn's stomach and one strong chop to his left side, he found himself below Sanborn with his face deep in the grass and his right arm twisted behind him and Sanborn's left knee in the small of his back.

From which Sanborn released him only when Mrs. Smith came to pick them up.

"You'd never make it," whispered Henry as they drove to Sanborn's house.

"You wouldn't make it without me," whispered Sanborn.

"I guess we'll never find out, since you won't know when I'm going."

"We'll find out," said Sanborn, "since if I don't go, they'll discover your dead body somewhere in the woods after looking for it for six months."

"You'd never make it," whispered Henry again.

At which Sanborn turned to him, and there was no laughter in his face: "Why don't you try to sound a little more like your brother, Henry?"

Which was the last thing they said to each other until they drove up to Sanborn's house and Sanborn's mother came out to console Henry's mother, who did not want to be consoled by Sanborn's mother but who endured it all pretty well—even Mrs. Brigham's weepy expressions of sorrow for the loss of your dear, dear Frederick.

Until they drove away, when his mother sighed, and sighed again, and then began to wonder aloud why everyone in Blythbury-by-the-Sea thought it was their right to know every little detail about Franklin's accident and every little detail about how he died and every little detail about how they were living now and when would they all finally stop asking how she felt because it wasn't their concern, anyway, because it was a private family matter.

Then she stopped to breathe. Henry decided that he probably didn't need to say a thing.

He especially didn't need to say a thing, because he had already said too much. Sanborn had been right. He did sound like Franklin.

Henry wondered why he didn't want to tell his parents about Katahdin. Maybe it was a private matter. Maybe, if he had asked himself, he wouldn't have been able to say exactly why he wanted to climb the mountain. Not entirely, anyway. To prove himself? To get ready for Trouble? Because he had been going to climb it with Franklin? Maybe. But there was something else, too. Something more.

He decided he'd better stop thinking about the mountain and get studying for finals week, which began that next Monday with his American History class and then rushed into Language Arts, then Government, then into Pre-Algebra—so getting worse and worse as the week went on until Friday, when he'd have Life Science and then PE—where the whole class had to run a 6:25 mile, something Sanborn couldn't do if his most dreaded nightmare was careening after him. He dreamed of someday being at Longfellow Prep, where classes were already done by the end of May. If Franklin were alive, he'd be giving Henry all sorts of grief, because he'd already be packed and ready to head up to Katahdin, and couldn't his little brother hurry up and finish his little classes so they could get going?

But Franklin was in the low swelling of the ground, and there was no one to give him grief. At least, not that grief.

On Monday afternoon, while Henry was rowing crew practice, he figured out one cause of World War I that he had missed on the American History final, but he calculated that he'd probably get an A- anyway—especially since he did a bang-up job on Lewis and Clark, those Great American Heroes.

Later, toward midnight on Monday, two bricks crashed simultaneously through the two first-story bedroom windows of the Chouan house in Merton.

On Tuesday, Henry wrote an essay evaluating the role of revenge in Chaucer's "Miller's Tale." He thought his analysis was unusually perceptive, because he used the word *bildungsroman*, figuring that the German would impress Mrs. Delderfield—even if it didn't really have much to do with "The Miller's Tale."

On Tuesday night, someone broke into the Chouan garage, tore off all the chrome from their pickup, and left it twisted and mangled on the front lawn.

On Wednesday morning, Henry heard before his Government final exam about the bricks and the chrome. Then he couldn't remember the process by which a federal bill becomes a law, or how Congress goes about overriding a veto, or whether governors had any role in drawing up the shape of congressional districts in their states. Since there were only ten questions on the exam and he had to make up three answers completely out of thin air, he figured that he hadn't done as well as he might have.

On Wednesday night, nothing happened at the Chouan house in Merton.

On Thursday, Henry, humiliated by his Government exam, found new depths of humiliation when he couldn't remember if he had to do the operations inside the parentheses first, or if the outside operations had to be performed on the interior numbers first, or if he should just go ahead and multiply through the parentheses, after all. Never in the history of Whittier Academy had there been so many erasures on a single sheet of paper. By the time it was over, Henry was amazed that his whole Pre-Algebra test hadn't dissolved into one big hole.

On Thursday night, nothing happened at the Chouan house in Merton. Henry checked the *Blythbury-by-the-Sea Chronicle* the next morning to be sure.

On Friday, Henry decided that there would be no more humiliation. He answered Life Science questions as if he had made up the whole science himself, and he thought the way he differentiated one phylum from another and then explained the operations of photosynthesis should make his teacher cry, it was so beautiful.

Afterward, he ran a 5:32 mile in PE. No surprise there, except that he had hoped to come in a little lower. Say, in under four minutes.

But there was one surprise that afternoon. Sanborn came in at 6:23.

"Two . . . seconds to . . . spare," he said to Henry after he crossed the finish line—and after he was able to breathe again.

"Sanborn, that's amazing!" yelled Henry. "Amazing. That's, like, five times faster than you've ever run it before. How did you do that?"

Henry had to wait a little bit for his answer. Sanborn was still trying to suck in air.

"Practice . . . and . . . discipline, . . . my . . . boy," he said. "Practice . . . and . . . discipline."

"I guess so," said Henry.

"I want to be . . . in shape . . . when we climb . . . Katahdin."

"I'm climbing Katahdin alone," said Henry.

"Why . . . don't you keep . . . on saying that, . . . Henry, . . . and then I'll grind . . . your sweaty . . . face . . . into the . . . track."

Henry decided that he wouldn't say it anymore.

But he *was* going to climb Katahdin alone.

Friday afternoon, Coach Santori called Henry aside after crew practice. Apparently, he thought he'd waited long enough for Henry to deal with his Outrage. Regionals were coming up, Coach Santori said. He wasn't sure that Henry's recent loss wouldn't be a distraction, he said. He was replacing Henry for Regionals, and probably for State, he said. But Henry would be welcome to come and dress for the meets anyway, he said. Go take a shower.

Friday night, two bricks went through the picture window of the Chouan house. The Merton police were waiting. After a short chase, they arrested two members of the Longfellow Prep rugby team for vandalism and trespassing, and that, according to the *Blythbury-by-the-Sea Chronicle,* was only the beginning of potential charges.

When Henry read the news while standing on the stoop, the wound on his palm began to throb.

When Louisa—who was finally coming down for some meals—looked through the thick glass of the door and saw Henry standing on the stoop, she came outside and took the paper and read the news herself. Then she ran back upstairs. She wouldn't open her door until Henry sent Black Dog upstairs, who pawed a couple of times, and whined, and then went inside when the door opened just enough.

Henry lay in bed that night, completely alone.

So he was awake after midnight when his father's slow slippered feet slid along the Oriental runner and down the steps toward the kitchen. He threw on a shirt and followed. He found him in the downstairs hall by the flintlocks, lit by a small lamp.

"You're up late," his father said.

"So are you."

His father nodded. He pointed to two of the flintlocks in the collection. "Those were in the wreck. I took them back from the historical society—we should have something, at least. They need some work. But they've been exposed too long. They'll probably never fire again."

"That's okay," said Henry.

His father considered them. He ran his hand along their stocks and trailed his fingers across their worn and pitted barrels.

"I never thought Trouble would come to this house," he said quietly. "Not really. Not to us." He paused. "I should have oiled these stocks better before I mounted them."

"We can do it another time."

"I suppose." His father took his hand down and slipped it into the pocket of his robe. His mouth worked for a bit before he spoke again. "Henry," he said. "Henry, do you think Franklin would have grown into a good man?"

Henry was so startled, he took a step back.

"I know," said his father. "How can anybody ask that? But lately, it's the only question I seem to be able to ask. Not: Why was Franklin taken from us? Not: What should happen to Chay Chouan? But: Would Franklin have grown into a good man? And I'm not sure I have the courage to hear a true answer."

"Dad."

"So I wander these halls at night, looking at old flintlocks, wondering, trying to understand, trying to figure out if all the time I thought Trouble could never come in, it was already inside, and I knew it, and I didn't want to know it. And then, Henry, then I wonder if Franklin being taken from us wasn't somehow . . . if Franklin was going to grow up . . . Oh, Henry."

He held out his arms. Henry filled them.

The flintlocks mounted on the wall in the downstairs hall of the Smith house glowed in the dimmed light. They had been in more than a few battles—at least four at Trenton, one at Lexington, two at the North Bridge, one fired as late as Antietam. But none had ever been in a battle as fierce as the one being fought that night, deep in a father and a brother whose hearts lay broken open—a battle whose outcome could never be fully decided.

* * *

He let his father believe that he had learned to be cold inside. With him, this was not hard. He did not show that he missed his dog. He did not speak of her to anyone. And he did not flinch when his father turned only to his brother.

But tears wept deep at night, alone, are not cold.

11

DURING THE FIRST WEEKS OF JUNE, Henry couldn't help wondering why the staff of the historical society was so concerned about the ship down in Salvage Cove. Front-page articles in the *Blythbury-by-the-Sea Chronicle*—with headlines in bold print—made it seem as if heaven and earth depended upon unraveling the terrific mysteries of a three-century-old wreck. Today!

Probably, the articles speculated, she had been a merchant trading ship traveling up and down the coast of New England. But, as Dr. Cavendish asked, if she had only been a trading vessel, why were so many cutlasses found? (And taken away, Henry thought.) And why so many muskets found? (And taken away.) And the cannon, which seemed much too large for a merchant ship. (Those, too.) The rings along the hull and the chains attached to them were another problem. They might, Dr. Cavendish said, suggest that this had been a slave ship, but this seemed unlikely. So what purpose did the chains and rings serve? And how had she burned? Henry wasn't surprised to see that Dr. Cavendish agreed with the bigger policeman: She was burned after she had been driven up on the shore. But who had burned her? If the crew had run her up on shore, why had they burned her? And why was there no record of her loss? And why were the cutlasses and cannon never salvaged? Or the chains, for that matter?

It was Dr. Cavendish's hope that the ship could be excavated and put on display in a new addition to the historical society's building. (Donations were now being solicited from the society's "gold members.") Meanwhile, a display of ship's artifacts would be ready at the historical society's museum for late summer, including its cargo and armaments, as well as examples of the troublesome chains. Perhaps by that time, more would be uncovered about the ship's history. "Until then," said Dr. Cavendish, "we just don't know."

Henry could not figure out why not knowing about a wreck mattered all that much—especially since now there was another wreck in Blythbury-by-the-Sea. And this one seemed a whole lot more important.

One calm, warm June night, Adams Auditorium in the Henry Wadsworth Longfellow Preparatory High School was, as the two Blythbury-by-the-Sea policemen put it, "devastated." Every year before the high school graduation ceremonies, banners that reached back to Henry Wadsworth Longfellow himself were hung in Adams; their gold braid and silver tassels would glisten against the high school walls. But the banners had been torn down and shredded. The deep-paneled walls had been smeared with white paint. The podium had been ripped from its moorings and toppled over into the front seats. The rich blue velvet of the auditorium chairs had been slashed, and all the footlights on the stage smashed in.

"No human beings of any conscience could have participated in such a desecration of a historical institution," the editorial in the *Blythbury-by-the-Sea Chronicle* claimed. "Only those undeserving of the privileges of American citizenship could be responsible."

Henry read the editorial while taking Black Dog down into the cove. When he came back up, he threw the paper into the garbage.

By mid-June—after the Whittier Academy crew team had finished so poorly at Regionals that they would not be going on to State—the sea had given back most of the beach to Salvage Cove. New sand stretched from the dark boulders as it once had, and the boulders themselves, scoured clean by the storm, began to grow back their long seaweed whiskers. Dark mussel colonies took hold in the new clefts the toppled rocks provided, and the sea turned bluer and warmer as green spring yielded to yellow summer. The water was so warm that even Black Dog sometimes let the green-white froth of a wave come up to her feet—though she would never, ever go in.

Little by little, Henry cleaned and polished all of the camping equipment—his own and Franklin's. He sorted it out, repacked it into his own backpack, hefted the thing up to his shoulders to feel its weight and balance, took it off and repacked everything, tried it on his shoulders again, and felt that everything was about right.

He bought a new tarp—always useful—and then splurged on a new Buck knife—also always useful—as well as a new short hatchet. This represented only a small drain on his savings account—and anyway, he needed all three. Late at night he studied Franklin's maps of Katahdin's trails, imagining himself hiking upward, catching his breath when the lines drew close together and the climbing steep, and then finally coming to the top of Katahdin and turning around full circle and finding that there was nothing between him and outer space but the blue atmosphere—and not so much of that—and then looking down at hawks shredding the clouds with their rigid wings.

There were times when Henry wondered if he should ask his father to climb the mountain with him—which would, of course, eliminate the problem of going to Katahdin without telling his parents, since there was no way in this entire green and yellow world that his mother was going to say, "Sure, go ahead. Have a good time."

As for his father—well, his father hadn't been to his accounting firm in Boston for weeks. He hadn't seen a single one of his Beacon Hill colleagues. He wouldn't go to St. Anne's anymore. He didn't drive into Manchester, or even into Blythbury-by-the-Sea. When he came to dinner, he hardly spoke. During the day, he stayed in the library. At night, his slippered feet stalked the halls. It seemed as if all that remained between his life now and the brooding 𝔖𝔪𝔦𝔱𝔥 stone was to wait for more Trouble.

Once, Henry almost did ask his father to climb the mountain. He came into the library and saw that there was no work on his father's desk. His pipe was cold and unsmoked, and he was sitting alone in the bay window, looking across Salvage Cove and the wrecked ship with his hands on his knees. Henry almost asked him then. But he wasn't sure that his father could even answer, because the other question was so fierce. Would Franklin have grown into a good man? Henry watched him brooding on this, and the other questions that went with it: What could have been different? Why had he not done something about the Trouble within?

So Henry did not ask him, but on some days he would stand beside him at the bay window, and together they would look out on the wreck. Then Henry would feel the fire of Katahdin grow stronger and hotter within his guts. He would climb it alone; he would handle it himself. But his father would be quiet and still, and when Henry left the library, he would leave him sitting silently in the fierce battle, looking out the window like a lonely ghost in an ancient house understanding his life too late, and now helplessly watching what he could not change.

Which was pretty much what Louisa was doing, too. Alone.

One late night when Louisa came downstairs—and when Henry and Black Dog were watching a Buster Keaton movie— Henry surprised her in the kitchen. She told him that she thought that everyone was asleep because she didn't hear anything downstairs. He reminded her that Buster Keaton made silent movies. And then Henry told her something that he had never told her before. He told her that he missed her when she wasn't around. She almost began to cry. Henry said that he knew what she was feeling, because he felt it, too. Real crying, Louisa's head low. And then Henry said that he was going to Maine and he was going to climb Katahdin.

She looked up at him as though he was abandoning her.

"Why go now?" she said.

"Because I was going to climb Katahdin with Franklin."

"That's not an answer."

"I'm not asking your permission, Louisa. I'm just telling you that I'm going to go."

"With who?"

"With no one. By myself."

"They won't let you go," she said. "Especially by yourself."

"Maybe."

"And that's not why you're going," she said. "You're going because he said you wouldn't make it."

Henry looked at her.

"Frank is gone, Henry. He's gone. But he was also wrong.

Henry, he did things to hurt people. He did. He told you that you couldn't make it to . . . hurt you. Doing something crazy like this all by yourself isn't going to fix that."

"Oh, and you're the expert on doing something crazy. Like not going to his funeral is going to fix that." Henry was breathing hard. He could hardly believe that he was saying what he was saying. "Like dropping out of your life is going to fix that."

Louisa stared at him. Her eyes filled again. Then she slapped Henry hard and abruptly across his face. "You don't know anything," she said.

She ran upstairs to her room.

And since that had gone so well, Henry decided that he would wait a few days before he told his parents he was going to climb Katahdin.

He figured that he would wait until after they had had a really good supper. Probably he'd tell them when they were in the kitchen, cleaning up, when Black Dog was sitting patiently near his mother, who would be feeding her leftover scraps of marinated flank steak.

But when that time came three nights later and he told them about Katahdin, things didn't go any better than they had with Louisa—maybe because it wasn't marinated flank steak. It was just plain fried chicken.

"Are you out of your mind?" was the first thing that Henry's father said.

"When there's all this Trouble?" was the first thing that Henry's mother said.

"It's what Franklin and I planned to do. You know that."

"That's the point," said Henry's mother. "It's what *Franklin* and you planned to do."

"It matters to me," said Henry. "A lot."

"We know it matters to you, Henry," said his father. "But not now."

"And you certainly can't go by yourself," said his mother.

"I'm not going by myself," said Henry.

His father looked at him. "Who were you planning to go with?"

Henry thought wildly. "Sanborn," he said.

"Sanborn's planning to go with you?" said his mother.

"Yes. Sanborn. And Black Dog, too."

"And you two have this already planned this out?"

"Yes."

"Then I'm sorry, Henry," said his mother. "But you'll have to unplan it. It's not the time for us to be splitting apart."

Henry did not say what came into his mind right away: We are already splitting apart.

Henry looked down at Black Dog. How could he explain to his parents that there was something about climbing Katahdin that was important? That it was so important, that it was the last word that Franklin had cried out before the darkness in his brain fell over him? That it was so important, that fire burned in his guts?

"Katahdin," whispered Henry.

And Black Dog barked.

It startled them all—a quick, loud, cutting bark. Once. Then she sat and looked at them with bright eyes and thumping tail. They stared at her, and she rolled over onto her back and arched her belly up to be scratched.

And that ended it. Henry leaned down to scratch her, and his parents turned back to clean up the remains of the fried chicken, and there was no more talk of Katahdin. Outside, the wind picked up, sweeping from the north, carrying on its back full-blown clouds that had scratched their billows over Katahdin's peaks.

That night, Sanborn called.

"So," he said, "you told your parents that I was going with you."

"I guess my mother must have called your mother."

"I guess she must have. So when are we going?"

"Your parents would let you go?"

"They don't care."

"Sanborn . . ."

"A mile in six minutes and twenty-three seconds, kiddo. I'll make it."

"Listen, Sanborn, this was supposed to be between me and my—"

"Yeah, I know it was. I'm just coming along to make sure that you don't get busted up in some ravine. You know, part of that mountain is called—"

"The Knife Edge, and you know exactly how high it is and how thin the trail is and how exposed we'll be and how many people have fallen thousands of feet to their doom."

"As a matter of fact, I do know all that. So when are we going?"

Black Dog stood. She cocked her head and stared at Henry.

The wind from the north swept by his window. It was full dark, so he did not see the scoured clouds running over the wreck and above the house.

"You are such a jerk, you know that, Sanborn? And we leave the second of July."

"Ah, the second of July, the third full week of summer break—not the first, but the third, when all suspicions will be allayed, and we'll naturally be gone all day anyway. Deceptive and devious, Henry. Ingenious, even."

"Shut up, Sanborn."

The Henry Wadsworth Longfellow Preparatory High School graduation ceremonies were held outside on the school's grassy common, instead of in Adams. Policemen ringed the crowd, and not just the two policemen from Blythbury-by-the-Sea. Henry had never before been someplace where he was being guarded by state troopers with rifles. Very big state troopers with very big rifles.

The Smith family was at the graduation by special invitation of Longfellow Prep. Henry and his mother attended. Henry's father did not come. Louisa did not come. And the two boys arrested in Merton could not come. Two empty chairs among the graduates heralded their absence. Someone had placed the school's torn banners across them.

Henry sat with the graduates in the chair that Franklin would have occupied. He watched Franklin's friends and worshipers and fellow rugby players graduate and head on to new Ivy League life—the life that Franklin would have headed toward after he had graduated. When it came time for his row, Henry stood with the other graduates—he was easy to pick out, since he was the only one without a blue-and-yellow robe—and he processed to the podium, paused while Franklin's name was read, and then walked across to take the diploma and shake a trustee's hand—all to the hearty applause of the standing audience.

Henry's mother, who was in the front row, was weeping.

*   *   *

The morning of the Katahdin trip dawned clear; it was warm already by seven thirty, when Henry's father—shaved and dressed—went out to the BMW to try to leave for Boston but then came back inside and went in to the library instead. It was hot by ten, when Henry's mother left for a meeting with Mr. Churchill. It was steamy by eleven, when Mrs. Lodge from the historical society came by to have some papers signed by Henry's father, who did not sign them because he couldn't see anyone just now.

After Mrs. Lodge left, Henry filled two water bottles. He left a note for his parents. He took out the leash he had bought for Black Dog and tried it on her. She thought that she was being punished and immediately fell to the floor and showed her belly. "No, Black Dog. Good dog. Good, good dog. It's fine. Get up. Good dog."

She got up, and they tried walking out of the kitchen using the leash.

Black Dog didn't make it past the counter. She rolled down and showed her belly again. She drooped her ears and whined.

Henry had to tell her all over again what a good dog she was.

While Black Dog tried to get used to the leash, Henry phoned Sanborn to tell him that they were on their way.

"You're really taking Black Dog?"

"I'm really taking Black Dog."

"Nobody is going to pick up someone who has a dog."

"Yes, they will."

"They'll think the dog is going to attack them or throw up or chew the upholstery or something. Nobody will pick us up."

"People like to pick up hitchhikers with dogs."

"And you know this because of your vast hitchhiking experience?"

"Shut up, Sanborn."

Henry hung up the phone, and then he pulled Black Dog along and out of the kitchen.

Black Dog fell to the floor and showed her belly twice in the hall.

"Listen," said Henry finally. "This is not going to work. It's just a leash, okay? A leash. Every other dog in Massachusetts knows what a leash is, so buck up. Okay?"

Black Dog tried to buck up. She only turned on her belly twice while walking down the driveway—where his father could not see them from the library, or Louisa from her bedroom.

At the road, Henry turned and looked back at his house. Black Dog sat and looked back, too. The timbers of the house were so solid, so heavy, as if they carried well down past the rocky ledges and on into the earth.

"Well," said Henry, "here we go." He hefted his backpack higher and tightened the strap around his waist. Then together, he and Black Dog went out onto the road and into the world.

Black Dog was not happy.

After about half a mile, she finally stopped falling down and turning up her belly. But every time a car drew near, she pulled and whined and got crazier and crazier until it rushed past and she could begin to come out of her desperation—until the next one came along.

Which, when they met Sanborn at his home, Sanborn said was going to drive them both nuts.

"She'll get used to it," said Henry. "Did you leave your parents a note?"

"No, O Devious One."

"No?"

"You have trouble with monosyllables?"

"Did you tell them where you were going?"

"Yes, I did."

"And that was fine with them?"

"I already told you, Henry: That was fine with them."

"Did they ask if you were going with just me?"

"No, they didn't ask if I was going with just you. They didn't ask anything. Okay? They're heading off to Verona or Florence or somewhere like that and they're busy packing. All they needed to know was that I was out of their way while they tested their colognes to see if they clashed. So are we going or what?"

"We're going," said Henry.

So they did, walking quickly onto Main Street, and through town, and then away from Blythbury-by-the-Sea, where Trouble was not supposed to find anyone; they stopped only to reassure Black Dog every time a car went by—she didn't get used to it—and then at a Stop and Go Hamburgers, since they were already hungry and they didn't want to use up the food they had packed. Afterward, full of grease and vanilla milk-shake, they headed onto the road again, north, until late in the afternoon. Then, when they were sure that no one who knew them would drive by, they began to walk backward, holding out their thumbs for a ride.

"No one is going to pick up two guys with a dog and big packs," said Sanborn.

"Backpackers will," said Henry. "You'd be surprised."

But Sanborn was not surprised. They took turns holding their thumbs out and walking backward for the rest of the afternoon, and then past supper, and then into dusk, as the light dissolved from the sky and hinted at the purple behind it, and Henry wondered if his parents really believed the note that said he was staying overnight with Sanborn for a few days—which wasn't, technically speaking, a lie. And he wondered, too, if they were going to have to find a place to camp soon before it became dark.

Then, when the purple was more than a hint, a pickup did stop. It paused, moved ahead, slowed, then pulled to the side of the road and waited for them. Sanborn was overjoyed. "Who knows?" he said. "Maybe he's going the whole way!"

Henry ran up with Black Dog, who wasn't shying away from this pickup at all. She pulled him toward it, barking in a frenzy. Maybe, thought Henry, she was pretty tired, too.

They reached the pickup and threw their two packs in the back—which is where Black Dog jumped in without any hesitating. She ran up front to the cab and let the driver know how much she appreciated his stopping for them by slobbering all over the window behind him, and when she wasn't slobbering, she was pawing at the window happily and wagging her tail. She must really have been tired of walking, thought Henry.

Henry climbed into the bed of the pickup and tied Black Dog close to the front so that she would stay in. Then he jumped down—Black Dog was still slobbering and barking—and walked around to the door. By the lowering light, he noticed that the chrome was missing from the side of the pickup. Sanborn had already gotten in, and Henry started to get in the seat beside him. The chrome was missing from the door, too, as though it had been torn off deliberately. He felt that this should mean something to him.

He got in and pulled the door closed. Then leaning past Sanborn, he turned to the driver.

"Thanks," he said—to Chay Chouan.

His father found the volume of Keats. He found what she had written inside. He burned it. "You bring the shame of your past on us. An American girl."

"There is no shame," he said.

"What do you know of shame? An American girl. Do you think I brought you here to meet one of them? I will not hand what I have built into her hand. And not into yours."

So he had given what his father had built, a heat that would not be forgotten. His father let him stay long enough to salvage what remained. And when they had done what could be done, his father told him he should go the next morning. With nothing.

He left that night. With the pickup.

12

SANBORN, who had not recognized the driver's face, chattered happily. "Yeah. Thanks for stopping," he said.

Chay nodded. He pulled the pickup back onto the highway.

"It was starting to get dark out there, and this jerk"—Sanborn nodded toward Henry—"this jerk figured that we would get picked up, oh, a couple of hours ago."

Chay nodded again. "The dog."

"That's what I said. No one is going to pick up two guys with a dog."

Chay nodded.

"Except for you."

Chay nodded again.

"We're heading up to Maine," said Sanborn.

No nod this time.

"Where are you heading?"

Chay waved his hand out to the open road. "North," he said.

"That's fine. That's where we're heading. North."

"Fine," said Chay.

Fine, thought Henry.

"We figured we could log a hundred miles or so and then find a campground. If you're going north anyway, if it's all right with you, maybe we could just keep going as far as you're heading. Until we get to Millinocket, Maine."

Chay nodded.

"Why don't you just pull over and let us out now?" said Henry.

Silence from Sanborn. The sounds of an old and worn pickup, pushing itself along on old and worn tires. The sounds of Black Dog, barking happily behind them, still wanting to thank the driver for stopping for them.

"Henry," said Sanborn slowly, "why don't you shut up?"

"Sanborn," said Henry, "why don't *you* shut up? Believe me, we don't want to be in this pickup. Because our driver doesn't have a driver's license." He leaned forward. "Do you? And why don't you have a driver's license? Because it got taken away. Because you ran into my brother and killed him."

Black Dog still barking from the back. Sanborn let out a long and troubled breath.

"Sanborn, have you met Chay Chouan? I met him in court. I didn't actually *meet* him, but we were both there. He was the one in the handcuffs. Chay, this is my friend, Sanborn. He's on this trip with me because my brother, Franklin—who I was going to go with—is dead."

Silence again.

"Besides your family," said Chay finally, "no one is sorrier than me about your brother."

"Go to hell," said Henry. "You don't know what it's like to lose a brother like that."

Chay drove.

"He had his whole life in front of him. He was just eighteen. His whole life. And he's dead because of you. I shoveled the dirt in myself. You should hear my mother late at night. You should . . . you should hear her. You can't imagine what those sounds are like."

Chay stared ahead. The road was empty, and the two headlights searched the gathering darkness. No stars in the sky yet. No moon.

"Your mother sounds like she is holding your brother, and he is bleeding to death, and she cannot do a thing to stop what is happening," Chay said, almost whispering. "She sounds like all she wants is to die before anything else happens, because already she can't bear to keep on living." Chay ran his hand across his eyes and through his hair.

"Because of you," said Henry.

Chay nodded.

They rode on. It seemed to Henry that a deep pause in his life had fallen abruptly upon him. Outside there was only this growing darkness. Inside there was only this silence, just as dark. Even Black Dog was still now.

"How do you know?" said Henry.

Chay said nothing. He stared straight ahead. His hand across his eyes again.

They drove on. They passed through a small town where a movie was letting out. Pretty soon, people would be heading to the ice cream shop. They'd talk about the movie. About whether they liked it or not. About whether the music was right for it or not. If it dragged in places. They'd wish there was more butterscotch in their shakes.

Henry felt himself fall so deeply into a crater of weariness, so deep, so black, that there was no use even trying to get out.

"This is the turn onto Route 95," said Chay. "To Maine. If you want to get out now, I'll stop."

Henry said nothing. He closed his eyes.

They took the ramp onto the highway. The sounds of the pickup's tires and engine grew steady.

Black Dog scratched at the back window, and when Henry turned and opened it, she stuck her snout in his palm. He stroked the side of her face. She licked his hand, then, satisfied, lay down into a happy heap in the pickup bed, as comfortable as if she had lain back there a hundred times.

"Where are you going?" said Henry.

Chay changed lanes for no particular reason.

"North," he said.

"Just north."

Chay nodded. He changed lanes again—for no particular reason.

"Do you know what you did to our lives?"

"Why do you think I'm heading north?"

"You're not even supposed to be driving."

Chay shrugged.

"What are you going to say if you get pulled over?"

Chay turned, and for the first time he looked full at Henry. "You think that is my biggest problem?" he said.

"I think your biggest problem is that you killed my brother."

"You said that already," said Chay.

"Yeah, I did. I'm going to say it a lot. Because you need to hear it a lot."

Chay shook his head. His hand went up through his hair again. "You keep saying things I already know," he said. "From my parents, I listened. From you . . ."

"From me, what?"

Chay said nothing.

"So you want me to tell you something you don't know?"

Chay laughed, so bitterly that Henry was startled for a moment. "Yes," he said. "Tell me something I don't know."

"Franklin was . . ." But Henry did not finish. He felt himself still in the crater of weariness, and whatever he had been about to say was even lower than he was.

Henry laid his head back against the seat.

They drove on. Still in darkness. Still in silence. The rhythmic sounds of the worn engine and worn tires. In the back, Black Dog was asleep. And Sanborn was asleep, too—the traitor—snoring louder than the engine. Henry looked out his window. The darkened night leveled everything out. Every mile or so, lights flickered, but in the almost-darkness, it was hard to believe that there was anything really beyond what he could see—even though he knew there must be.

He turned back to Chay.

"How do you know how my mother sounds?"

Again, his hand through his hair. "In Cambodia, we lived in a refugee camp for three years."

"So?" said Henry.

Chay looked at him, then back at the road. "The Khmer Rouge came into the camp while all the fathers were in the fields. They lined up all boys over twelve to fight for them. My older brother was taken because he was so big. But he was only ten years. My mother tried to tell them. She begged the soldiers. They would not listen. When she would not let go, a soldier shot my sister. My mother ran to her. The soldiers dragged my brother away. He was screaming for her."

Henry remembered the hearing. "*So, many of your students have had their sisters shot in front of them? Or their brothers taken by force?*" How had he forgotten?

"That is how I know what your mother sounds like," said Chay.

The tires hummed on the road, and Henry turned back to the dark window.

They crossed into New Hampshire, and because Chay was driving at the exact speed limit—which meant that he was being passed by every truck on the road—sixteen minutes later they were crossing the bridge into Maine. Henry had driven across many times when his family was heading up to the resorts of Kennebunkport. But he had never come across at night, when the lights of the industrial plants below were strung like jewels along the water's edges, and all the grittiness and dirt and smoke were hidden.

Henry closed his eyes.

He saw his brother, pale and white on the hospital bed. He saw the tubes stretching into one arm. He saw the stump of the other, and the bandage with blood and gore leaking through. He saw his brother breathing in time with the machine behind him. He saw his mother with her wide, unblinking eyes. He saw his father with his hands up to his face.

And suddenly, it wasn't his mother. It was Chay's mother—and nothing was white.

He heard their sounds.

They drove on through the night.

Henry kept his face to the window, and they passed one exit after another until the sky ahead reddened and suddenly there were bright lights high above the road. Henry saw them reflected in expanses of the sea that had pushed into the coast and come right up by the highway. The water shone black obsidian, and streaks of red cut across it—the reflections of the lights of Portland.

"I'm getting off here," said Chay.

Henry didn't look at him.

"I haven't eaten anything."

"You don't have to explain," said Henry. He looked at his watch. Almost ten o'clock.

What is it that makes a city look so beautiful at night? he wondered. Probably it's the lights that come unexpectedly out of the darkness. To the east, they glowed brilliantly in buildings that may have been insurance or accounting offices but now were made magical and exotic by their white and orange and yellow lights. It was like something conjured up, so rich they were, and mysterious.

Black Dog woke up when they slowed and rounded off onto the exit. Henry heard her bark, and when he turned around, she was stretching with her back end way up in the air—and trying to keep her balance.

They drove into Portland—mostly deserted this late—and then turned onto Commercial Street to follow the coastline. Here it was not deserted. Small cafés and restaurants still shone their bright lights, and Henry could hear light music playing. Couples were eating at tables outside the restaurants. He rolled his window down. He could smell the piquant sea.

Henry remembered it all—though it had all been in daylight. He remembered walking this street with his family, year after year, visiting the same gift shops and toy shops and kite shops and—because his father thought there was no better thing in the world to do on vacation—the old book shops, just to see if, by chance, there might be a lead on another medieval manuscript with another *ad usum*. He remembered the first time his parents let Franklin and Louisa take him by themselves through the city, and how his mother reminded them to watch out for him, and how Franklin had said, "Henry's old enough to watch out for himself. He's not a baby," and how he thought he would lift off into heaven because his older brother thought that he could watch out for himself. He wouldn't even take Louisa's hand when they crossed the busy downtown streets, because he wasn't a baby.

Chay reached the end of Commercial Street. He looked in the mirror, then made a quick turn and drove back the same way. He looked hungrily into the restaurants.

"There's a chowder house down at the end of the street, before you turn back toward 95," said Henry. "On the wharf. It's probably still open."

Chay didn't say anything. They drove slowly.

"There," said Henry. "It *is* still open. You park past it. Right there."

Chay pulled into the half-dark parking lot beside another pickup—this one rusted, and dented, and filled with beat-up duffle bags, and sporting a torn bumper sticker that shone in Chay's headlights: AMERICA FOR AMERICANS DAMMIT! Chay turned the lights off, but he did not turn off the engine. He held his hands rigidly on the wheel and stared into the rearview mirror.

"If you're waiting for someone to come out to take your order, they're not going to do it," said Henry. He smacked Sanborn—"Wake up!"—and reached for the handle of his door.

"Wait," said Chay.

Henry turned and looked through the back window. Nothing. And then, slowly, a policeman drove by at a crawl. Henry felt Chay tighten beside him. He could almost hear his heartbeat. He saw the policeman's brake lights come on, saw the patrol car slow.

Chay's tightness almost exploded. He's barely holding himself together, thought Henry.

Then the brake lights went off and the patrol car drove by.

"It's only a policeman," said Henry. "He doesn't have any reason to stop you—except maybe for a stupid U-turn where you weren't supposed to pull one."

Chay took his hands off the wheel and looked at him, and Henry wondered whether, if the lights had been on, he would have seen a face as white as his brother's had been in the hospital. "Policemen don't need a reason to stop me," Chay said.

"Sure," said Henry. He hit Sanborn on top of his head. "Hey, Sleeping Beauty. You want something to eat?"

"Bring back a shake," Sanborn said—if that was what he was really saying. It was all mixed up with a yawn.

"What kind?"

No answer.

Henry got out of the pickup and climbed up into the bed, where Black Dog was straining and eager. As soon as he untied her to put her into the cab with Sanborn, she jerked the lead out of his hand, vaulted over the side of the pickup, and jumped up on Chay—who was also out of the pickup—her ears up, her tail wagging, her mouth panting and barking and whining and wheezing—and all just because Chay had stopped to pick them up! Henry thought she was overdoing it. And it was humiliating, especially when Chay stood rock still, his face set, his hands high in the air, until, as if he had made a sudden decision, he knelt in the lot and let Black Dog, in utter rapture, lick him all over his face while he rubbed her sleek sides.

Henry had never seen her tail spin so wildly.

He grabbed Black Dog, half-pulled, half-carried her into the cab, and closed the door on her. "Lie down," said Henry, and Black Dog looked beyond him once again to Chay. "Lie . . . down," said Henry again. And because she sometimes wanted to be obedient, she did. Sanborn, who could apparently sleep through about anything, rearranged his unconscious self and cuddled up next to Black Dog, probably because she was soft and warm. Black Dog looked at Henry, then at Chay, then at Henry. "You stay," Henry said.

She looked at him with half-closed eyes, annoyed.

"I'll bring back some fried clams."

Black Dog looked as though she might forgive him if he did.

Chay hadn't moved at all. He was still kneeling and his hands were held out as if he was still stroking her sides. "All right?" Henry asked. Chay nodded, and Henry turned toward the chowder house. He really didn't care whether Chay followed him or stayed in the parking lot.

The Chowder Mug was the kind of place that was surprising to find on Commercial Street, because it didn't look as if it was fixed up for tourists. It looked as if it served real food to real people, and they couldn't care less if tourists came in to spend their money. The chairs were metal and vinyl, the tables were old Formica, and the menus were chipped plastic. They hadn't been changed in a long time—except for the new prices taped over the old ones. The place smelled of cooking oil and fried fish and clams.

Henry loved it all. He sat down at one of the tables and didn't even look at the menu; he knew what he wanted. But when Chay came in—after all—and sat down across from him, Henry handed him a menu. "You should try the chowder," he said. Then he stretched and waited for the waitress, who, when she came, looked as if she wasn't about to take any nonsense this late at night, thank you very much. And that was fine, since Henry wasn't interested in nonsense. He ordered a large bowl of clam chowder and fries and an Admiral Ames root beer.

"And for you?" said the waitress to Chay.

Chay studied the menu again, then looked up. "What's a chowder?" he asked.

"What's a chowder?" the waitress said. "You come into a chowder house and you want to know what's a chowder?" She turned back toward the kitchen. "Hey, Willy, we got a customer out here wants to know what a chowder is."

"So tell him," yelled the unseen Willy.

Chay waited.

The waitress sighed. "Chowder is a milky soup. It's got potatoes and onions and clams. If you lived in New England, you'd know this."

Chay handed her the menu. He ordered a hamburger and fries and a Coke.

"Daring, aren't you?" said the waitress.

Chay did not answer.

The waitress looked at Henry and shook her head. She slapped Chay's menu beside the other one already on the table. Then she went to the counter and hollered the order back to Willy: "Chowder, fries, and a blue plate!"

"What's a chowder?" Willy yelled back.

"I'll show you what a chowder is," the waitress said, and shook her head again.

There was hardly anyone else in the restaurant. An old couple wearing matching berets. They held each other's hands as they sipped their tea. They looked as if they had built their house far enough away from Trouble.

In the back, a couple of fishermen, maybe lobstermen, lining up bottles—and they weren't Admiral Ames root beers—lining them up on the edge of their table. They laughed loudly and suddenly, and then fell into sullen silences. They glared around at the restaurant, and once Henry caught their eyes, he didn't look their way again.

Henry and Chay didn't say anything the whole time they were waiting for their food. When their clam chowder and hamburger came, they ate in silence, too. Henry saw Chay glance at the chowder. He doesn't know what he's missing, thought Henry. He ate his chowder, hot and thick, quickly. He used his French fries to clean the sides of the bowl, and in between long drafts of Admiral Ames root beer he sighed happily, since there is nothing like a bowl of clam chowder and a good root beer to make a person happy.

And then he stopped himself.

He looked across at Chay. Who had murdered his brother, Franklin. And he felt his anger rise in him and sour the chowder in his stomach. And he felt guilt for sitting at the same table. And it was too bad that Chay had lost his sister, but he wasn't sitting at the same table with the people who killed her.

He pushed his bowl away. He didn't finish his fries.

He had not known how much he looked like her. How he moved like her. How he held himself like her. She had said it was so, but he had not known.

And the dog! The dog! Keats was right about aching Pleasure. But why would anyone eat a chowder?

13

CHAY, MEANWHILE, ate little by little. His head hung low. His eyes were half-closed, and his hands seemed made of weights, he raised them so slowly to his mouth. He's going to fall asleep, thought Henry. His face is going to fall right into his blue plate.

But his face didn't fall. Chay kept eating.

When the waitress came to take away Henry's bowl and to leave their bills, Henry ordered a basket of fried clams to go. And a milkshake. Vanilla.

"This is a chowder house," said the waitress. "Chowder houses do not serve vanilla milkshakes. If you want a vanilla milkshake, there's an ice cream place down the street, but it's probably closed by now."

Henry ordered another bottle of Admiral Ames root beer instead.

When the fried clams and root beer came, he went up to the counter to pay his bill. The two fishermen came up to pay theirs at the same time, and they stood largely on each side of him. He could smell the sea on them, and the stale scent of beer.

The waitress took his money. "Where you boys headed?" she asked.

"Katahdin," Henry said.

"My brother climbed it once," she said, making the change.

"He always said it was overrated." She handed the coins to Henry.

"You climbing with your friend?" said one of the fishermen, nodding back to Chay.

"He's not my friend," said Henry.

The other fisherman laughed abruptly. More stale beer smell.

"So why hang around with a VC?" said the first fisherman.

Henry had never heard anyone called a VC, and he had no idea what it meant. He figured that it probably didn't mean "Very Cool."

"He's my ride," said Henry.

It wasn't the best moment for Chay to come up to the counter. But Trouble comes when it wants to.

Chay took out his wallet. Henry could see that it didn't have much in it.

"You should've tried the chowder," said the waitress.

Chay didn't say anything.

"Maybe he don't like American food," said the first fisherman.

Both fishermen watched Chay carefully. The second took a last drink from his last bottle, and then cracked it down on the countertop. The first tipped his bottle up to his mouth again. He sucked loudly on it.

"C'mon," said Henry. He picked up his bag of fried clams and his bottle of Admiral Ames, and he nodded to Chay to go on ahead.

The fishermen followed them out of the chowder house. Henry felt them walking behind him when they got onto the street. He felt them turn into the half-dark parking lot with them. And he felt the beer bottle crash past his feet, shards of glass skittering away on the asphalt.

"Hey, gook, where do you think you're going?"

Chay stopped and turned around. He looked past Henry.

Even in the dark, Henry could see in Chay's face an anger greater than he had ever felt. It startled him. It came from a place deep inside. Then Henry turned, too.

"Mack, this one don't look like he's going to run away," said the first fisherman.

"Maybe he knows kung fu or something. Is that it, gook? You know kung fu?" He held his hands up in front of him and crouched. "Are you Bruce Lee?"

The fishermen thought they were hysterically funny. They both laughed uproariously.

"What do you want?" said Henry.

"Maybe you should go away, little boy. This doesn't have anything to do with you."

"Unless you love gooks."

The two fishermen laughed again. Then they both stopped, almost as if they had rehearsed it. They stepped closer.

"We don't want any trouble," said Henry.

Mack punched the other fisherman on the arm. "They don't want any trouble." He turned back to Henry. "But you got trouble. And you know why? Because *he's* trouble." He pointed to Chay. "Him and all the others from Vietnam, coming over here like they have every right to. Taking jobs. Bringing in new fishing boats and taking up all the licenses."

"He's not from Vietnam," said Henry.

"Good fishermen getting laid off and new fishermen can't get a place—unless they're from Vietnam, and then they got the whole federal government of the U. S. of A. sending them checks to help out. They get the spots on the boats, and real fishermen—"

"Like us!"

"Yeah, real fishermen like us got to leave their homes and come up to Portland to try to hire on. Or sit around and drink cheap beer."

They laughed uproariously again. Then stopped.

"You should never have left Vietnam, gook. We're going to teach you why."

Chay was very still.

Henry looked around them. On one side of the parking lot was a row of metal-fronted warehouses and lobster fisheries—as closed as vaults. On the other side, the parking lot ended at a wharf. Henry could hear the water lapping up against it, and he imagined its dark, oily surface—and what it would be like to fall into it.

A door opened and shut.

Sanborn stood beside them.

"Looks like the gook's got another friend," said Mack.

"Henry," said Sanborn, "for the record, you don't handle things very well on your own." He pointed at the Admiral Ames. "Is that for me? I told you to get a vanilla shake."

"They don't serve shakes in a chowder house," said Henry. "It's root beer."

Chay reached over and took the Admiral Ames from Henry. He held it by the neck, then bent down and smashed the bottle. He stood up, holding the shattered and sharp top half out.

"I guess that means I'm not going to get my root beer," said Sanborn.

Chay took a step forward toward the fishermen. He still didn't say a thing. But he took the keys out of his back pocket and flicked them to Henry.

It did not take Henry long to figure out the plan.

In a second he had sprinted back to the pickup and pulled the door open.

"We don't care about you anyways!" yelled Mack.

Henry got in, pushed Black Dog's snout away, looked around for the ignition, found it, put the key in, couldn't turn it, pushed Black Dog's snout away, took the key out and put in the right key, pushed Black Dog's snout away, started the pickup, whipped it into reverse, and stomped on the accelerator.

Which cascaded a yelping Black Dog into the windshield—and scattered Sanborn and Chay and Mack and the other fisherman like bowling pins.

Henry stomped on the brake, and Sanborn got in and Chay threw the broken root beer bottle and got in beside him and together they hollered things that Henry couldn't make out but it wasn't at all hard to figure out what they wanted. Henry stomped on the accelerator again and they flew out of the half-dark parking lot into the empty streets of downtown Portland.

Still in reverse.

On the street, Henry stomped on the brake again, shifted into drive, stomped on the accelerator. He drove into the first left he could find, down a long and narrow wharf.

"No, no!" screamed Chay. "Wrong way!"

Henry, in a second, thought this was obvious, too. He knew what was at the end of wharves. He stomped on the brake again, shifted into reverse, stomped on the accelerator, and shot out from the narrow wharf just as the two fishermen appeared. Startled yells.

Chay yelled, too—something sounding like a Cambodian battle cry, Henry figured.

He stomped on the brake again, shifted to drive, and stomped on the accelerator. He turned a quick right this time, then drove up into the narrow streets. He was breathing two or three times every second. He had now driven the combined distance of all the other driving he had ever done in his life—which meant once down his driveway. And he had lost the bag of fried clams.

Black Dog looked at him with her ears down.

"Sorry," he said to Black Dog, then turned to Chay. "I'll find a place to stop and you can—"

"Don't stop!" yelled Chay.

"Those guys were running for their pickup," said Sanborn.

"That left!" said Chay.

Henry wheeled quickly to the left. Black Dog shot into the windshield again.

"You can slow down a little when you take a turn," said Sanborn.

"You can shut up," said Henry.

"Right!" said Chay.

"Do you know where we're going?" yelled Henry. He took the right too fast and Black Dog gave a sudden and irritated yelp—but Chay was holding her.

"No," said Chay—which was not comforting. "Right!" he yelled again.

"A little slower this time," said Sanborn, "unless you want us barfing up."

Henry, who definitely did not want them barfing up, took the next right a little slower—into a street where all the cars parked on both sides were heading toward him.

"You turned down a one-way street," said Chay.

"You keep saying things I already know," said Henry.

The street was so narrow that their side mirrors almost touched the parked cars beside them. Henry prayed that another car wouldn't turn in ahead and drive toward him. And he prayed that if the two fishermen were looking for them, they wouldn't look down this street, since a truck going the wrong way down a one-way street would be a pretty clear giveaway.

"Take your next turn," said Chay.

"Which way?"

"Any way." Henry took the next left and slowed down. He looked in the back mirror—no one behind him. "I think I can stop now," he said.

"Please," said Sanborn.

He stopped, and then all at once, they began to laugh. Even Chay. And if Black Dog could have laughed, she would have laughed, too, sitting on Chay's lap and grinning and looking all giggly, all of them laughing as if they had been laughing together all their lives.

"Great driving, Henry," said Sanborn.

"I've never taken turns on two wheels," said Chay.

"Neither has he," said Sanborn.

"You're both very welcome for me saving you from getting beat up," said Henry. "I'm going to get out now—as soon as I can get my hands to let go of the wheel."

More laughter, and Chay reached up past Black Dog to pry Henry's hands from the wheel. And as soon as Chay touched him, Henry felt again the electric volts of his grief. He recoiled against the door, and all laughter stopped.

Silence, suddenly.

Henry and Chay got out of the pickup. They passed each

other silently. Chay got in behind the wheel, and Henry climbed in the other side and gathered Black Dog into his lap to see if he could calm her down. Then they closed the doors, and they all sat, breathing a little hard.

Henry wondered how it was that he could ever have found himself in the same pickup, laughing to die, with his brother's killer. He thought that he might be the one barfing up.

He looked out the window, holding Black Dog. He leaned back and brought Black Dog's head against his chest.

"Do you know how to get to the highway from here?" asked Sanborn.

Chay shrugged.

"All you have to do is start driving," said Henry. "You're going to hit the highway, or you're going to hit the water, and if you hit the water, then you turn around the other way and you'll hit the highway."

Black Dog suddenly raised her head.

A patrol car—maybe the same one they had seen before—cruised up beside them and stopped. It looked as if something in Chay stopped, too—maybe his heart. He started to sweat. Beads appeared on the side of his face.

The policeman lowered his side window and leaned over toward them.

Henry watched Chay force his arm to move. He rolled his window down.

"You boys all right?" called the policeman.

Chay nodded.

"Answer him," whispered Henry.

Chay nodded again.

"You're not lost, are you?"

Chay shook his head.

"Just a minute," said the policeman. He rolled up his window, put his car in park, and got out. Henry saw terror grip Chay; sweat now rolled down the side of his face.

The policeman stopped at the back of the pickup and wrote down the license plate number. Henry thought Chay was about to pass out.

Henry opened his door and got out. "Actually," he said, "we are lost. We were down at a chowder house on Commercial, and we took a left to try to get back to the highway."

"That was your first mistake," said the policeman. "You go left and you end up in the drink. You needed to take a right. Then all you have to do is take your next left at the light and follow the signs to 95. If you turn around here, there's a one-way street that will take you right back down." He pointed the way.

"Okay," Henry said. "A one-way street."

The policeman walked over to Chay and leaned down to the window.

"Are you all right, son?" the policeman said.

Chay nodded.

"You talk about as much as the Statue of Liberty, don't you?"

Chay shook his head.

The policeman considered something. And he might have considered something like "Can I see your license?" if Black Dog hadn't decided that she wanted to find out what the policeman smelled like. She stuck her head past Chay and out the window and sniffed.

The policeman scratched her behind the ears, which she loved, and which she showed she loved by making every cuddling sound that a dog can possibly make, all at once.

And that was enough. "You sure you know how to get to 95?" the policeman asked.

Henry got back into the pickup. "We're sure. Thanks," he said.

"You sure?" the policeman said to Chay.

Chay nodded.

The policeman walked back to his car, and Chay turned the pickup truck around and headed toward the one-way street. Ten minutes later, they were on Route 95 again, heading north, the stars growing more and more visible as they left the lights of the city.

"I never did get my shake," said Sanborn.

14

THEY DROVE ON into the darkness. Every star in the universe watched them.

"You handled that policeman really well," said Sanborn.

Chay looked in the mirror and changed lanes.

"Nodding, shaking your head, keeping quiet—*that's* not going to make him suspicious."

"Policemen mean trouble," said Chay.

"That's why you answer them very politely," said Sanborn. "Sometimes they mean trouble in America, too."

A low laugh from Chay, who glanced over at him. "What kind of trouble does a policeman mean to someone from Blythbury-by-the-Sea?"

"I don't know. He could have given you a ticket."

Chay laughed out loud—and it was not a sweet laugh. "A ticket. Could they strap your father to a plow and make him work the fields like an ox? And when he falls down, could they kick him until he stops moving?"

"This isn't Cambodia," said Sanborn.

Chay shook his head. "You've never been arrested by someone who doesn't look like you."

Henry looked out the dark window. He imagined his own

father, strapped to a plow, dragging furrows while soldiers sat in the shade nearby. He cut the image out immediately.

They turned off onto Route 1; a sign said, "Coastal Route," which seemed likely to take them north. They passed through Brunswick and wound along the Androscoggin and then up to Bath and over the Kennebec River, and after some blank rocks and dark touristy gift shops, they meandered through pretty Wiscasset and over a long, low bridge that left the town twinkling behind them. They did not speak. The quiet humming of the tires spoke for them. And they might have gone on like that forever, except that Henry noticed Chay's head nodding, and he wasn't too happy when the pickup drifted over toward the guardrail—beyond which there was nothing but darkness. And water.

Henry looked at Sanborn, who was asleep—again.

Black Dog squirmed. She was sitting up on Henry's lap with her ears held out to the sides, and the look on her face told Henry that she was trying to be polite, but if Henry didn't do something quickly, then Black Dog couldn't be held responsible for the humiliating consequences coming very soon.

"We have to stop," Henry said to Chay.

Chay gestured out into the black night. "Where?" he said.

"Right now, anywhere."

But before anywhere came, they heard a siren shrilling behind them, still far away. They both looked back. Against all that blackness, Henry could see red and white lights revolving and coming toward them quickly. He remembered the color of the lights.

Chay began to speed up.

"You have to pull over," said Henry.

It was as if Chay hadn't heard him.

"This won't help," said Henry. "If they're going to stop us, they're going to stop us. So slow down. Maybe it's not even us they want."

Chay took his foot off the accelerator. The humming of the pickup changed, and soon it was drowned out in the oncoming wail—which grew louder, and closer, and louder, and sharper, until suddenly the wail and the red and white lights were right upon them, whipping around their barely moving pickup and at their side. For a moment, Henry could see one of the policemen in front, looking over at them. And then the policemen were past, and the siren took on a new and lower tone.

Chay did not speed up until the red and white lights had disappeared around some bend ahead of them.

Black Dog whined.

"We still have to stop," said Henry.

"Doesn't your friend ever wake up?" said Chay.

Henry didn't answer. He scratched Black Dog behind the ears. She figured that this was enough of an invitation to whine even louder, which she did, because she wanted to let Chay and Henry know a little more clearly how urgent was her need.

The road had grown smaller now—there was only one lane heading north, and other than the policemen speeding ahead, there was no one else on it. They drove past small gatherings of buildings, and farms, and the antique-used-junk-whatnot shops, all closed and dark. Occasionally, headlights came toward them on the southbound lane, but even those began to come less and less frequently, and then they were gone altogether. It was as though they were driving alone on the planet.

"There," said Henry. "Turn in there."

"A graveyard?" said Chay.

"Very good," said Henry.

"You're going to let her out in a graveyard?"

"No, you're going to park by the graveyard, and I'll let her out across the road."

Chay turned in and stopped. The headlights shone along a low stone wall that divided the road from the graves to keep their sleepers peaceful. This did not interest Black Dog, since she had other urgencies to consider. Henry held her by the collar until he got her leash on, and together they got out and Black Dog pulled Henry across the road and into some dark pines. They were old; Henry could tell by the depth of the needles under his feet. Their sappy scent came up to him as Black Dog circled and pulled until she found the right spot—which didn't take long.

Black Dog did not want to hurry back, and Henry figured that since she'd been stuck in the pickup for such a long time, she had a right to run around now. And so he let her pull him through the trees, even though his face kept snapping off small, sharp twigs, and twice he had a branch whip back against his knees. But Black Dog found a whole lot to explore, and it wasn't until Henry thought he was starting to smell something distressingly like a skunk that he dragged on the leash and headed back through the pines toward the shining headlights. Three more sharp and brittle branches smacked him in the face before he got out of the woods.

He took off Black Dog's leash and let her into the cab seat, where she climbed onto Sanborn, who did not move. Then Henry got in as well. "All set," he said to Chay.

But Chay didn't answer. His head was back and his mouth open. He was as deeply asleep as Sanborn.

Henry looked at Black Dog on top of Sanborn, circling into comfort. Then he yawned, and reached over to turn off the lights and the ignition. All sound died. Chay did not move. Henry put his hands between his knees to keep them warm, and closed his eyes.

He slept lightly.

He woke every time Black Dog got up and curled around Sanborn and into sleep again.

He woke up when Sanborn snored—which wasn't just a few times.

He woke up twice when Chay moaned.

He woke up sharply whenever he dreamed—but he didn't remember any of the dreams.

At first light, he woke up for good.

Chay was gone.

Black Dog, too.

Henry rubbed the heels of his hands against his eyes. He was surprised that Chay had been able to open and shut the pickup's door without waking him. He sat up and wiped the condensation from the windshield. A wispy fog drifted over everything, as white as a hospital room. He stretched and felt the kind of weird tiredness that comes with sleeping while sitting up in clothes he'd been wearing too long; he supposed there was no chance he'd be brushing his teeth anytime soon.

Henry got out, climbed up into the bed of the pickup, and opened his pack. "Black Dog!" he called. He pulled a new shirt out and changed into it as quickly as he could, slapping away a handful of mosquitoes. He could see his breath in the chilled morning air. "Black Dog!"

"She's here," he heard Chay call. Henry looked toward the

voice. He could just make out Chay on the other side of the stone wall, walking slowly through the graveyard, looking carefully at each of the gravestones. Black Dog walked beside him, stopping when he stopped, waiting for him to finish reading and to walk on. In the fog, Chay looked like a drifting ghost, searching for the spot where his body had been laid.

Henry tightened.

"Is it morning?" Sanborn called out from the pickup's cab. He asked this very slowly.

"If you open your eyes, you'll be able to tell," Henry said.

"It's too early to open my eyes."

"What do you do when your mother tells you to get up for school?"

"My mother has never once in her life told me to get up for school," said Sanborn.

Henry figured that Sanborn could take care of himself. He climbed down from the pickup's bed and went around to the front to watch Chay, still drifting slowly among the graves of the dead. Sometimes the fog that blew across him grew so thick that he disappeared entirely, as though he had suddenly descended into the earth to join the rest of them there. But then, another breeze, and there he would be, his arms held around himself, resurrected until the next descent.

Black Dog stayed beside him.

Henry leaned back against the front of the pickup, and felt immediately the deep dent in the grill and the hood. Even down to the bumper. He stood and looked at it, his eyes wide, suddenly nauseous. He put his hand where the hood had been pushed in, and then let it down slowly to the wide crease in the bumper. Then, hardly believing he was doing it, he turned around and filled the dent with his own body, pushing in against the metal.

They had built their house so far from Trouble. But Chay Chouan had found them anyway.

He looked across the stone wall at Chay again. With Black Dog. With his dog. And he hated him as Franklin would have wanted.

He heard Sanborn get out of the car and head over to the pines. Black Dog lifted her head, saw Henry, and barked happily. Her thwacking tail disturbed the patterns of the streaming fog.

Henry left the pickup and climbed over the stone wall. Slowly he walked through the fog and the gravestones, passing generations of the dead sleeping deep beneath mossy swellings of the ground. All the stones were tall and thin and white—everything in the fog seemed white. Here and there he could make out a name: Holcomb, Barnard, Kittredge, Sawyer, Hollis, Griffith, Hurd. How many times had families come to this graveyard and lowered someone they loved into a dark hole forever? For him, once had been enough.

Henry looked up and saw Chay, not far.

He walked toward him.

The last few yards he took at a sprint.

Black Dog barked once, not understanding.

Then Chay turned around. At exactly the right moment.

He didn't even raise his hands.

Henry smashed his fist into the side of Chay's face.

Chay toppled to the ground and rolled over, his back coming up against one of the gravestones. Black Dog began barking desperately. Henry stood above Chay, breathing heavily. "Get up," he said.

Chay felt his jaw, and winced when he tried to see if it still closed the way it should. "You waited a long time," he said.

Henry leaped over Black Dog and threw himself on Chay, pushing him against the gravestone. Chay held him off while Henry pounded at him wherever he could, connecting time and time again, and each time, he felt something satisfying deep within him, but it maddened him all the more, and so he pounded all the more. He could hear Chay's breath when he knocked it out of his lungs and guts.

He did not know how many times he had hit Chay before he felt his arms weaken and grow weighty. It was harder and harder to lift them up, so that when Chay pushed him off, it was harder than anything he had ever done to go back into him again. But he did. And he pounded until he felt Sanborn pulling at his shoulders, and he swung once more at Chay's face and opened the skin above his cheek before Sanborn pulled him away and threw him onto the wet ground beside another gravestone.

Black Dog stopped barking.

They all stayed that way. Henry, on the ground, covered with a shroud of fog, the heat of his sudden sweat clammy with the wet of the fog. Chay, on the ground too, his hand up against his bleeding face, watching Henry with dark, indeterminate eyes. Sanborn, standing, poised between them to stop the next assault. Black Dog, looking back and forth among them all, ready to bark again if it would help. Ready to do anything if it would help.

And they were all watched over by the white winged skulls that peered from the gravestones beside them, hovering in the fog that was starting to shred with the rising of the new sun.

"Well," said Sanborn, "I guess it's good to get that out of our systems."

No one answered. Henry and Chay lay against their grave-stones and stared at each other.

Until Chay finally stood, grimacing as he got up. He walked past them, saying something sharp and Cambodian to Black Dog as he went by. She lay down quickly beside Henry, and Chay moved along the stone wall until he came to an opening. He went across to the pickup and started the ignition. Then he waited.

Henry watched him the whole time. He put his hand out to Black Dog, and she began to lick it. She was probably licking off Chay's blood.

"You going to spend the morning lying on a dead guy?"

"Shut up, Sanborn."

"You don't want to start with me, Henry. You're so winded, you wouldn't stand a chance. Not that you ever stand a chance."

"Looks like I stood a chance with him. He's the one with the bloody face." Slowly Henry got to one knee.

"Henry, you're a Great American Hero. You can beat up a guy who isn't fighting back."

"What do you mean, he wasn't fighting back? You saw him."

"I saw him. He was letting you beat on him, Henry. He didn't throw one punch—and the way you fight, he could have."

"You need glasses, Sanborn."

"I see fine, you jerk. Maybe you should try wearing some." Sanborn helped Henry to stand up.

"I don't care if he wasn't fighting back. It's about time some-one beat Franklin up. He deserved it, after what he's done."

Sanborn looked quickly at Henry.

Henry whistled to Black Dog, who bounded up and around them. "So what do we do now?" said Henry.

"Well, since our packs are in the pickup, and since he's the only ride we have, and since he's waiting for us, and since no one is going to stop for two guys and a—"

"Yeah, yeah, yeah," said Henry.

They walked across the graveyard and to the wall. The stones were dark with the dew, but already the sun was laying its beams on some of them, and the mica embedded in the granite was spangling the light back. Henry didn't think he could climb over them just then. He suddenly felt as if the air he was breathing was too heavy; he had to work hard at shoving it down into his lungs.

He felt, almost, nothing.

Sanborn took his arm and led him along the wall until they came to the opening that Chay had gone through. When they got to the pickup and Sanborn leaned over to open the front door, Black Dog jumped up into the cab and thrust her snout into Chay's face and licked it.

"Black Dog," said Henry. "Black Dog, down." Which did about as much good as if he had asked her to sprout wings and fly overhead. So Henry reached in and pulled her out of the cab, and then he dragged her back into the pickup's bed. She fussed and wagged her tail and licked him while he tied her up, because she wanted to be sure that he knew she could watch over him better if she was up in the cab and she thought he tasted good.

Henry finished, and when he went around to the cab, he saw that Chay had taken his shirt off, balled it up, and was holding it against his bleeding cheek. Already two bruises were starting to darken along the line of his rib cage. Henry thought that should have been satisfying, and maybe it was a little bit. But not much.

"Just a minute," he said.

Chay looked at him.

"I need something in my pack."

Chay turned off the ignition and Henry went around back again, opened his pack, and dug in for the bag of first-aid supplies he'd included—not because he thought he would ever need them, but because Franklin had always insisted. He took out a tube of antiseptic cream and a wide Band-Aid. He stowed the bag away, and then, as a last thought, took out a clean shirt. The largest one he had, since Chay was bigger than he was. One of Franklin's rugby shirts, with the blue and yellow of Longfellow Prep.

He got back into the cab. "Let me see," he said. Chay waited a couple of seconds, then dropped his hand and shirt. The cut wasn't long, but it was bleeding well enough. Henry took Chay's shirt and wiped away what he could, and then he put some of the cream on the end of Chay's finger and told him to wipe it into the wound—which he did. Then Chay took the Band-Aid that Henry opened for him and used his mirror to put it on. Henry handed him Franklin's shirt, and Chay, after a moment, leaned forward a little bit and quickly pulled it down over his head.

"Thanks," he said.

"Stay away from my dog," said Henry. Then he and Sanborn got in.

Chay said nothing. He reached out and turned on the ignition again. As they drove onto the road, Henry looked at the grave-yard one more time. The last shrouds of the fog were dissolving into the brightness of an early summer day.

15

THE AIR GREW BRIGHTER and brighter as they drove—heading north. They passed stands of maples with boldly green leaves, and bright quivering aspens, and wispy white birches, and pines looking proud of their sturdy winter endurance. They drove by long stretches of rock that engineers had once cut through to make the highway; the deep scars of the drill bits that explored them slanted down into stones that had never seen the light of anything but a primeval sun.

After one very long rocky stretch, the rocks opened up and let a hayfield slope gently to the road. Its long grass was beaded and tamped down by the dew, but here and there it was already drying and standing up high again, ready to be mowed. And right by the road stood a white clapboard diner with a small sign hanging on its outside: MIKE'S EATS—which was good enough for Sanborn, who suggested that if they didn't turn in for breakfast, he might die, which would be homicide by refusal to allow breakfast, and they'd have a whole lot of trouble hiding the body.

So Chay parked beside a huge pile of split wood, a pile much taller than the pickup. They got out, and Henry went around to scratch Black Dog behind the ears and tell her what a good dog she was and to promise her some bacon—though after the failure of the fried clams, he wasn't sure she'd believe him. But he promised as sincerely as he could, then followed Chay and Sanborn inside.

The diner wasn't a big place—half a dozen tables—and no one was sitting at them when they came in. All the windows were opened, so Mike's Eats smelled of fresh grass and sunshine and butter. It was the kind of place that probably hadn't changed much since it was opened fifty years ago—about the same time as the Chowder Mug. There were wooden tables and chairs with green-striped tablecloths and cushions, black and white linoleum tiles worn by the table legs, yellow curtains with white decorative frills at the bottom, red plates on a rack that ran around the room. Even Mike turned out to look as if he was playing the part of the cook from a 1950s rerun: white pants, white shirt, white apron, white hat. He waved at them from the door to the kitchen, telling them that they could sit anywhere, that he'd be with them in half a second, that there was a three-egg omelet and bacon and orange juice and toast and coffee special today, and that if they didn't see something on the menu that they wanted, just tell him because he'd heard it all and there wasn't anything he couldn't make if it could be made on a griddle.

Sanborn actually licked his lips.

They sat down and looked at the menu, and Mike was as good as his word—he came over in half a second, wiping one hand on his apron and holding a green pad in the other. "You boys look a little worse for wear," he said. "Like you slept in a car last night."

"Yeah," said Sanborn.

"And that looks sort of nasty," Mike said, nodding at Chay's Band-Aid. "Just happen?"

Chay nodded. "Little while ago," he said.

"How about you boys order, and then"—Mike bent down

and looked at Chay's cheek—"I'll get you a proper bandage. That one's already soaked through. Anyone for the three-egg omelet special?" He took a stubby pencil out of his apron pocket.

Sanborn ordered the three-egg omelet special but asked if he could make it a four-egg omelet special, and Mike said he could for another seventy-five cents, and Sanborn said fine. Henry asked for something more human—two fried eggs with some link sausage and orange juice. And maybe some toast on the side.

"I got English muffins."

Henry took the English muffins and added a side order of bacon to go.

"You got a dog waiting on you?"

"A dog who loves bacon."

"Most do," said Mike. Then he looked at Chay.

"Coffee," Chay said.

Mike paused before he wrote on his pad. "You got to be more hungry than coffee."

Chay shook his head.

"Okay," Mike said. He wrote down Chay's order and headed back to the kitchen. But before he got there, he turned around and called, "Hey, I got this load of winter wood delivered yesterday. Five cords. I don't have time to stack it proper, and almost all of it still needs splitting. And the pine's got to be sorted out, because no matter how much I holler about it, there's always some of that cheap pine that gums things up. Anyway, three boys like you, you could probably do it all in a morning and part of an afternoon. Four bucks an hour. What do you say?"

"No, thanks," said Sanborn. He was still licking his lips and probably thinking about his four-egg omelet and wondering if it came with link sausage instead of bacon.

"I'll throw in breakfast and lunch, too, if you do a good job."

Henry shook his head. "We've got to get going. We're heading up to Katahdin."

"Oh," said Mike. "Climbers?"

"Yeah," said Sanborn, who was wishing Mike would go back to the kitchen.

"I'll do it," said Chay.

Sanborn and Henry looked at him.

"Great," said Mike.

"I'm not going to do it," said Sanborn.

"I'll get your bandage," said Mike, and went back into the kitchen.

"I'm not going to stay here and stack wood all morning," said Sanborn again.

"I didn't say you would."

"Then why did you say you'd do it? If you stack wood, then we have to wait around until you finish."

"He knows that," said Henry.

"So after we eat, we're gone," said Sanborn. "You can stay around and kill yourself, if you want."

"No one is going to pick up two guys and a dog," said Henry. "We found that out yesterday."

"Actually, one of us knew that a long time before the other one of us showed up with his dog."

Mike came back in with the bandage. "You boys know the difference between pine and oak?" Henry and Sanborn shook their heads. "You ever split wood before?" More shaking of heads. "Okay. Well, if you two decide to help out, I'll get you started. Then we'll see how it goes. You can change that bandage in here. And here's some antiseptic cream you should use."

190

Chay followed Mike back to the bathroom.

Sanborn leaned across the table.

"Listen, Henry, I'm not working around here all day. If we have to walk the rest of the way to Katahdin, we're going."

"He doesn't think we can do it," said Henry.

"Who? Mike? Of course he doesn't think we can do it. I've never split a piece of wood my whole life. You, either."

Henry shook his head. "Not Mike."

Sanborn sat back and looked at Henry. "So you have to prove to him that you can."

"No."

"Yes, you do. And so we're going to spend the day stacking wood behind Mike's Eats instead of driving up to Katahdin. What a jerk you are."

"I love you too, Sanborn."

"Jerk."

They didn't talk much after Chay came back, and it wasn't long before Mike brought Sanborn his four-egg omelet and Henry his fried eggs. But Mike brought Chay what looked like a five-egg omelet, its edges reaching the sides of the platter and covering the sausages stored beneath. "You're going to need something sticking to your bones if you're going to work," Mike said. Henry thought that what was on Chay's plate could have fed all three of them, plus anyone else who came in to Mike's Eats that morning. But Chay had no trouble with it.

He was finished when Mike came back with the side order of bacon and the bills for Sanborn and Henry. "You going to want these or not?" he said. He handed Henry the brown bag of bacon. The grease was already coming through.

Henry took the bag and looked at Sanborn. "I guess we're going to work," he said.

Chay didn't say anything. He didn't even look up from starting his last bit of sausage.

The door to Mike's Eats opened.

"You boys let me know when you're ready, and I'll show you what needs doing. How are you two this sunny morning?"

Mike said this last part to his new customers. Two policemen.

"We'll be fine as soon as we get a cup of your black coffee," one of them said.

Chay looked up, froze for a second, and then looked back down at what was left of his sausage. Henry felt his sudden and full fear.

"Looks like you got a load of wood to stack," said the other policeman.

"Yup. And I just hired these three boys to split and stack it for me."

"That right?" said the first policeman.

Henry felt their eyes shift toward them. He hoped that they didn't look at Chay and get suspicious. He figured that he should say something that would show that they had nothing to hide—like driving on a suspended license.

"Hey," he said.

Both the policemen nodded. "So where's that coffee?" the first one said.

When Mike went to get the coffee, Chay stood up—slowly—and turned and walked toward the door. He looked as though he was walking without any knees. Henry and Sanborn followed him out. "You be careful out there," said the second policeman.

"We will," said Henry, and tried to walk as if he didn't care—or at least more naturally than Chay.

When they got outside, Chay was already sitting in the pickup.

"Why were you walking so funny?" said Sanborn.

"I wasn't walking funny," said Henry.

"You were walking like you had to go to the bathroom."

"I was not."

"Oh, there's a brilliant comeback. 'I was not.' What's next? 'Oh, yeah?'"

Chay turned on the ignition.

Henry looked at Sanborn, then walked over to the truck and motioned for Chay to roll his window down. "What are you doing?" he said.

"If you want to come, get in."

"Chay, we didn't pay. If you drive away now, what do you think Mike will say to the two policemen in the diner?"

A long moment. Chay reached out and turned off the ignition. Henry could see that his hand was trembling.

"Let's just get to work," said Henry.

Chay looked up at Henry and laughed. Again, not a sweet laugh. "You're telling me to get to work. When is the last time you worked for something you ate?"

"Ask me in a few hours," said Henry. He went around back and climbed into the pickup bed. Black Dog was sitting up, wagging her tail because she'd been waiting for the promised bacon as patiently as a dog could. Henry tore open the bag, and she happily did the rest.

Henry climbed back down when she had finished eating the bacon and licking the bag, and then he heard Chay's door open and close.

Just as the two policemen came out of the diner.

Henry looked over at Chay, whose body had locked. He was staring down at the ground.

"Let's get going, Chay," said Henry. "Chay."

The two policemen sipped at their cups of coffee and watched them as they walked by. Then the second policeman strolled behind Chay's pickup and looked at the license plate. When he got back to his patrol car, he set his coffee on the roof, took out a pad, and wrote something down.

Mike came out, wiping his hands on his apron and letting the screen door slam behind him. He met the boys by the pile of wood—the suddenly huge, impossibly big pile of wood.

"Okay," he said. "Okay. Over here's where I want it stacked. You see where I've driven these posts in? Between them. Bark side up. Nice and flat and even, since I'm particular about how it looks. If you find any pine, it goes over there, between *those* posts." He looked in the pile and picked out a piece. "You see this? It's lighter than anything else, it's got a straight grain, kind of yellow, and it's got this piney smell." He held it out for the boys to smell, which they did. "That's for tourists who don't know any better and just want to sit out under the stars with a campfire and pretend they're roughing it. We split on this stump over here." He looked at Sanborn. "You want to split first?"

Sanborn—who was not a happy Sanborn—shrugged.

Mike picked up a length of wood and a maul that was leaning against the stump. "This is oak. See how it's too big for a wood-stove? You set it up here on the stump and—" He swung the maul in a circle overhead and landed it on the end of the oak, which suddenly lay on the ground in two pieces. He looked up at Henry and Chay. "Oak always splits so nice," he said. "Why don't you boys get started on the stacking. Throw anything bigger than this"—he put his two hands together to show proper woodstove width—"throw those over here to the splitter. Once he gets tired, you can change around. And before you do any of that, you'd best get your dog tied somewhere over in that shade. There's rope inside the back door of the house up there"—he pointed up the hayfield—"if you need it. Just knock on the door and holler for one of the kids, and he'll find it for you. Tell them I told you to ask for a bowl of water, too."

Henry walked up to the house and knocked at the back door and hollered for one of the kids, who appeared with his mother, who figured out what he needed. But instead of going to find it, she yielded to the kid, who really, really, really wanted to help, and so it took a while until he found the rope and brought it over to Henry with the bowl of too much water, his mother smiling broadly the whole time. Henry took it from him and tousled the kid's hair—which the kid loved—and then walked back down to the diner and tied Black Dog in the shade while the kid held the bowl of water for her. After she finished her drink—which she really needed after the bacon grease—the kid sat down in the shade to pet her. Black Dog was overjoyed.

Henry started to stack with Chay while Sanborn tormented a piece of wood for about ten minutes or so until he finally got the knack of it—sort of. They worked that way for an hour, and then another hour, sweating in the growing heat of the bright day. Mike stopped them a couple of times with some sour lemonade, and once he split while they drank, splitting in a few minutes about as much as Sanborn had split in an hour. Then he handed the maul back to Sanborn. "Don't aim at the top," he said. "Aim at the block and go through the wood." Understanding dawned on Sanborn's face as if he had just figured out that the world is round and not flat. After that, the splitting went better.

And maybe it helped too that three more of Mike's kids came first to watch and then to help, which slowed things down considerably but which made splitting and stacking a lot more fun. Even Chay smiled.

By noontime, when the kids were called back up to the house and Sanborn announced that his four-egg omelet had worn off and that Mike had better have something good to eat for them soon, Chay and Henry had stacked almost two-thirds of the woodpile in rows as neat as anyone could ever want them. If it hadn't been for crew practices, Henry figured, his hands would have been all blisters. As it was, he felt as though he had gone through a couple of workouts. He watched Chay for a moment, turning the pieces bark-side-up on the top of the stack. His black hair was as wet as if he had dumped a pitcher of water over himself. So was Franklin's rugby shirt.

Henry handed a piece up to him and Chay turned to stack it—neatly. "So," said Henry without looking at him, "how come you didn't fight back this morning?"

Chay took the next two pieces from Henry's arms. He fitted those two as well.

"Suppose I had hurt you?" he said.

And Henry felt that he really was what Sanborn had been telling him all along—a jerk. Of course he couldn't fight back. How could Chay have won?

They walked together to the woodpile—which was a whole lot smaller now.

"Maybe a graveyard wasn't the best place to settle things," Henry said.

"The graveyard," said Chay. He began to take a load of wood into his arms, piece by piece. Henry did the same, throwing out some pine. "My family has nothing like that. I do not even know where they took my sister. They buried her in the refugee camp, but I don't know where. No place. A refugee camp is no place." He laughed his unhappy laugh. "That's where I'm heading now," he said. "No place."

They finished loading up their arms and walked back to stack the wood.

Henry thought of the cold stone brooding over his brother's grave: 𝕾𝖒𝖎𝖙𝖍. He thought of Franklin's empty room with no light turned on. He thought of the late-night dark of his own room, and of the wide emptiness of a cold sea.

"What happened to your brother after the soldiers took him?" Henry asked.

Chay stood still.

There was no need for any words. A heart that has lost knows every other heart that has lost. Late and soon, loss is all the same.

They stacked the wood in their arms neatly, and then went back together to pick up another load, Chay looking up at Mike's house the whole time.

16

WHEN MIKE CALLED THEM IN for lunch, he had thick chicken salad sandwiches with mayonnaise and onions and tomatoes and sweet pickles, mugs of clam chowder that were swearing hot, and tall lemonades that were frosty cold all ready for them. Chay studied the clam chowder, testing it with a spoon and pulling up the potatoes and clams.

"You don't eat it by looking at it," said Mike.

So Chay tried to eat it by tasting it, which went pretty well, probably because he was so hungry from stacking wood.

Henry finished first, and he left Mike's warm apple crisp with spiced whipped cream on the table so that he could run Black Dog; this was not an easy decision, but she had been crying outside the whole time they had been eating the chicken salad sandwiches inside. Sanborn finished his own warm apple crisp, considered for a moment, and then ate Henry's, too. Henry noticed this when he came back in, and as he later told Sanborn, there would have been blood on the floor if Mike hadn't come with another warm apple crisp. And Mike brought another one for Chay, too.

Afterward, Mike's kids came running back down, screaming with joy that there was still more stacking to do. For the afternoon work, Mike showed Chay how to do the splitting—which

Sanborn was glad about since he was getting blisters every place on his hands that could get blisters—even *between* his fingers. Mike and Chay spent a lot of time over it, and when Chay got the stroke right for the first time and sent the maul cleanly through some straight oak, he laughed aloud—a happy laugh—and turned to Mike with a smile—a real smile—crossing his whole face. It was almost as big as Mike's.

Mike's kids clapped and cheered.

The splitting went quickly after that, and when Chay had finished all the thick pieces, he helped Henry and Sanborn and Mike's three kids with the rest of the stacking. They were done by midafternoon.

Mike came and looked appreciatively at the neat wood. "You're good people. I guess I'd hire you again," he said. He turned to his kids. "You looking for a job?" he asked.

"C'mon, Dad," said the oldest—about seven.

"Well, I guess not." He looked at Henry and Sanborn and Chay. "Any of you three ever looking for a job, you come back. We'll be here." He handed them each twenty-five dollars and a heavy brown bag—"So you have something to put on your bones for supper."

Henry shook his hand. "We can't—"

"Take it," he said. He looked at Chay's cheek. "Let's go in and clean that up one more time. It could stand a new bandage." They went inside together—Mike's kids, too, so that they could see the terrible wound—and when they came out, the bandage was new and white. Two of the kids were holding onto Chay's hands.

Chay knelt down, and he kissed each of the kids on the top of their heads. "Goodbye, Little Mike. Bye, Ernie. Bye, Petey. Bye,

Freddy." Then he got into the pickup—Henry and Sanborn were already waiting inside, and Black Dog was tied up in the back— and they all waved their blistered hands, and Mike's kids waved, and Mike wiped his hands on his apron and he waved, too. He looked at Chay. "Remember what I said. You got a job here whenever you want." Then he stepped back into the crowd of kids and waved again. Chay turned on the ignition, but he didn't drive away. He stared at Mike and Mike's Eats for a long time, and Henry wondered what was going on in his heart.

"Are we going to head out or not?" said Sanborn.

Chay put the car in gear and they headed out.

"Goodbye! Goodbye! Goodbye!" from the kids.

They headed out slowly. Going north. Mike's kids waved behind them.

Sanborn fell asleep almost immediately, his head back, his mouth open wide to let out snorting snores. "He can turn himself on and off," said Henry.

Chay shrugged.

Black Dog did not fall asleep. She sat upright in the pickup bed, her ears held high, looking out toward the west. Every so often her ears would flatten down and she would whine loudly enough for them to hear, and when Henry would reach back through the panel window to stroke her, she would show that she was very, very concerned—but Henry had no idea what about. "She's upset about something," he said.

Chay looked quickly back at her. "She hears thunder," he said.

"I don't hear any thunder," Henry said.

Chay shrugged again.

Henry slouched down. He was achy from the day of lifting and stacking and thought how nice a very hot shower would feel; then he figured it would be a while before he had one. He looked out his window and watched the pines grow taller and darker and thicker. Then he looked over at Chay and looked at the bandage tight against the side of his face. Only a tiny stain of blood showed.

"How's the cut?" he said.

"Okay."

"I shouldn't have hit you. It doesn't change anything."

"You needed to do something," he said.

"So what would you do, if you needed to do something?"

Chay fingered the steering wheel.

"You didn't fight back. So what would you do?"

"I'd burn down Merton Masonry and Stonework," Chay said.

Henry sat up. "You burned down Merton Masonry and Stonework?"

Chay fingered the steering wheel again.

"*You* burned it down?"

Chay nodded.

Henry looked at him. "You burned down your parents' business?"

"It was partly mine, too."

"You know, everyone on the whole east coast of Massachusetts thinks that it was someone from Blythbury that did that."

"They're wrong."

"You should let people know."

"Why?"

"Because people should know."

"What people?"

"People."

"It's not their business."

"You should let your parents know, at least, so they don't blame someone else."

Chay looked over at him. "They never did blame someone else," he said.

Out to the west, a dark and roiling purple streak had cut across the bottom of the sky, and now it was bloating itself up, puffier and puffier, swirling and then, suddenly, crackling with lightning. Henry counted seven, eight, nine, ten, eleven seconds before the rumbling came, deep and low.

"You burned down Merton Masonry," Henry said again. He whistled.

Chay didn't say anything.

"How come?"

Chay shook his head.

"How come, Chay?"

Chay changed lanes around a slow dump truck. "It has to do with my family," he said.

"I guess so, since you burned down the family business."

Chay nodded.

"So probably it wasn't about the music you listen to."

Chay shook his head.

"Or a curfew."

Another shake of Chay's head.

"A girl?"

Chay's hands tightened on the wheel. "Enough," he said.

Another deep and low rumbling. Henry counted ten seconds.

Black Dog whined. Chay pulled over, and Henry went back to untie her and bring her into the cab. When he opened the door, she clambered up onto the seat and tried to climb in Chay's lap, but he pushed her back over to Henry and she settled for him, even though she might have been able to tell that Henry was a little irked.

Sanborn was still asleep. Of course.

Henry scratched Black Dog behind the ears, but still she wouldn't settle down. She squirmed in his lap, looking out the window, whining, perking up her ears and lowering them.

"Did you ever have a dog?" Henry said.

Chay sighed. "Do you need to know everything?"

"Not everything. Did you ever have a dog?"

Chay looked at Black Dog, then back to the road. "Once," he said.

"What happened to her?"

"Cambodian sons don't need dogs. Dogs are for American boys who don't work hard for their families." He looked at Black Dog again.

"That sounds like it's from a poster," said Henry. "Cambodian sons good, American sons bad. Cambodian sons don't need dogs, American sons do."

Chay nodded.

"So what happened to her?" said Henry.

A long minute passed. The asphalt whirred beneath the pickup's tires.

"My father penned her up. He didn't give her any food. He made me watch when he beat her—to make me strong and independent. Then he took her someplace and drowned her."

Another crackle of light in the west, and Henry counted three seconds. The clouds were all big-bellied now, and the purple had spread over half the sky. When Henry looked to the east, he saw that the yellow air of the July day looked like a patient with a deep fever.

Chay reached out and put his hand over Black Dog's head. Black Dog reached her snout up to Chay's hand, and slowly he lowered it so that she could lick it. Then Chay let his hand come down on the top of Black Dog's head. Black Dog laid her ears down, and Chay scratched behind them. Black Dog closed her eyes with pleasure.

Another sharp crackle of lightning; this time, the thunder was right on its back. And then the rain hit, sudden and shocking, so hard against the windows of the pickup that Sanborn woke up. The windshield weltered into a waterfall of white water and Chay slowed, flipped on the wipers, and leaned forward to peer through the cascade.

"A little damp out," said Sanborn.

"Have a good sleep?" said Henry.

"I always have a good sleep. Are we there yet, or did we drive into the ocean?"

That was about how it looked. The rain plummeted so fast that the wipers splashed hopelessly into the sheets of water. The torrent on the roof and sides of the pickup sounded as if someone was rattling chains against them. Black Dog tried to make herself as small as possible on Henry's lap as the thunder and lightning came on, shattering the darkness—again and again and again. It was as if an entire range of purple clouds had slipped down from the mountains in New Hampshire, picking up friction as they went. And then, full of momentum from their sliding, they had rolled on into Maine and were taking it out on the coastal lowlands.

Chay finally pulled off to the side of the road and set his flashers on because he couldn't see a thing in this midnight of a storm, and they all waited, saying nothing, feeling the pickup rock back and forth with the winds that began now to buck up, the rain still so loud that Black Dog looked as if she wanted to put her paws over her ears—which Henry finally helped her do.

"No storm is forever," Henry said to her. And he was right. No storm is forever. And so the lightning began to come a little less often, and the thunder to seem a little farther away, and the winds stopped wanting to flip the pickup over and began to wheeze—though the rain kept on just as hard as ever. Finally, the sky paled toward the west, and then paled more and more quickly. Chay drove back onto the road and headed north again, and the late-afternoon sun came out, lower than before, and sparkled the trees, the grass, every leaf, every particle of air.

Henry turned and looked at Chay.

His hands—both hands—were tight on the wheel, his knuckles mostly white.

And he was crying.

One thin, shining line cut down his face and ended in a drop glistening at his chin. Nothing else in his face gave it away. His mouth was set, his eyes unblinking. But there was this tear, and one tiny beam from the new sun shone on it, one tiny beam that had crossed millions and millions of miles of dark, cold, lifeless space just so that it could shine on this tear on Chay Chouan's chin.

Black Dog saw it, too. She leaned over, puzzling, and leaned over some more, until she crossed over Sanborn—"Hey," he said—and craned her neck up to Chay's chin, and licked.

Henry turned and looked out his window.

Henry's father had told him that if they built their house far enough away from Trouble, then Trouble would never find them.

But Trouble had found them. More than Henry could ever have imagined.

They stopped at a gas station and bought three root beers—not Admiral Ames root beer, because they were too far from Portland now. They all three chipped in for gas, and then they were on the road again—which is where they ate the suppers that Mike had packed for them. Black Dog showed more than a little interest in these—so much interest that she snatched all three of the dollops of apple crisp that Mike had put in.

The sky was trying to decide it if wanted to be a deep gold or blush into something redder when Sanborn finally asked what they were all thinking: "Do you guys know where we're going?"

"To Katahdin, Sanborn. Remember?" said Henry.

"Thank you, Albert Einstein. I meant what you know I meant: Do we know how to get there, or even how far away it is, or even if we're going to get there before dark?"

Henry had to admit that he had no idea. He had been planning on leaving that part up to Franklin.

"Franklin isn't here, Henry," said Sanborn—as if Henry had forgotten. As if Henry could ever forget.

"So we need to stop somewhere overnight and get directions in the morning," said Sanborn.

"We can sleep in the truck again," said Henry.

"No," said Sanborn, "we're not going to sleep in the truck again. You guys didn't sleep with a dog on top of you—so we're not going to sleep in the truck again. Find someplace that has real beds and real pillows. And showers. And a real bathroom where things flush. And did I say showers? I've got my father's credit card."

"It'll have to be a place where we can take in Black Dog," said Henry.

"Of course," said Sanborn. "It was my top priority. It has to be a place that will take in Black Dog."

"You have your father's credit card?"

"Don't you?"

"No."

"I do."

"How come you have your father's credit card?"

"So I can get what I want without having to ask him. It saves a whole lot of trouble."

Henry thought about what his father would say if he asked him for the credit card. Somehow, all he could imagine his father doing, if he asked, was shaking his head and walking into the library to be alone. Henry rubbed his palm against the side of his leg.

The sky had decided on the deep gold. It gilded all the sharp edges of the red pines, and the straight granite rock faces cut out along the road, and the wispy clouds still being pulled in long streamers after the storm front. The air itself was dashed with flecks of gold, and they drove through a shining haze—though they could hardly see it. The shining seemed always just off to the side, almost invisible, but there. And it was while trying to catch hold of it somehow—to fix it in focus—that Henry first saw the lake that lay between two dark green hills.

The golden sky had coalesced in its water and its flat surface shone dully, like the gold of a medieval illumination. Down the center of the lake was a long incandescent streak, streaming like a path for the Resurrected to march hand in hand to Glory. They all three stared at it—Black Dog, too—and when the road turned to follow the abrupt bend of the lake, the sun off the gold water shouted into their eyes. Chay slowed down. None of them wanted the shouting to end.

Slowly they traveled around the shoreline, and as the angle grew less, so the light grew less, and the water changed from gold to a duller flat sheen. Black Dog whined—Henry figured he knew what she felt, the lake was so beautiful—except that pretty soon she let him know that he really didn't know what she felt, which was more in the way of her getting out of the truck and finding a soft, grassy place than appreciating the view. No matter what happens, there is always the business of the world to attend to, Henry remembered.

And so, just before they reached the end of the lake, Henry asked Chay to stop at a dirt turnoff, which happened to be the driveway to the Rustic Lake Resort Cottages—which really did not look like cottages that you would attach the word "resort" to, and which turned out to be owned by a short and balding man in a Florida-bright shirt with palm trees at the shoulders and pockets who came right out holding an egg salad sandwich and said that he didn't appreciate someone stopping by his Rustic Lake Resort Cottages to run their dog. He might have pointed out a lot more that he didn't appreciate about the three of them except that he saw the quicksilver flash of Sanborn's father's credit card. Henry, who didn't see a single car near any of the Rustic Lake Resort Cottages, figured that Mr. Florida Bright Shirt would put up with a dog and a whole lot more if a credit card was flashing. And he did.

But not without fussing when he got them into the resort office.

"Last time I rented out one of my cottages to three guys, they wrecked the place. Lamps pulled off the walls, shower curtain torn down, water everywhere, the whole deluxe carpet soaked, top bunk crashed down on top of the bottom bunk. I never have figured how someone didn't get killed in there."

"We'll be careful not to get killed," said Sanborn.

"You'd better be careful not to get killed," said Mr. Florida Bright Shirt. "And if you do, don't break anything while you're doing it."

He took an imprint of Sanborn's father's credit card, and Sanborn signed below it. The man looked at the signature, then at Sanborn. "You twenty-one?" he said.

"On my last birthday," said Sanborn.

Mr. Florida Bright Shirt, who was obviously thinking about all the empty parking spaces in front of the rest of the cabins and the big VACANCY sign in his resort office window, didn't ask any more questions. He handed them a key. "You got to jiggle the handle on the toilet to make it stop running," he said. "If you don't, the thing'll run all night long."

"Thanks for telling us that," said Sanborn.

"Breakfast is over there in the morning." He pointed to a bare counter with coffee stains. "And don't come too early."

They went to find Cottage 4.

"Be sure to watch the sky tonight," he called after them. "There's supposed to be a meteor shower. Not like in August, but enough so it'll be worth watching."

"We'll do that," said Henry.

"You're lucky you're this far north," Mr. Florida Bright Shirt said, "where you can see so clear."

Henry turned to look out over the lake—which no longer

shimmered with gold, but glowed to match a sky that had finally decided to blush into red after all. Still, the red didn't really look like a blush, Henry thought; it was deeper, more ominous than that. Henry could imagine that sky appearing somewhere in a folktale, just before a huge battle or the death of a king or the sinking of a ship. Or before the end of a great and noble people.

17

COTTAGE 4 WAS DOWN BY THE WATER, and when they got there, they stood by the canoe beached on the rooted shore. Black Dog nosed around to see what had come up at the lapping edge.

"It doesn't look like a bad lake to swim in," said Henry.

"You go swimming," said Sanborn. "I'll take the hot shower."

"It looks like a village is burning somewhere past those trees," said Chay quietly.

Silence. The lapping of the water. The snuffling of Black Dog, who was getting close to the water without wetting her toes.

Henry looked out over the lake and tried to imagine what Chay was seeing—what he had seen—in a world where Trouble lived. He looked at the red sky and the red water underneath it, and he tried to see the ocean outside his own window, the vermillion sunsets, so bright that he could almost taste the colors that streamed over the waves.

But that wasn't what Chay was seeing, Henry knew.

Henry and Sanborn left him at the lake, went back to the pickup, hefted the two packs out, and carried them into a cottage that smelled of old and damp pine—because that is what it was mostly built from. Cottage 4 had one room, not big, with an old red couch, an upholstered chair with a deer pattern to match the small and broken rack of antlers mounted on the wall above it, and a tiny television on a spindly table with rabbit ear antennae sitting on top of it—not connected. A table and four chairs— from three different kitchen sets—grouped themselves beside a counter with a sink and an electric oven, trying as hard as they could to look like a kitchenette. More coffee stains. An old *Field & Stream* left on the counter for evening reading.

Sanborn pointed to the bed on one side of the room. "Chay can have that. We'll take the bunks over there. I've got bottom."

"You're like some sort of general, Sanborn."

"That's me. In control and on patrol."

"Cute."

"Thank you." Sanborn opened his pack, found some clean clothes, and went into the bathroom. "Too bad there's only one towel in here and I got it first," he called out. Then he turned the water on. It sputtered for a while before it finally settled into something like steadiness.

Henry glanced out the picture window. They should have put the table and chairs there, he thought, where you could watch the lake while you ate. The sun was gone now, its last dark light faint; he couldn't see the far shore anymore. He opened his pack and found a Hershey's chocolate bar, and remembering what happened with the apple crisp at lunch, he unwrapped it and started so that he could be finished before Black Dog could take it from him. Then he glanced out the window again.

Chay was swimming into the black-red of the lake. Sort of swimming. His stroke wasn't strong, and he was keeping his head out of the water as far as he could. Black Dog stared at him from shore, but she wasn't going to follow—even though everything in her tense body showed that she wanted to. Twice she turned and looked back at the cottage.

As Henry watched, Chay kept going—straight out.

Henry left his chocolate bar on the window ledge and went out and around Cottage 4. Black Dog ran to him, and then she ran back to the shore, then back to him, then back to the shore, whining. Henry walked to her. On the stump by the canoe, Chay had left Franklin's blue-and-yellow rugby shirt, folded neatly. The rest of his clothes were dumped into a pile.

Chay was still swimming straight out, swimming now with his head low in the water. Henry could barely see him.

He looked at the canoe. It had one oar in it—a rowboat oar. A length of dirty clothesline tied the canoe to the pine stump. There were at least two inches of water pooled inside; leaves and sticks and muck floated on top. He thought he could make out some rusty fishhooks.

Henry looked out again at Chay and panicked for a moment when he didn't see him, until he saw a stroke farther into the dark water. Chay's head was so low now that even the tiny ripples on the lake must have been splashing into his face.

Henry bent down and worked at untying the knot of the clothesline—which wasn't easy, since who knew how long ago it had been tied and how many times it had been rained on and snowed on and rained on and snowed on. He worked at it slowly at first, then frantically, until the pain his palm began to throb, and then to pierce. He ran back into the cottage—the shower was still going, steam coming from beneath the bathroom door along with some horrible song that Sanborn was mutilating—and he found the Buck knife in his pack and ran back out. The light was almost fully gone.

He sliced through the clothesline, grabbed the oar, and shoved the canoe out into the darkening lake. But before he could jump in himself, something happened that was almost, Henry thought, a miracle.

Black Dog splashed through the water and, with an impressive leap, jumped into the canoe.

It wasn't graceful, and she almost tipped the canoe over as she desperately splayed out her feet to get her balance. But after Henry settled it, she carefully went up to the bow, sat down, and turned back to Henry to tell him that she was ready, and what was he waiting for?

Henry drove the canoe out until the water covered his shins, and then he jumped in, shoved the rowboat oar against the rocky bottom to get them started, and headed out after Chay, thinking thoughts that Father Brewood would not approve of about one so-called resort owner who didn't know a rowboat oar from a canoe paddle, and wishing he was in a kayak instead.

He did not let himself paddle desperately. He paddled with precision and rhythm, following the disturbance in the water, since Chay's head was now invisible. He paddled with all the muscles that crew practice had given him—and even though he was using a rowboat oar, the canoe cut through the ripples on the lake with a speed that might have impressed even Coach Santori.

Henry felt as if the only thing aware of him was the starry host, which had come out not one by one, but all of a sudden, and that host was watching him indifferently, not particularly caring if he reached Chay or not. They wouldn't change their cold shining if he flipped the canoe over and disappeared himself. Mr. Florida Bright Shirt would care more, since he'd lose the canoe and the oar, and people aren't supposed to drown at rustic lake resorts. Trouble isn't welcome at rustic lake resorts.

Then Henry did start to row desperately, since he couldn't see any water splashing up—either because of the darkness or because there wasn't any water splashing up anymore. And in the silence under the cold stars, Black Dog barked, a single bright bark, sharp and filled with worry, and even though it seemed so small, it filled up the space of all that blackness upon the surface of the lake—where every sign of the splashing was gone.

"Chay," Henry hollered. "Chay!"

Henry paddled ahead with everything in him.

"Chay!"

"Hey," a voice called, off to his left.

Black Dog barked again.

Henry thrust the stupid rowboat oar back into the water and veered left. To Chay. Who suddenly in the darkness threw a tired and dripping hand out of the water and over the side of the canoe. His cold fingers grasped at it, and almost let go—until Henry grabbed his wrist.

Black Dog fell over herself as she tried to turn around in the narrow bow. For a moment, the canoe tipped far over, and Black Dog backed up as far as she could against the high side with a desperate yelp.

Henry leaned back, too. "Come around by the stern," he said, and when Chay didn't move, Henry drew him by his wrist along the canoe, until Chay grabbed on with his other hand, and heaved once, and then again. He flopped his chest over, and Henry reached and dragged his legs in as well. Then they sat in the canoe, both breathing quickly, Chay with his arms across his chest. It was too dark to see if he was shivering, but if he was, there wasn't much that Henry could do about it.

He told Chay to move forward, and he did, sidling past Henry and so to Black Dog, and then Henry turned the canoe around and headed back, trying to figure out which were the lights from the Rustic Lake Resort Cottages, and finally just picking one set and heading toward it.

And Chay, facing ahead, sat with Black Dog against his chest—probably to keep warm. He wrapped both his arms around her.

A loon called its eerie and lonely call, and it echoed across the lake. It called again, and all was silence—except for the chorus of bullfrogs offering their grainy chorale. Only the lightest wind breathed down on them. Darkness. Low ripples troubling themselves against the sides of the canoe. Water dripping from the stupid oar when Henry raised it from the lake.

Henry felt himself quivering.

He heard Chay begin to weep.

And then, the wail that came out of Chay was as eerie and lonely as any wail that has ever come from any throat of any loon that has ever swum on a dark and cold lake in all the world.

Henry had never heard any sound that was so fully and completely lost. Not even the sounds of his mother deep at night.

And when Chay stopped to breathe, the wail echoed and echoed and echoed around the lake, and when the echoes finally fell away, there was only silence on the water. Even the wind died down, so that they sat in a canoe that did not seem to move, and the water was so still that Henry could count the reflected stars hovering in its depths. He almost reached out to touch one, so close they seemed, and real.

"Chay," said Henry, "I was an idiot to fight you this morning. What happened was an accident. I know that. Maybe most trouble is an accident and it doesn't help to blame anyone. When the blaming is all over, you have to start living again."

In the darkness, Henry could feel Chay turning to look at him. "Is that your wise American saying for the poor Cambodian immigrant? 'Trouble is an accident'? 'Start living again'?"

"I don't have any wise American sayings," said Henry.

A warm breeze picked up behind Henry's back. He could feel it on his neck and then mussing up his hair. Black Dog snorted in its wake.

The boat drifted under the cold stars.

"You know what it is to lose someone," said Chay. "But you do not know what it is to be lost. So lost that you want to burn down your family's business. So lost you get in a pickup and head north—anywhere."

"So lost you swim out into a lake?"

No answer.

"You're not lost, Chay."

Chay laughed. It was hard to tell, in the dark, what he meant by it.

"If your brother brought home a Cambodian girl and told your parents he loved her, what would they say?" Chay asked.

"What's that got to do with—"

"What would they say?"

"They would say 'Great.'"

"Would they?"

Henry considered. "It would take some getting used to."

"If I brought home an American girl, my family would not get used to it. They'd say American girls are immoral. They'd say an American girl would disgrace the family. They'd say they could never go back to Cambodia with honor and respect."

"What would they say when you told them you loved her anyway?"

The warm breeze again, pushing them toward shore, and turning them a little until it soothed Henry against his cheek like a caress.

"They would say . . . they would say that they had known all along that no good would come from me, because of where I came from. And then I'd say, 'Where did I come from?' and my mother would start to cry. My father would look at me like he hated me. Then he'd send my little brother away, and he'd tell me what soldiers do to pretty girls like my mother when they come into refugee camps. He would say that he was not my father. *My* father was the man who raped his wife. He would say that my birth was a curse to him. Every time he looked at me, he was ashamed that he did nothing to stop the soldiers. And he'd say I disgrace them. I should go somewhere far away so that his eyes do not burn because of who I am. And then I'd ask why I never heard any of this before, and my father—who isn't my father anymore—would tell me to go away and not. . . . He'd tell me to not come back."

If you build your house far enough away from Trouble, then Trouble will never find you.

That is what Henry's father had said.

It had been true for so long. Trouble could never really find them.

But Henry knew that the world his father wanted to live in— the world that he had wanted to give him and Franklin and Louisa—could never be real when there was the swelling of the ground over his brother and the brooding stone—𝕾𝕸𝕴𝕿𝕳— and a lost Chay Chouan, swimming out into a dark lake.

"Chay," said Henry quietly, "who was the girl?" But he already knew.

Somewhere behind them, far, far out on the lake, the loon called again—so sad, so lonely, so impossible to console. Like a sea turtle who'd lost her eggs. Like a Canterbury pilgrim who'd lost the way.

But Black Dog knew just what to do. She held up a single paw, lightly—a single paw out to Chay. And when he saw it in the gloom, he drew Black Dog even closer to him, and he held her even more tightly, this dog who had braved the water to come to him. He held her face close to his, and she licked and licked, and her tail thumped in the bottom of the canoe, and Chay wept. He stroked her fur, and he wept.

Henry put the stupid rowboat oar into the water again, set the warm wind at his back, and began to paddle. They were close in now, but Henry had to turn and follow the shore, passing cottages where the lights were warmly lit as the cool air of the evening began to make herself known. Some kids still squealed at the water's edge under the bright lights of a dock, jumping in and climbing out and shivering and jumping in again. They waved happily to the canoe, and Henry waved back. They passed by some tall pines, darker than the night, hanging out over the water and covering the shore rocks with thick tendrils of roots. And then, finally, by a weak orange light, they came back to the Rustic Lake Resort Cottages, where Sanborn was sitting on the shore, waiting for them and swatting at the mosquitoes attracted to his fresh cologne.

Mr. Florida Bright Shirt was waiting, too.

Henry paddled hard for the last few strokes and ran the canoe up onto the shore. He wished it hadn't grated so much on the rocks, especially when the resort owner yelled "Careful!" and held up the cut clothesline. "You've already got this cable to pay for, you know."

Chay stood, a little unstable. Then he turned and hefted Black Dog up into his arms—because she showed pretty plainly that she had already gone into the water once that night and she wasn't going to go in again. He carried her to shore and set her down. Then Chay went to the stump, gathered up his clothes, threw Franklin's rugby shirt over his back, and walked to the cottage. He paused under the weak porch light, waved with one hand, and went in.

Black Dog shook herself, sniffed at the stump, sniffed at the resort owner, and then meandered to Sanborn to have her ears scratched—which she had to wait for since Sanborn was holding the canoe steady while Henry got out.

"Is this what you call taking care of someone else's property?" said Mr. Florida Bright Shirt.

Henry took the clothesline from his hand and tied up the canoe. He stowed the oar inside it.

"And that fella shouldn't be walking around in his birthday suit," said Mr. Florida Bright Shirt. "This isn't some hippy commune, you know."

"It's beginning," said Sanborn.

Henry turned to him.

"What's beginning?"

Sanborn pointed high over the lake.

Henry looked up, and he gasped.

One by one, the stars were falling out of the sky, streaking to their fiery ends.

The loon sounded once again—and then was silent under the fire fall.

18

THEY DID NOT CRASH the top bunk onto the bottom bunk that night. They did not pull the lamps off the walls, or tear the shower curtain down, or soak the whole deluxe carpet—which looked and smelled as if it had been soaked more than once anyway. When they got up in the morning and went over to the resort office for the Full Continental Breakfast that Sanborn's father's credit card paid for—a frozen muffin, a bowl of corn flakes, plastic cups of warm orange juice stacked on the stained counter—they left Cottage 4 pretty much as they had found it, and left Black Dog to watch over it for them.

But she was not in Cottage 4 when they finished their Full Continental Breakfast.

She was waiting for them outside the resort office.

Henry looked at Black Dog, then at Sanborn. Black Dog looked at Chay and wagged her tail. Chay looked at Henry, and then at Sanborn.

"She must have thought we were leaving her," said Henry.

Chay looked over at Cottage 4. "Oh, no," he said.

Henry was right: Black Dog must have thought they were leaving her—and she did not want to be left behind. And Chay was right, too. In her frenzy to get out, she tore down the curtains by the picture window. She scraped most of the paint off the front door. And when she climbed on top of the kitchenette counter, she pushed over the electric oven, whose shattered front window showed that it was done for.

Who knows what else she would have done if she hadn't found the vulnerable screen over the top bunk?

There wasn't much to say as they stood at the cottage doorway, still hungry, Black Dog eating the extra frozen muffin that Henry had carefully filched. And it was hard to blame her much, since she had been trapped in a strange place, and she was so very glad to see them, and the grin on her face as she ate the muffin was so endearing that no human being with a beating heart could help but forgive her—especially hearts that had fought their own fierce battles.

Chay rehung the curtains, which might hold if no one touched them and no breeze blew through the window. Henry used pages from the old *Field & Stream* to sweep up the glass from the electric oven window and the paint chips from the front door. Sanborn tried to piece the ripped screen together. And after they did as well as they could, Henry and Sanborn carried their packs out to the pickup. "You didn't bring much along, did you, Chay?" said Sanborn.

Chay shrugged.

Sanborn shrugged, too.

When they finished, they went back in and looked around the Cottage 4 one more time. It wasn't too bad. "He'll charge us for the electric oven and the scraped-up door," said Henry. "And the screen, too."

"He's got my father's credit-card number. He'll put it on that."

"And your father won't mind?"

"He won't even notice," said Sanborn. "He hands it over to his accountant, and everything gets paid without him worrying about it. Remember?"

They followed Chay to the pickup.

Henry looked over the lake before he climbed into the cab. The storm the afternoon before had wiped the sky so clean, he felt as if he could reach up and rub the blue pane with his fingers and it would feel like dry and cold glass. And on the other side of the pane there was nothing right up to the edge of the atmosphere, so the sunlight shone through it like Glory and fell happily onto the three of them, mixing with the green and pitchy scent of the pine needles above them and the smell of water—a smell, Henry suddenly realized, that has no word in the language to describe it. Somehow he was glad about that; sometimes, you just have to know without words.

He took a deep breath.

Black Dog was not glad to get in the back of the pickup again. She put her front paws on the gate and left her hindquarters on the ground for a long time, and no amount of coaxing by Henry could get her to jump. It took Chay's starting the engine to get her in—probably because she was still worried about being left behind—and when she did, it was pretty clear to Henry that she would rather be in the cab with them than out in the pickup's bed. He decided he wouldn't add the final humiliation of leashing her.

Mr. Florida Bright Shirt, who had not yet seen what Black Dog had done to Cottage 4, had told them how to get to Katahdin during the Full Continental Breakfast. They should've taken Route 1A out of Stockton Springs, he said, but lots of people make that mistake, and before you know it, you're heading east instead of north and looking for a place to stay overnight.

His whole business depended on dumb tourists, he said—which didn't make Henry want to be his best friend. Anyway, since they'd come this far, they should go on to Ellsworth and then take the *other* Route 1A on up to Bangor. From there they'd see the signs for 95 and they could head straight north again and watch for the Millinocket exit. Or it might be called the Molunkus exit—he never could remember.

So they headed to Ellsworth, stopping at a diner to get another breakfast. When the waitress came with the bill, Sanborn whipped out his father's credit card. "No more splitting," he said. Afterward, they found Route 1A and headed north, the pines so scented that Henry leaned out of the truck to catch their smell on the breeze—which is what Black Dog was doing, too, which led Sanborn to remark that they looked like they were related, which led Henry to reach over and punch him, which led Sanborn to grab his arm and twist it until Henry hollered.

At Bangor they got on 95; it looked the same here as it did in Massachusetts and probably as it looked the whole way down to Florida—except for palm trees, of course. They got off at the Millinocket exit—which was the same as the Molunkus exit—and from there, everything changed.

Because in the distance, they saw the mountain.

It wasn't like any mountain that Henry had ever seen.

Katahdin was a bulk, huge even from this distance; it rose out of level lands and spread itself out leisurely in great swoops of slopes and peaks. Most of it looked bald—sheer living rock that lay under the sun for warmth and light, ready to slough off any birches or pines that might try to grab hold. The peak on the south rose highest and most pointed—if it could be called a peak. It was as if the mountain had stretched itself out beyond them toward the west and drawn the peak along with it. As soon as he saw it, Henry knew it was the Knife Edge.

To the north, the mountain took its time sweeping down in a long, slow line and dropping off into sharp walls. Farther to the north, the mountain rose again, not quite so high, angling to square itself against the horizon. At its very top, the mountain had rubbed itself raw against the sky until it was so scoured that it shone white—or maybe, Henry thought, he was seeing the last of the stubborn snows.

Chay slowed down, and then pulled over to the side of the road. They were astonishing, this run of peaks, carved so sharply against the bright sky, so bold in jutting out of the land and standing against snow and ice, winter after winter. Henry leaned forward, staring up at the mountain. Cloud shadows rippled across Katahdin's bold face.

Finally, reluctantly, Chay reached to put the pickup in gear— just as a policeman drove past them, slowing down a little to glance inside their pickup, and then going on toward Millinocket. Before he rounded a stony bend, they saw him look into his mirror, back at them.

Henry looked over at Chay—who was predictably white. "It doesn't mean anything," he said. "He's not going to give you a ticket for stopping on the side of the road to look at a mountain."

Chay put the truck in gear and drove back onto the road. Very slowly.

It was almost noon now; the brightness of the day had paled into a lighter blue, and the air had whitened until it held all the promise of a still, savannah heat. Already Henry's back was sweating against the leatherette seat, and he could hear Black Dog panting—which only made things hotter.

"So is air conditioning only for lazy Americans?" Henry said.

Chay shook his head. "It doesn't work," he said.

Henry lowered his window as far as it would go.

By all rights, Henry thought, there should have been a cool breeze. The road to Millinocket wound past shadowy pines and by stones that led down to blue water on both sides. It seemed made for a cool, breezy drive. But under the noonday sun, the stones were heated and the air beneath the pines was breathless.

Henry unstuck his back from his seat and sighed.

There were other cars on the road to Millinocket—all of which were passing them, since Chay was driving slowly so he wouldn't catch up with the policeman. Those cars had their windows wound tightly up, and everyone inside looked cool and fresh. A lot had young kids in them, some with balloons, and more and more of the cars were decorated with red, white, and blue bunting flapping in the hot breezes, flying straight out from antennas, dragging back from rear bumpers.

"It looks like the Fourth of July," said Sanborn.

"It *is* the Fourth of July, you jerk," said Henry.

"Thank you, Mr. Calendar Man," said Sanborn. "I'll be sure to consult you for all the high holidays."

"Sanborn, everyone in the country knows it's the Fourth of July except you."

"Oh, you took a poll this morning?"

"Quiet," said Chay. A policeman drove past them, going the other direction. The same policeman.

Chay's hands went white again. His face, too.

"Keep going," said Henry. "We're just part of the crowd."

Which they were. In fact, they had to drive more and more slowly as the traffic started to back up, and the bright and brave bunting that had been flying in the breeze from the cars began to go limp. And that was the way it stayed for the next half hour, as Chay rode his brake behind bumpers on into town.

Millinocket was as decked out for the Fourth of July as any of the cars—even more so. Every building that had a second floor had a flag draped from it. Starred-and-striped bunting leaped across the street from one pole to another. Red, white, and blue balloons held on to anything that they could. The scent of cotton candy and corn dogs and grilled frankfurters filled the air. Henry heard the bright notes of a brass band warming up somewhere.

Most of the side streets were blocked off with orange cones, and when Henry looked down them, he could see people in bright yellow T-shirts directing cars and floats and bicyclists—all sporting red, white, and blue streamers—and waving their arms at milling trombonists and trumpeters. On the sidewalks along the main street that they were driving on, people were walking with folding chairs and blankets, probably to find the best seat for a parade.

Henry turned around to see how Black Dog was handling Millinocket. She looked fascinated. She seemed to figure that the streamers were made just for a dog to chase, and she was willing. She watched them all, her ears going down for a moment when they passed one streamer, but then perking up again with the next one. Her mouth was open, and she was drooling in her excitement.

Then, ahead of them, a police siren wailed suddenly. And a second, and a third.

The children walking along the road clapped and cheered; some put their hands over their ears and laughed.

But Chay did not clap or cheer or laugh. He looked around quickly, from side to side, and then in a spasm of panic, he turned

227

the pickup into one of the blocked-off roads, squashing three orange cones and heading toward one of the men in the bright yellow T-shirts—

"Chay!" said Henry.

—and stopping abruptly when the man held up his arm.

"*That* way," the man in the yellow shirt said, pointing. "Classics are supposed to be two blocks over and one block down." He waved Chay on. "Go down there, and they'll show you."

Chay went down there, and more people in bright yellow T-shirts showed him. While Henry and Sanborn sank lower and lower in their seats, and while Black Dog began to bark at the more exciting streamers, Chay drove the two blocks, turned left at the waving yellow arm, and then stopped close behind a green DeSoto that looked as if Cleanliness and Purity had descended upon it; it gleamed coolly, even in the hottening sun. Henry peeked behind them. A white DeSoto had closed in.

"I suppose you know," said Sanborn, who was also looking out behind them, "that we are now a part of the Millinocket Fourth of July parade. And we don't even have any streamers."

"We can turn off as soon as we get moving," said Henry.

Chay nodded.

But since no parade ever gets under way quickly, moving took some time. And there were more than a few people in bright yellow T-shirts who passed them and looked sort of wonderingly at them, until Sanborn finally got out of the car, went over to a fire hydrant that had three red balloons holding on, pulled the strings from the hydrant, and tied the balloons onto the tailgate of Chay's pickup—which Black Dog thought was wonderful.

When the line of classics did get moving—very, very slowly—

Henry and Chay looked for a side street to duck into. But the people with the bright yellow T-shirts lined the route, waving their arms and directing them, so that there was nowhere to go except to follow the green DeSoto in front of them—almost on the DeSoto's bumper, since the yellow-T-shirted people kept hollering that they were supposed to "close ranks," and the white DeSoto was right on them, pushed a little by the large float from the Great Northern Paper Company filled to overflowing with potted pines destined for lumbered forests.

"We might as well start waving," said Sanborn. So Henry and Sanborn waved as they came onto the main parade route, and everyone lining the street cheered each new classic and waved small paper flags and blew on small plastic horns and shot water pistols up into the air.

Black Dog could hardly contain herself.

They crawled along, waving, and Black Dog barked, and the balloons on the tailgate bobbed, and Henry realized that he was starting to melt.

"Does this classic have anything to get up a breeze?" he said to Chay, and he looked at the temperature controls.

Chay had turned them up to blow out heat into the cab.

Henry looked at him. "Are you crazy? It's got to be a hundred degrees in here."

"A hundred and fifty degrees," said Sanborn.

Chay pointed to the temperature gauge for the radiator, whose needle was almost, *almost* touching the red zone that did not mean anything good.

"So what are we going to do?" said Henry.

"Overheat," said Chay.

"Does blowing the hot air in here get it down?"

"Sometimes."

Henry looked at the gauge, whose needle was now clearly in the red zone. "What happens if it overheats?"

"More of that," said Chay, pointing to the front of the pickup, where Henry could see a wisp of white steam escaping from beneath the hood.

"And what happens if there's a lot more of that?"

"It means," said Sanborn, "that there's going to be a lot of unhappy parade people behind us."

19

WHAT HAPPENED NEXT happened very quickly, and none of it was really anyone's fault, since classics have already given everything that can be expected of them and are bound to complain sometimes. Especially when it is very hot.

Black Dog was leaning farther and farther out from the pickup's bed—probably to escape the heat coming through the cab window. But whether it was the heat or not, when she saw a red balloon that was suddenly let go, she barked twice and leaped out. Henry, who was still trying to wave at the crowd even though he was melting, hollered, then opened his door and ran out after her.

At the same time, the wisp of smoke from under the front hood suddenly turned into a gusher with a surprising volume. Henry heard the hissing of the steam and the "Oohs" of the crowd—who thought it was part of the parade—and then he was gone after Black Dog, who was weaving in and out of the parade route, jumping up anytime the hot air blew the balloon back down, and barking in between times. Henry ran after her, yelling "Black Dog, Black Dog," and no one knew if Henry was warning them or calling to the dog, so they took the safer option and began backing away from a dog that was running wildly and jumping like a lunatic. When she stopped for a moment and thrust her nose into a dropped cone of cotton candy, the frothy pink on her snout looked like the kind of foam anyone who was worried about rabies might be suspicious of, and now the backing away took on a look of panic.

Meanwhile, the entire parade had stopped, and Henry thought he knew why. The driver for the Great Northern Paper Company's float was standing on one of the potted pines to see what the holdup was. The pilots for the Millinocket Municipal Airport float were clambering up onto their plywood control tower to see. The Millinocket Junior High School Marching Band was playing the theme from *The Bridge on the River Kwai* and marching in place—until Black Dog ran right through them and knocked the percussion section completely off their rhythm, which got everyone in the band out of step. Then, still pink-snouted, she charged into the Veterans of Foreign Wars and through the Cub Scout troop behind them, and so past the Millinocket fire engine that was spouting a spray of water to cool everyone down, but, since it was now blocked, was simply soaking the same people over and over again.

Henry tracked Black Dog by following the confusion she left behind—and the red balloon that now and then rose above everyone's head. If it hadn't been for the spray of the fire engine catching the balloon solidly and throwing it down to the ground, Black Dog might have kept on running. But when Henry finally got to her, she had taken the balloon into her mouth and killed it well enough. She held it in her jaws and showed it to him proudly when he came up. She grinned and wagged her tail.

What could he say except "Good dog"?

Henry looped his belt around Black Dog's collar and wiped

most of the pink froth off her snout. "C'mon," he said, and turned to head back into the stalled parade.

But when he turned around, he wasn't so sure he wanted to head back into the stalled parade. Ahead of him he could see the brilliant orange feathers on the tall hats of the Millinocket Junior High School Marching Band gathering together. The percussion section was flocking toward them purposefully. Trouble.

Henry looked around. Every store up and down the block had closed down for the morning. None had a light on or an open door.

Except one. And over its screen door was one word: KATAHDIN.

Henry did not believe in Fate. But sometimes, believing has nothing to do with acting. The sign said "Katahdin," and that was enough. He drew Black Dog close to him and, trying to walk like someone whose dog hadn't just run through the entire Millinocket Fourth of July parade, he crossed the street and opened the screen door. A tiny silvery bell tinkled happily as he and Black Dog went in.

Henry could see that what they had come into wasn't actually a store. It looked like a museum. Sort of. Mounted prints torn from old books covered one wall; on the other side of the room were pictures of Katahdin, showing every angle of the peaks and labeling the major trails in bright red lines: the Russell Pond Trail, the Chimney Pond Trail, the Northwest Basin Trail, the Baxter Peak Cutoff, the Helon Taylor Trail, the Dudley Trail, the Appalachian Trail—all the trail names that he had studied. Photographs of the mountain taken from overhead were taped to the ceiling, so that Henry could look above him and see straight down into Katahdin's Great Basin. It was dizzying.

Lights between the ceiling photographs shone on neatly arranged and labeled artifacts on three long tables. Henry, still holding Black Dog close, followed rows of arrowheads, whose chipped edges and tips looked fierce enough to pierce deeply into whatever they hit—still. "The Work of the Great Abenaki Nation," read a sign between the rows, and Henry tried to imagine himself striking at a thin stone until only this lethal thing was left in his palm—in his probably bloody palm.

"Those there I found mostly myself," came a voice from the back of the room.

Henry looked up.

"Eighty years of looking's in that case," said the voice.

The first thing Henry noticed about the man was his mustache, mostly because it covered so much with a startling white. Henry wondered how his voice got through it all—or food, for that matter. Everything else in his face arranged itself around the mustache. It was a base for the broad nose that ran well up into his forehead, and provided symmetry for the thick white eyebrows that spread out from its top like spume from a fountain running down into pale eyes—which were looking at Henry, and harder at Black Dog.

"Don't usually allow dogs in here," he said.

Henry turned quickly at the sound of the Millinocket Junior High School Marching Band's percussion section, which seemed to have fanned out through the streets. The dead birds on top of their tall hats bobbed back and forth like Polynesian birds of prey.

"'Course," said the man, "there's always the exception for a good old dog."

Black Dog looked up at the man, and Henry could tell right

away that she liked him and that she wanted him to know that she *was* a good old dog. Henry let go of the belt and she trotted across to him, her toenails clicking on the planks of the wooden floor.

"Thanks," said Henry. "I think my dog destroyed the Fourth of July parade."

"That so?" he said. "Wasn't much of a parade to begin with. But I don't guess that you came from wherever you came from just to see a Fourth of July parade in Millinocket. You going up Katahdin, just the two of you?"

"I'm going up with Black Dog. Me and two others."

Henry was startled by what he had just said. When had he figured that Chay would be climbing the mountain with them?

"You picked the wrong day for it," said the man.

"I did?"

"Yup, you did. You want to share the trails with four hundred other folks climbing right next to you, stopping to eat salami sandwiches and pickles and throwing beer bottles all over the trail afterward? This your first time up?"

Henry nodded.

"This isn't how your first time on Katahdin should be. Three is fine—and a good old dog is fine, too," he said, smiling because Black Dog was smiling. "One is better, but three will do. But not four hundred." The man leaned back against one of the long tables. "There should be quiet, and some high clouds that you can walk up into, and then through."

Henry and Black Dog watched the man. The eyes over the enormous mustache were almost closed.

"And the sky is bluer than you can ever hope to see on the ground. And above you, the mountain is all bright stone, looking like God hasn't gotten around to putting the trees on it yet. And then you get to the top, and you realize why the Abenaki thought it was a sacred place." He leaned forward. "You realize they were right."

Henry let out his breath.

"That's what your first trip to Katahdin should be like," said the man. "Not with tourists carrying pickles. You only go up for the first time once. And that's the climb you remember best."

"Maybe we should wait a day," said Henry.

"Maybe you should. Stay tonight and see the fireworks. Millinocket goes all out with its fireworks—for seven days, starting tonight. The last night is the grandest night of them all."

"Black Dog will hate fireworks," said Henry.

"All dogs hate fireworks."

"My name's Henry."

The man smiled and nodded. "A good name for someone about to climb Katahdin. I'm Thaddeus Baxter of the good old Baxter clan that gave the land in this park to the state of Maine forever. And this"—he waved his arms over the collection—"this is what I've done for the first eighty years of my life."

"Since your first climb?"

Thaddeus Baxter laughed. "Look at this."

Henry and Black Dog followed Thaddeus Baxter along the exhibit tables, which were filled with . . . well, stuff. Stuff that, Henry figured, people had thrown away on the mountain. Stuff that people had thrown away for good reasons, almost all of which probably began with "It's broken." Most were artifacts from the old lumbering camps: a fry pan with its handle snapped off, a pulley system lacking one of its wheels, a two-handled saw missing both of its handles and something close to all of the teeth along its blade, and tin plates and pans and mugs rusted through in five or six places. Another table held a post from the old Hersey Dam, part of a trestle that held the suspension bridge over the Penobscot River, and more two-handled saws from the logging days—still without handles and teeth. They must have been pretty hard on them, thought Henry.

"And this," said Thaddeus Baxter, "this is my pride and joy."

It was a bicycle wheel, without a tire, mounted on the wall.

Thaddeus Baxter reached up and spun the wheel. It revolved slowly, its spokes going around and around, spinning over an exhibit of faded red flannel long johns used by the loggers—which wasn't a pretty sight.

"Impressed?"

Henry nodded. It never hurt to be polite.

"This is the wheel that Myron Avery used way back in 1933 to measure the trails up the mountain. This very wheel. Here's where he held it, right here." He put his hand reverently on the handle that angled out from the hub. His face looked as though he was touching a relic. Then he looked at Henry. "You don't think it's all that much, do you?"

Henry decided that being polite and lying were about the same thing here. "No, no. I think it's amazing."

Thaddeus Baxter laughed again. "Never kid a kidder, son. You think it's a bunch of junk some good old coot dragged down from the mountain and put under some lights."

Henry smiled and reached down to scratch Black Dog's ears. She was trying to lick some cotton candy fluff off her snout.

"But let me tell you something: Everything here's got a story. See that saw? It doesn't look like much now, sure. But there was a day when two men climbed a pine tree seventy-five feet off the ground—maybe eighty, maybe more—and they strapped themselves to that tree and to each other, and they sawed through until they topped it, and two hundred feet of pine board tipped over about six inches away from their chests and crashed down, and they looked at each other and laughed while the sun came down on them in the new hole they made in the sky. And see that fry pan? That there? That's cooked twenty thousand pancakes and spilled five hundred gallons of grease to feed the men who topped the trees. And that pulley? That helped to drag logs all the way down the mountain to the river so they could be floated out, and if you were good and knew what you were doing, you could get on top of one of those logs and ride it like you were on a bronco, except no good old western bronco was ever that fast. Or ever that dangerous, come to think of it."

"How about the long johns?" said Henry.

"Those long johns, son, are what kept many a good logger out of the Millinocket graveyard. They were the only thing that stood between him and Katahdin's cold. And let me tell you, if you weren't wearing these—and I mean, getting sewed in come late August and staying in them all the way through late April—you'd be found out in a drift some morning, and you wouldn't be moving."

Henry raised his eyebrows. He wasn't sure that not being found in a drift was worth wearing the same underwear for eight months.

"So all this is about surviving on the mountain," said Henry, waving his arm across the tables of stuff.

"More than surviving. You don't go up the mountain just to survive. You go up the mountain for a whole lot more. Why are you going up?"

"Just to climb."

"Oh, good God, boy, you're not just another tourist, are you?"

"I'm going up for my brother."

"And what the heck does that mean?"

"What does what mean?"

"That you're going up for your brother."

But Henry wasn't sure exactly what it meant. "We were going to go up together, but then he died. Now I'm going up in his memory."

"Sort of like a eulogy, you mean."

"I guess."

"That's a fool reason to climb Katahdin."

Henry stared at him. "What?"

"You don't climb the mountain for a eulogy. You don't climb it to take photographs with fancy cameras. And you don't—you really don't—climb it for someone else."

"So why did you climb it the first time?"

"Because I was seventy-five feet up in a pine when the top we'd just cut through sheered off and took the fellow sawing with me down with it, screaming all the way." Thaddeus Baxter looked out the window, far away through it. "Makes you think it could be you. That's when I first climbed Katahdin."

Henry looked at Thaddeus Baxter. "Did it help?" he whispered.

Now Thaddeus Baxter looked at Henry. "Did it help? Jehoshaphat, if these old bandy legs of mine still worked, I would take you up onto Katahdin and show you places that no one knows about except God and me. I would show you places so beautiful, it's where angels linger on a July afternoon, because there isn't anything in heaven to touch it." He reached up and spun the bicycle wheel. "It helped." The wheel spun slowly, as though it were ticking off time.

Henry leaned against one of the tables.

"Maybe I know why I'm going up," he said.

Thaddeus Baxter spun the wheel again. "That so?"

"To find out how to live with trouble."

Henry turned and set his back against the exhibit table. He looked across to the old engravings on the other wall.

And then, he was looking at one engraving.

The print of an old two-masted ship. Drawn up on the shore. Aflame. Beside an old house. With a sea captain looking out the bay window.

Henry knew the house.

He knew the black boulders that circled the burning ship.

Salvage Cove.

And beneath the print, a caption in bold letters read, "Captain Smith and the Burning of the *Seaflower*."

20

"SHE WAS A BEAUTY in her time," said Thaddeus Baxter, "a sight for sore eyes when she sailed into a harbor."

"The *Seaflower*," said Henry.

"Isn't she elegant? Even when she's burning, her lines are still pretty."

Henry moved closer to the print.

"You know her?" Thaddeus Baxter asked.

Henry nodded. "A little."

"Then maybe you know more than I do. She's one of the local stories that gets forgotten until someone digs up a print that's been stuck away in somebody's attic for two hundred years. Someone like me. Then I find out what I can about it. That's so of every one of the prints on that wall." He waved his hand at them. "I collect what I can."

"She was taken ashore and burned," said Henry.

"By her captain."

Henry looked at Thaddeus Baxter. "Her captain?"

He pointed. "That's him watching her, out of his own house."

Henry looked at his own house in the print. At Captain Smith, standing in the bay window of the library. Henry leaned in closer. It looked as if the captain's hands were up to his face.

"Why would a captain burn his own ship?"

"Maybe because of what he'd done with her after King Philip's War. You know what cargo she carried?"

Henry thought of the chains and manacles. He thought of the swords and flintlocks. He put his hand up to his neck and rubbed the sudden hurt.

"Slaves," he said. "Slaves from Africa."

"Slaves is right," said Thaddeus Baxter, "and you might think it'd be slaves from Africa. That's what I thought first. But you'd be wrong. The slaves were from here. Indians. Indians who lost the war and got arrested by the good governors of Plymouth and Massachusetts Bay. They said that the Indians committed 'notorious and execrable murders, killings, and outrages,' and condemned them to slavery for the rest of their lives. One hundred and eighty people. Men, women, children."

"And they used the *Seaflower*."

Thaddeus Baxter nodded. "They did. Captain Thomas Smith took them away from New England forever. That's how he made some of his fortune. He chained those Indians below decks and shipped them down to the Caribbean. But no one in the Caribbean wanted to buy them, because no one wanted trouble-makers. So he sailed across the Atlantic and took them to West Africa, but no one wanted to buy them there, either. You didn't know any of this, did you? That's what comes of finding an old print like that."

"What happened to them?"

"Thomas Smith left them in Morocco. Sold them off in a place about as far away and different from New England as you can get. And there they stayed."

"That doesn't explain why the ship was burned."

"Doesn't it? Suppose you was Captain Thomas Smith and you left one hundred and eighty people on a foreign shore with nothing. Slaves. And then you sailed away, back to the only home they knew, the home that you'd helped take from them. God only knows what happened to them." Thaddeus Baxter paused, and together they looked at the old print. "What do you think you'd feel if you looked out on that ship day after day, sitting pretty in your harbor?"

"So he burned her."

"Maybe. Or maybe the *Seaflower* slipped her cable in a storm and drove up on the rocks, and he burned her because she was wrecked. No one knows. But if you look at the print, he isn't trying to salvage her, is he?"

"And that's how the cove got its name. Salvage Cove."

Thaddeus Baxter shook his head. "Not Salvage Cove—not then, at least. Back when the *Seaflower* was burned, 'salvage' was the spelling for 'savage.' The *Seaflower* was beached and burned in *Savage* Cove."

The palm of Henry's hand suddenly sprang into pain.

Trouble. It was there in the flames leaping off the bow of the *Seaflower,* as high as the masts, coming out of the hold that had once held one hundred and eighty slaves bound for Africa. It was there in the face of Captain Thomas Smith, standing in the library and looking out over the cove, his hands up to his face, his mouth open in horror at what he had done. It was there in Savage Cove.

"They say he never left his house after that," said Thaddeus Baxter. "He died there, alone, all shriveled up, afraid to come out into the kind of world he'd helped to make."

Henry shivered, even though the air in the museum was hot and still. Black Dog looked up at him and gently licked his throbbing hand. Then she rubbed her snout along his leg to get a little more of the cotton candy off.

"How do you know about the *Seaflower?*" asked Thaddeus Baxter.

"I picked up bits and pieces of it," Henry said.

Thaddeus Baxter waved his arm over his collection. "That's just what I do," he said.

Henry nodded and held out his hand. "Thanks," he said.

"Glad to have you. You take care of yourself up on the mountain—and the good old dog. But if I was to give advice, I'd tell you to wait a day."

Henry grabbed his belt, and he and Black Dog headed out. The sound of the tinkling bell followed them. Henry was still shivering a little.

How can you ever hope to build your house far from Trouble if Trouble is there already?

Henry felt shaky, but the first thing he decided after he got back onto the main street of Millinocket was to find Sanborn and Chay.

The second thing he decided was to start looking for them on the side streets. He decided this mostly because—completely because—some of the members of the percussion section of the Millinocket Junior High School Marching Band were still roaming up and down, peering into alleys and the now-open stores.

So Henry ducked down the first street he found, walked a couple of blocks, and then headed in the direction he had left the pickup. Black Dog, who had finally gotten all of the pink cotton candy off her snout, strained at the belt beside him, pretty unhappy about having to walk on a leash because there were all these gray squirrels that were running up into trees and laughing at her from the branches. But Henry wasn't going to let her get into any more trouble.

The day had gotten hotter while he and Black Dog had been touring Thaddeus Baxter's collection, the kind of hot that droops all the leaves on the maple trees and starts to make the air above any asphalt road wavery. Here and there Henry saw a few people walking back from the parade with folding chairs under their arms. Some were sitting on porches, rocking, holding fans. Charcoal fires starting up for grilling. Sprinklers on. Flags drooping like the maple leaves. A radio turned to golden oldies. A bicycle riding by, still with its red, white, and blue streamers woven through the spokes.

Henry walked five or six blocks, then turned back toward the main road—which he approached very slowly, looking both ways. There were no marching band members that he could see, so he turned and began walking up the street. The sun covered everything with the white sheen of her breath. Henry had to shield his eyes from the glare off the street and the shops. So it was Black Dog who saw Sanborn and Chay first—which Henry figured out when she started pulling hard at his belt.

"I think in the trade they call that 'running away,'" said Sanborn.

"I wasn't running away. I had to get Black Dog."

"Did you see that the engine was overheating?"

"What was I supposed to do?"

"Did you see that we had to stop?"

"I figured that you had to stop, since the whole parade behind you had to stop."

245

"Yes, Henry. We stopped the whole parade. You can't drive on an overheated engine."

"And that's why nobody was moving."

"And that's why there aren't many people in Millinocket who are happy with us."

"I know the feeling. Where's the pickup?"

"Let's see. Where did we leave the pickup? Well, after we got out and had to push, I think we only had to go four blocks. Or maybe it was five blocks. And then we took that right to get out of the parade, and we had to push it another block before we could find a space to leave it. And, Henry, if you look along the street there, you'll see that most of it is uphill from here. And a pretty steep uphill, wouldn't you say?"

"And so that's why you're carrying the backpacks. Because you figured that if you carried those, then the pickup wouldn't be so heavy. Smart, Sanborn."

"No, no, my friend who left us to push the truck alone, not so. I am carrying my backpack and Chay is carrying your backpack because Chay's pickup doesn't lock. In fact, he has no memory of even having a key that fits into any of the locks."

Chay shrugged.

"So we were searching all over Millinocket for the guy who ditched us, and looking for a hardware store that might be open to buy a gallon of radiator fluid, and hoping that we would find the hardware store first so that we could ditch the ditcher."

They found a hardware store a block down from the way they had come, and—a miracle—it was open. Sanborn made Henry go in and pay for the radiator fluid while he kept Black Dog outside. When Henry came back out, three Millinocket

Junior High School Marching Band members were standing across the street, watching them carefully.

"I guess they like dogs," said Sanborn. He waved.

"I don't think that's it," said Henry.

The three marching band members suddenly turned and ran off, glancing behind at Chay and Sanborn and Henry—and Black Dog—and quickly turned into a side street.

"I think we'd better go," said Henry.

They walked back up the main street, Henry carrying the radiator fluid. The sun was so hot now that he could feel the back of his neck reddening. He rubbed at it as they turned at a corner toward Chay's pickup.

"Let's find someplace to eat," said Sanborn.

"No," said Henry.

"Who made you the lunch monitor?"

Chay walked on a little ahead.

"Unless you want the whole percussion section of the marching band beating on you, which is going to happen pretty soon, I think we need to get out of here."

"Henry, why would the percussion section of the marching band want to beat on me?"

Chay came walking back, quickly. He took both their arms, turned them around, and directed them toward the corner. Henry felt that he was in one of those dreams where you run and you run and you run and you don't get anywhere, and your legs are so tired that it feels as if you're running through oatmeal, but you keep on running because something is behind you that you don't want to let catch up.

He looked behind himself to see what it was that was trying to catch up.

There, parked crookedly on the side of the street, was Chay's chromeless pickup. At least, Henry thought it must be Chay's pickup. It wasn't too easy to see, since three police cars were surrounding it, all with their red lights swirling overhead.

"You must have parked it illegally," said Henry.

"Maybe if you had been here to help push, we could have found someplace else," said Sanborn. "But you weren't here, were you?"

Chay propelled them both forward and around the corner. He was breathing very heavily. He was sweating even more heavily.

"Chay," said Henry, "did you tell your father that you were taking the pickup when you left?"

Chay didn't answer.

"Your father wouldn't report it stolen, would he?"

Chay walked on ahead of them.

"I think the answer to that is, 'Yes, he would,'" said Sanborn. Chay was half a block ahead of them now. "I guess that means we're going to thumb the rest of the way."

Henry looked at him. "Three guys and a dog, thumbing the rest of the way to Katahdin. Who's going to pick up *three* guys and a dog?"

"Not to mention that the police will be looking for one of them, who is Cambodian, and who is probably right now breaking some kind of parole," said Sanborn. "And I don't think it's going to be hard to pick out the Cambodian from all the people living in Millinocket, Maine."

"So if we did thumb, we'd have to do it at night and hope that a policeman doesn't drive by. And who's going to pick up three guys and a dog at night?"

"No one ever said anything about *three* guys and a dog," said Sanborn.

Ahead of them, Chay looked back. He waved for them to come on, then crossed the street. He leaned slightly forward against the weight of Henry's backpack.

"Are you talking about ditching him?"

"No one ever asked him along. He was going in the same direction, but we never asked him to climb the mountain. And what are you doing, getting all chummy-chummy with him anyway, Henry?"

"I'm not getting all chummy-chummy with him. He gave us a ride, and I don't want him to get into any trouble because . . . just because of that."

"This is the guy who killed your brother. You take him out for a canoe ride on a lake. And now you want to bring him along to Katahdin. *He killed your brother, Henry.* Yesterday morning you were ready to tear his guts out, and now you're all worried that the police might find him because he stole his father's pickup."

"So we go get my backpack and we tell him, 'Thanks for the ride. Go away now.' Is that it?"

"Yeah, that's it. Then we climb."

Henry looked north. Katahdin shimmered in the heat waves of a Fourth of July. Its white and purple stones rippled, and the rim of peaks hazed in the humid air.

It was almost tropical.

Like he might be in Cambodia. Looking up from a burning refugee camp. The mountains cool and impossibly far away. His father plowing the fields with a strap across his shoulders. Like an ox.

And the soldiers are laughing.

And then they see your mother.

Trouble.

And then they take your brother.

Trouble.

Your sister.

Trouble.

Trouble that you cannot build your house far away from.

Not even if you cross the Pacific Ocean. Not even if you cross a continent. Not even if you learn a new language. Not even if you go to a school with yellow-and-blue shirts where no one has ever been a refugee, and you try to forget that you ever were— even though they won't let you.

Not even if you meet an American girl who laughs easily, cries easily, is one of the best female athletes in Massachusetts but doesn't talk about it because she doesn't want to show up her brothers, who eats Rice Krispies with bananas and brown sugar, who watches Saturday morning cartoons and then takes the afternoon to get ready to go to the Boston Symphony because she likes Stravinsky.

And suddenly, Henry knew everything about the accident, knew it with a sureness and precision as sharp as a geometric axiom. He could see it all like a story, every moment full and slow, every look, every glance, every cry. And all the long nights that followed that were so horribly alone—he knew about those, too.

He knew.

He looked around and set the gallon of radiator fluid beside a parked car. Then he began walking after Chay, who was waiting for them on the other side of the street. "We're not ditching him," he called over his shoulder. He heard Sanborn sigh. Henry turned. "We're not ditching him. He got us all the way up here, and it's only another few miles to the mountain."

"It's eighteen miles, Mr. Rand McNally."

"It's not eighteen miles, Sanborn."

"So the sign that said 'Katahdin 18' must be talking about how old the mountain is."

"That's right," said Henry. "Are you coming?"

Sanborn hefted his pack higher up on his back and came on. Henry felt the disapproval he wore, but he waited for him to catch up, and together they followed Chay, who took the first side street to avoid any policeman-like eyes. Which was just fine for Henry, too, who still wanted to avoid the percussion section of the Millinocket Junior High School Marching Band. They turned at the end of the block and paralleled the main street until they came to another road that headed straight for Katahdin. They set their feet on it together, and so began the eighteen miles that would take them to the base of the mountain.

21

WHICH IS NOT TO SAY that they walked along the road.

They did follow it for a short while. They passed old farms, worn and beaten up by too much winter, and lumbered land where tall pine forests once grew, while dozens of cars, more than dozens, passed them, some still wearing their red, white, and blue bunting from the parade, all headed up for light picnics on Katahdin's once-holy trails.

Chay watched the road nervously, and Black Dog shied away every time a car passed. Finally, Chay nodded off to the left, and they crossed when a break came in the line of decorated traffic and hiked out into a fallow field, away from the road, crunching down the stumps of cornstalks harvested last autumn.

"In case you haven't noticed, that big rocky thing over there—that's the mountain, and we're not heading for it," called Sanborn.

Chay pointed ahead. "No one will see us in the trees," he said.

"Those are three miles away," said Sanborn.

"A quarter mile," said Henry.

"This according to the guy who's not carrying a pack."

"So give me yours for a while," which Sanborn agreed to, and Henry let Black Dog off his belt and put it back on. Then together, with Black Dog joyously running on ahead, they crossed the rest of the field and so came into the cool shade of pines.

It really had only been a quarter of a mile, at most, as Henry pointed out to Sanborn, who was very polite about being corrected, of course.

Once inside the woods, they turned again toward the mountain. The smell of the piney resin was all around them, so strong in the cooler air under the trees. The sounds of the decorated cars on the road were gone completely; now they heard only the small snapping of the branches as they clicked them off the trunks with their passing packs. There were more mosquitoes in here, but not so many that they couldn't wave them away while they were climbing the ravines, trying to keep heading toward Katahdin.

Still, there were enough mosquitoes for Sanborn to fuss about. There wouldn't be any along the road, he pointed out. And why hadn't Henry brought along some repellant? And now they were getting up his pants! When Chay suggested that he should pull his socks over his cuffs, Sanborn ignored him. Sometimes it is more satisfying to suffer than to take advice.

But Black Dog loved it all. She loved sprinting up the sides of the ravines, and then clambering down, using her back legs as unsteady brakes, and nosing into the bottoms, hoping that some were still wet and muddy so she could stick in her snout and then roll in the muck and keep the smell for later. It wasn't long before she was a bouquet of forest smells so varied and thick that she would have confounded any botanist.

She dashed out and around and among them, as Chay led and Henry followed Chay and Sanborn followed Henry, all three quiet in the effort of staying on track toward the mountain, all three sweating with the strain of climbing up and down, and none of them wanting to be the first to call for a stop. But finally Henry did, mostly because Black Dog had gotten a sharp pine twig between the pads of her paw that he needed to get out but also because it was so nice to shift the weight of the pack off his shoulders.

Chay nodded ahead of them. "Up there," he said, and they climbed up another ravine where there was no water for mosquitoes, and where a small, very small, breeze blew through the pines.

From the top of the ravine, Henry looked up at Katahdin.

In the late afternoon sun, it was steely and severe. The green that it showed on its shoulders wasn't the green of spring moss and maple leaves. It was the bare green of survival, as beaten up as the farms that dwindled within sight of the mountain. The rock itself was scarred, as if God had drawn a strap over his shoulders and plowed the rock into long furrows.

Henry looked at Chay and wondered if he saw it, too.

Henry turned to the mountain again and scratched behind Black Dog's ears even as she was trying to lick his hand to let him know how grateful she was that he had taken out the sharp pine twig. Henry watched the high clouds sculling across the mountain. The breeze clacked the tops of the pine trees together and Black Dog panted. She was ready to move on.

So they started out again, keeping the road barely within sight on their right, looking out from the top of the ravines to be sure that they were still heading for the mountain. They kept going until it was long past the time they should have stopped for supper—or so it seemed to Sanborn—and the land leveled out, and then dropped down, and the pine woods opened and showed them a lake whose shore meandered as far to the east and to the west as they could see in the waning light. Its waters were still, and showed the darkening blue of the sky as if it were a painter's palette. They headed east along the shore as it undulated toward the road—where now the cars were heading back in to Millinocket, most of their streamers and bunting all blown away by the wind.

"We'll cross over at night," said Chay.

"So why don't we eat now?" said Sanborn—which they did. They stopped by the shore and Henry pumped Franklin's Coleman stove while Chay opened three cans of beef stew. Henry heated them, and they ate ravenously. Then Henry cleaned out one of the cans and took some water from the lake. He boiled it, and then cooked up a mix of French cut beans and dried onions, and they ate that, too. And then Sanborn took out a fry pan and emptied a plastic bag of asparagus spears into it—and then a tin of sardines on a whim—and it all smelled so wonderful that they ate with their fingers right out of the fry pan.

Black Dog got her share as well—not of the asparagus, which she smelled but wouldn't touch, but of the sardines, which she ate whole.

As they sat eating Fig Newtons, the sun going down beyond the mountain, Henry figured that it had been, all in all, one of the best meals he had ever eaten.

They cleaned the fry pan in the lake, crushed the cans and stored them, and tied up the packs again—there wasn't any food left over from the meal to save—and in the darkness thrown off by Katahdin, they headed out. Behind the mountain, the sky was a deep red, though the peak was still fully lit and yellow. They watched the sky grow darker and darker as they came down to the road, waited until they could see no headlights in either direction, and then climbed onto the asphalt—which seemed remarkably hard on their feet after an afternoon of walking on pine needles—and crossed the low bridge over the lake, seeing in its waters the last light of the dying day. Ahead of them, the peak of Katahdin was still lit.

On the far side of the bridge, they turned back west and walked alongside a stand of old hardwoods as the light fled utterly and the mountain slowly disappeared into the night. When they could tell Katahdin was there only because it blocked out the stars behind it, they stopped. They found some low dead limbs to hack from the trunks and downed wood that wasn't too damp and gathered it into a loose woodpile. Chay put the fire together while Sanborn and Henry spread the tarp, opened their sleeping bags, hung their packs on some stout branches, and took out sweatshirts and another of Franklin's rugby shirts for Chay. Even with a fire, you should still wear an extra shirt when you camp out, Franklin had said. Henry could almost see Franklin's hands on his own as he unpacked.

The first spark of flame in a campfire is a sign of hope, but that wasn't what Henry was thinking about as Chay knelt low to the ground and blew on the reddening edge of the birch bark. The bark glowed more sharply with each of Chay's breaths, until suddenly it caught hold in a pale yellow flame, and then the twigs leaned into it and started crackling, and the tiny flame illuminated the column of smoke coming up. The flames lit Chay's hands and face as he added thin sticks and blew at the bottom of the pile. And it wasn't long before the crackling was constant and Chay was adding thicker wood, and all the light that the sun had put into these branches came blazing back at them. They settled around it, watching the fire turn red and white and blue.

They were quiet, listening to the crackles. Henry felt the presence of the mountain behind him, so large that it could block out wheeling stars. And he wondered how it was that he felt like nothing so much as crying in a world that seemed so beautiful, and yet had so much Trouble. Tomorrow he would finally be at the mountain. Suppose, when he reached it, he found nothing at all?

And what was he expecting to find there, anyway?

Chay added a long piece of wood to the fire. Sparks flew up a few feet, and then died. "The mountain is bigger than I thought," he said.

Quiet. Henry looked into the darkness.

"Maybe there was a time when people who lived here thought it was sacred, a place to go when there was trouble." Chay almost whispered.

"I think it was like that, once," said Henry.

"It's where I would go, if I was in trouble," said Chay. He looked behind him. "I'd go and wait there. Something would happen. Someone would come." He added another piece to the fire and it flared up. "Probably Mike," he said.

"Yeah," said Sanborn. "Because he'd have another pile of wood to stack."

Chay didn't say anything. He found a branch on the ground and peeled off its bark. Then he threw it all into the fire.

Behind them, the mountain loomed.

"Tell us about the refugee camps," Henry said.

Chay looked at him.

"What do you remember?"

Chay sat down close to the flames. "Hunger," he said. "I remember hunger. Eating grass. My mother making me eat fish that stank. I remember a soldier taking me when my mother was gone and making me crawl on my hands and knees through a field, and my mother coming after me because he was making me check for land mines. She ran through the field to pick me up. That was the night we left the camp. I remember walking. There were red flowers on the trees. We got to the sea and found a boat with other refugees. Everyone was screaming to get on the boat."

Chay crossed his legs and spread his arms out over them. He stayed that way a long time. A cold breeze blew down on them from the shadow of Katahdin, and Henry moved closer to the fire.

"So did you get on the boat?" Sanborn asked.

Chay nodded. "Yes," he said.

And suddenly it was all there in Henry's mind, refugees on the shore, leaving everything—like pilgrims setting out to seek strange places that they didn't know much about. Or worse, like the imprisoned Indians below the decks of the *Seaflower*. A crowd of people scared. All desperate. All afraid.

Trouble.

Chay told them as if the story had been writhing inside him like a dark tiger, and he was finally going to release it in the shadow of Katahdin. How they had forced themselves onto the boat. How the boat had left the dock with families split in half, and how some of them swam out until they sank into the water. The ocean red. There was no food onboard, no water, and the engines sputtered and belched smoke and sometimes stopped altogether, and they drifted in the heat and stink of three hundred people crammed together. Some jumped over the side. Some were pushed over the side.

"We saw a lot of other ships," said Chay, "and we signaled to them." But none of the ships answered, and when the engines finally coughed themselves to death, they drifted with the wind and his mother was crying. Finally, a fishing boat saw them. They tied up, and then they came aboard with guns and axes. They'd take what they wanted in payment for a tow, they said, and the refugees gave them rings, clothing, necklaces, and then the fishermen boarded their own boat again and cut loose, sending bullets and laughter back at them.

So they drifted, and drifted, and drifted, and if it had not been for a Danish ship that found them and towed them to Hong Kong, they would have drifted until they capsized and drowned, and been glad of it.

But the Chouans were lucky. They weren't stuck forever in Hong Kong. They were put on a ship to Guam, and then on another ship to San Francisco, America, and they lived in a Presbyterian church basement for four months. They could smell freedom. Then they took a bus all the way to Merton, Massachusetts, and the first morning that Chay woke up there—in another church basement—it had snowed. He had never seen anything like it before. He took his little brother outside, and they let it melt on their faces. And when they breathed, they could see their breath! Like dragons! Only cold.

"From then to now, there was one rule," said Chay. "Remember you were Cambodian before you were American."

"So what does that mean?" said Sanborn.

"It means you speak Cambodian at home. You go to Cambodian markets and not A&P. You honor your ancestors and the Buddha. You send what you can back to those still in Cambodia."

"And you don't fall in love with American girls," said Henry. Chay said nothing.

"Which is why your father was angry."

Nothing.

"Because of Louisa," whispered Henry.

Chay looked at Henry, and was as still as the mountain behind them.

"Louisa?" said Sanborn.

The fire cracked loudly, and more sparks shot into the air and died.

Back on the road, a car's headlights came along quickly, and then slowed. The car went on, then turned and came back, sweeping its beams in their direction. It stopped and its lights went out. Two doors opened and closed. In the darkness, Henry couldn't tell if anyone was coming toward them or not. He couldn't see anything—but he figured that it wouldn't be hard for whoever got out of the car to see them sitting by the fire.

"It's probably the guy who owns this field," said Sanborn. "Maybe he thinks we're trespassing or something."

"We *are* trespassing," said Henry.

"Isn't this some sort of state park? We're camping out. That's not the same as trespassing."

"What's the difference?"

"It's got something to do with malicious intent."

"I think it has to do with being on someone else's property, Sanborn."

Whatever it was, they looked out into the darkness over the field for the Trouble that was coming toward them. Chay did not move at all—until Black Dog suddenly perked up her ears.

Henry reached up to put his hand on her collar—as two men

came into the firelight and stood beside the pile of wood they had gathered.

One of them held a shotgun over his forearm.

The other held a broken glass root beer bottle. An Admiral Ames.

The two fishermen from the Chowder Mug.

"Hello, hello," the one with the shotgun said cheerfully. "We weren't sure if we'd find you or not."

22

CHAY DID NOT MOVE, but Henry, Sanborn, and Black Dog stood up. Henry couldn't take his eyes from the reflection of the red firelight flickering on the long barrel of the shotgun. He held Black Dog's collar tightly.

"Good thing you said where you were going," said the one with the shotgun.

"And good thing there's only one road here," said the one with the Admiral Ames bottle: Mack.

"I guess that would make it easier for someone low on the Darwinian scale," said Sanborn.

Henry thought that might not have been the best thing to say.

The man with the bottle swung it slowly toward him. "So smart," he said. "I sure do wish I was as smart as you, kid. But when I was your age, I was heading over to Vietnam to fight for my country against him." He pointed at Chay.

"No, you weren't," said Sanborn.

"Sanborn," said Henry quietly. He thought that Sanborn might not understand that they were in trouble here and he wasn't helping.

"Yeah, *Sanborn*," said Mack. "Why don't you shut up? We're not here for you."

"What do you want?" said Henry.

Mack held the bottle out so that its jagged and splintered shards caught the firelight. "To return this." He turned to Chay. "You dropped it in the parking lot. We think you were going to use it on us, because that's the kind of sneaky trick that a VC pulls. So we thought we'd bring it back to you and see how you like it yourself. . . . So how do you like it, gook?"

At the word, Chay stood, too.

"Oh, you don't like it. Or is being called a gook what you don't like? Is that it, gook? Because that's what you are. A gook." The man took a step in and held the broken bottle toward Chay. "So what are you going to do about it, gook?"

"We're not asking for trouble," said Henry.

"We weren't, either," said the man with the shotgun. "And then a few of them started coming. And no one cared—until they started taking our jobs. You know how many years my family fished out of Gloucester? You know how many?" He jerked the shotgun at Chay. "And then *he* comes and I'm laid off my boat, and Mack here, too, and they hire . . ." He pointed with his chin at Chay. "It's time we handled things ourselves," he said.

"He's not a fisherman," said Henry.

"Then we won't cut him up as bad as we did the others," said Mack.

"He's not even from Vietnam."

"How do you know?" said Mack. "Were you squatting in a stinking rice paddy watching guys like him shooting at you? Were you there? Did you have a buddy scream for you because he's shot in the belly and you can't get to him because the VC are using him as bait?" He drew up the sleeve of his left arm. Even in the quivering light of the fire, Henry could see the round scars pocked up in a line from wrist to elbow. "Did you ever get shot up?"

Chay took a step closer. The man with the shotgun leveled it at his chest.

"The war was in Cambodia, too," Chay said. "Only in Cambodia, it didn't matter which side you were on. They all wanted you dead." He nodded at the two men. "They were like you."

Except for the crackling of the fire, everything was silent beneath Katahdin. Not even the wind rustled her long tresses. Black Dog whined once, and was still.

Chay reached up and drew off Franklin's rugby shirt, and Henry saw for the first time the long welts that lay across his back. New welts. In the firelight, they blazed red.

Even in the middle of Trouble, Henry wondered where they came from. Because of Louisa? Because Chay could dare to love—and be loved by—an American girl?

Chay threw the shirt to Henry. "Henry, Sanborn," he said, "go. Go far away."

Henry looked at the two men, holding their bottle and shotgun toward Chay.

If you build your house far enough away from Trouble, then Trouble will never find you, Henry's father had said.

He was wrong, Henry thought.

You have to live where Trouble is.

He bent down to pick up Franklin's shirt, which had fallen by the fire. He let go of Black Dog's collar. He reached for one of the branches, a thick one, burning at one end. He stood. He drew his arm back.

"Hey," said Mack.

All that took about half a second.

In the next half second, Chay turned and saw what Henry was doing.

Black Dog leaped in front of Chay.

Sanborn reached down to the fire for another burning branch.

And with a cry that sounded like something out of Savage Cove, Henry threw his branch, end over end, at Mack, who held up his pocked arm but missed the branch as it hurtled into his chest and face, sparks flying all around him.

He dropped the broken bottle.

Then the man with the shotgun held up his arm to avoid the branch that Sanborn threw.

He wheeled the shotgun around.

And pulled the trigger with his eyes closed against the sparks that dashed around his face.

And slammed fourteen white-hot pellets along the lines of Henry's exposed rib cage—his arm still held high from his throw.

Henry felt himself blown back and down. At first he thought it was the sound of the gun that was still booming in his ears. But that was only for a moment. Every nerve in his right side carried the piercing heat that tore at him. He tried to scream, but the pellets and the fall together had shocked the air entirely out of him and he gasped as though someone was holding a forearm against his throat. He gasped to draw some air back in, but there didn't seem to be enough.

Suddenly, Chay and Sanborn were over him, and he could see their eyes opened into wide circles. They looked almost funny, like clowns, their eyes were open so wide. Like something you'd see in a cartoon. "I think I got shot," Henry finally said.

Chay had Franklin's shirt again and was pressing it against Henry's side. "Don't get it bloody," Henry said. Then he threw up. With every retch, he thought his whole body was being torn to pieces.

All this time, the man with the shotgun stood transfixed, the smoke still coming in a wisp from the gun barrel. "I didn't mean anything," he said. "I didn't mean anything. We were just going to scare him. That's all."

Henry, between waves of raw pain, thought they had done that just fine.

Chay took Sanborn's hand and pressed it against Franklin's rugby shirt. Then, quickly, he stood up, knocked down the shotgun, and had his hands up around the man's throat. "Give me the keys!" he yelled. Lying on the ground, Henry was astonished. He didn't think that Chay had ever yelled in his whole life.

"What?" said the man.

"The keys!" Chay screamed. "Give me the keys to your car!"

Henry watched as the drama acted out, with the fire as the footlights and the invisible dark Katahdin as the backdrop. Everything seemed to be playing in slow motion and someone needed to adjust the focus, until he remembered that you don't need to adjust the focus at a play. He tried to blink his eyes, but his eyelids went down and came back up very slowly. He thought that if he tried it again, they might not come back up and he would miss the play. And he didn't want to miss the play, because here's the part where the second bad guy—Mack—is sneaking around behind the first good guy—Chay—who is holding the first bad guy—the one who dropped the shotgun—and trying to get the keys out of his pocket. From far away, Henry heard the second good guy—Sanborn, who was sitting next to him and probably getting Franklin's shirt all bloody—holler something out. But he was too late. The second good guy is always too late, Henry thought. Because the second bad guy had picked up the fallen bottle and swiped it against the first good guy's back and left a staff of new, sharp, bright red lines.

Henry tried to blink again, and he was right—it *was* hard to get his eyelids back up. And when he finally did, he saw that he had missed something. Chay was kneeling beside him, stiff and twisted. And both the bad guys were gone. But Henry could still smell the metallic smoke of the shotgun. And though the pain in his side was getting sharper, he decided that the nauseating ache that was pressing in through his whole chest was a whole lot worse.

"Henry," Sanborn was saying. "Henry."

It took a little while for Henry to shift his head so he was facing Sanborn.

"We've got to get him some help," he heard Sanborn say. Henry felt him pull away Franklin's rugby shirt from his side. "He's bleeding a lot."

Chay nodded.

Why aren't they talking to me anymore? thought Henry. He tried to sit up, and wasn't sure if Sanborn was holding him down or if something heavy was lying on top of his chest—like Chay's unchromed pickup.

Then Chay was standing up and the play started again: He said something to Black Dog—something not in English—and Black Dog looked at him as though she understood, and then they disappeared together into the dark wings.

Suddenly, all the lighting changed for the next scene. Henry, his head on the ground, tried to keep his eyes open because it was done so well, with all the smooth rhythm of a perfectly synchronized crew team. It began with a spotlight that backlit Katahdin, starting with a soft glow and then growing whiter until the rim of the mountain was burning with the white light. And then the spotlight tilted up even more, and then more and more, quickly, rising in a huge, impossibly huge ball above the mountain and dropping its light all down the front of Katahdin, settling silvery gossamer folds between the ridges, the trees, the stones, so that everything on the mountain shivered into wakefulness and threw shadows that shrank back as the spotlight rose higher, then higher, so that now its light folded down even to their campsite, and then came across Henry and Sanborn, so that Henry could see everything with perfect clarity.

"Sanborn," he said.

"You should be quiet, Henry."

"Thanks, Mom."

"Shut up, Henry."

"Sanborn, did you know that you have this huge zit on your nose? It's throwing a shadow."

"Thanks for pointing that out, Henry."

"Maybe we should call some book of world records."

"You know, the only reason I'm not smashing your face into the ground right now is that I'm holding your insides from spilling out."

"Don't get Franklin's shirt bloody."

"Sure, Henry."

Henry turned back to the spotlight. It had changed its color to the lightest yellow. I wonder how they did that, Henry thought. He watched the drapery on the mountain change color, too—all except for Katahdin's rim, etched with dark precision against the starry sky.

"Henry, do you think you could hold this shirt against your side? No—with your other hand."

Henry felt himself moving—slowly.

"Good job."

"Thanks, Coach. I gave it all I have."

Sanborn went over to the woodpile and drew out some more branches. He loaded them onto the low flames, and they quickly caught, the little branches snapping into flame and sparkling up into the sky. He went back again and loaded the fire once more. Then he went to his pack and found the water bottle, brought it to Henry, and held up his head—and let it down again when Henry screamed.

"Okay, okay," he said. "That wasn't exactly the right thing to do."

Sanborn tried tipping the water bottle to Henry's lips, and Henry tried to turn his head to catch some without his body shrieking. But he decided that he would do better just by staying still—absolutely still. Maybe he'd concentrate on the flames that were crackling merrily, as if nothing at all was wrong in the world and he didn't have a shotgun blast buried in his ribs.

The spotlight drew higher—and dimmer. Maybe it's running out of batteries, Henry thought.

Whatever the reason, as the spotlight dimmed, the air grew colder and Henry's legs began to shiver a little. Sanborn brought one of the sleeping bags over and laid it on top of him. But Henry still felt his legs shivering, even though he was starting to sweat, too. "Sanborn," he said, "we could try that water again."

They did, and Sanborn managed to get a little into Henry's mouth. When Henry swallowed, he could feel the ripple of pain follow the water all the way down his esophagus. He threw it all up again, and whatever else was left in his stomach, and by the time he was finished, he was crying.

"This," said Henry very, very slowly, "is embarrassing."

"Then we'll only tell people who've been shot by a shotgun," said Sanborn. "And, boy, when I find them, I'll tell them how Henry Smith couldn't even get shot without throwing up."

"You . . . jerk."

"Shut up, Henry."

And he did. They both did. The moon rose big above them, dimmer but still bright enough to fade out most of the stars. Bright enough to light all Katahdin, so that it shimmered against the darkness behind it. And still bright enough to light the campsite around them. And the trees. Why had he never noticed the texture of tree barks? How they showed the way these trees had faced the weather that swept down from the mountain and had come out full of scars—but still okay. What a miracle the tree barks were in the moonlight.

Sanborn got up to put more branches on the fire. And he brought back another shirt. He folded it into a pad and replaced the rugby shirt against Henry's side.

"You got it bloody, didn't you?" said Henry.

"*You* got it bloody," said Sanborn.

"You never get a rugby . . . you never get a rugby shirt clean after it gets blood on it."

"You use bleach," said Sanborn.

"That's why you go around with pink rugby shirts, you jerk. You don't use bleach on colors."

"You can use bleach on colors if the water is cool enough. And they're not pink—they're just faded."

"They're pink because you use bleach."

And that's what they were talking about—whether or not you should use bleach with your colored laundry—when a row of flashing lights came screaming up the road and stopped opposite the field. Lights came on as doors were opened and Henry could hear voices. Sanborn stood and called and waved his arms, and Henry felt as if the last act of the play was finally coming on to the great climax. It had been a long play, and it was time to go home to bed, because he was awful tired.

So when the first new member of the cast came on and knelt beside him, Henry looked up at his face—he tried to keep it in focus, but it was blocking out the spotlight and the crisp edges of Katahdin—and he closed his eyes.

"Henry," a voice said.

Now Henry was sure he was in a play. It sounded like his father.

"Henry!"

Louisa?

Something licked his face and whined.

"You're going to be all right," said his father's voice.

That sounded like his cue. Henry turned his face away from the licking and let his eyes close. He did not try to open them again.

23

HENRY DREAMED STRANGE DREAMS. His father's face was in many of them. Sometimes it was Captain Thomas Smith's face, held with his shaking hands and lit by firelight. High and shrill noises. Shrieking pain. Too many blankets. Bright lights. White. Chrome. Strange and heavy odors that gagged him.

His Buck knife—he wondered where his Buck knife had gotten to. And Black Dog.

His father's face. Louisa's face. Sanborn's face. His mother's face.

Then more of the strange and heavy odors. He tried to stay awake. He tried to straighten his eyes to figure out why he kept seeing these faces. And then the odors got too heavy, and he fell asleep. Deep and dreamless, like the mountain.

And when he woke up, he saw his father's face again. And his mother's. He blinked, and blinked again. His arms were too heavy to raise up to wipe his eyes, so he blinked once more to clear them.

His parents were still there after all the blinking, faces and all. They were slumped in two chairs they had pulled together at the end of Henry's perfectly made white bed. Their arms were around each other, their faces side by side, as if they had fallen asleep cheek by cheek. This probably wasn't easy for his mother,

Henry figured, since it looked as if his father hadn't shaved in at least a week—which, once upon a time, had been unusual. His mother's face was not as pale as Henry's sheets, but it was heading in that direction, and it wasn't helped by her uncombed hair above or rumpled clothes below. Henry blinked again. He could see their breathing, their mouths so close that it seemed as if they were giving vital air to each other.

He tried to stay as still as everything else in the room. He didn't want to wake his parents. He watched them. He watched their love.

Then quietly, because they were so deeply asleep, he raised his right hand slowly, and then his arm to see if he could do it without hurting himself. He couldn't—but it wasn't a bad hurt. More like the kind of hurt you feel the next morning after a hard crew workout. He twisted his body a little to see what that would do—and decided he wouldn't twist it again for a while.

He tried raising his legs, and that went well—which was good, because he'd have to go to the bathroom soon and the apparatus on the table next to him that looked designed for the purpose wasn't anything that he intended to use.

He let his legs down, then raised them again.

And that was enough to waken his parents—whose eyes opened. Who stood up in their rumpled clothes. Who automatically tried to straighten their clothes, which were past straightening. Who gave up and were on Henry's bed. Who opened their mouths.

And who had no words to say.

Henry watched his parents catalogue him. They laid their hands against their son's face. They looked down at his two good arms. They listened to his breathing, in and out. They saw the brightness of his eyes.

"I'm all right," Henry said. It was hard to talk. He could still smell the strange odors, still feel their heaviness in his throat. "I guess I'm all right."

His father nodded. They took each other's hands. Then Henry closed his eyes and went back to sleep.

He slept for about a day.

Sometimes he woke up a little.

When he did, he saw his parents. Once he thought he saw Sanborn. Twice he thought he saw Louisa.

But mostly he slept dreamlessly, the kind of deep, deep sleep that a body needs for everything to reset. He did not turn on the bed, and hardly noticed when a nurse came in to check on him, or when an orderly went by to collect an uneaten meal, or when his father kissed him lightly on the forehead, or when his mother or sister held his hand. So when he finally did wake up, he woke up half-startled, as though he had come up out of a deep and long ravine and suddenly he was on the summit, and the air was brilliant and blue, and the wind low and smooth, and the smell in the air . . .

Well, that was when he realized he wasn't up on a mountain. That, together with the throb in his ribs. And his father and mother in their chairs, slouched against each other, asleep again. Holding hands. Smiling. How long had it been since he had seen them together, smiling?

Henry did not stretch. He lay still and watched his father and mother. His father. Who had come out of the house after all these weeks.

"Dad," he said.

His parents' eyes opened immediately, as if they had been waiting for the word. And then they were on the bed again, every line in their foreheads slanting down until Henry smiled, then laughed because of the slanting lines, then held his side because laughing hurt so much, but laughing anyway.

And his father and mother laughing, too, so that the lines disappeared and their faces opened into broad expanses of Happiness.

And then Louisa coming in with all the commotion, and Louisa on the bed as well, and laughing all over again—his side hurting more and more, but still laughing. And his father reaching over to put his hand against Henry's face.

"You're a lucky kid, you know that?"

Henry felt the bandage along his rib cage. "I got shot," he said.

"And any one of the fourteen pellets that hit you could have jumped off your ribs and gone into your lungs. But of the fourteen, guess how many did that."

"It feels like fourteen."

His father laughed again. "None. That's why you're a lucky kid. Even one pellet could have been no end of trouble."

"How did you find us?"

"That was easy. I cabled Sanborn's parents to let them know that neither you nor he were where you were supposed to be—which we are going to talk about. Then we followed the Brighams' credit card. Louisa and I were already in Millinocket when Chay came running into the police station. Your mother was at home making more phone calls than a private detective. Between the three of us, we figured things out."

"Let me guess. Sanborn's parents didn't cable back."

"No."

"Where's Black Dog?"

"At the hotel. Sanborn is hiding her, since there are signs everywhere forbidding little children and dogs."

"And Chay?"

A pause. Henry looked at Louisa. "We don't know where Chay is," said his mother.

"How could you not know where Chay is?"

"When Chay came in that night, I recognized him immediately. So did Louisa. We were more than a little surprised, as you might guess. He told us what had happened, and Louisa and I got in a patrol car and they called the ambulance from the station. When Chay tried to get in with us, one of the policeman saw his back and took Chay to the emergency room in Orono. He was all cut. And there were some . . . older . . . "

"I know," said Henry.

His father nodded. He told Henry about getting him to the hospital, too. About Henry's mother arriving in Orono before dawn after a frantic drive in the Fiat, which only a miracle had preserved from a dozen speeding tickets. It wasn't until Henry was out of danger that his father had thought about Chay again. By then, Louisa had gone back to the emergency room to look for him, but he was gone.

"You called his parents?"

"They've changed their number to an unlisted one. I called the Merton police and they went over. They called back this morning. His father told them that he didn't want anything to do with him anymore." Henry's father looked down at his hands. "Henry," he said, "I know you must hate that boy. I understand that. But if it hadn't been for him, we might have lost . . . We owe that boy a lot. Despite what happened with your brother."

Henry looked at Louisa—and then back at his father.

"I know," he said. "Since you can't build your house far away from Trouble, it's good to know people like Chay Chouan."

His father nodded.

Henry closed his eyes. He thought of his sister that night, driving with Chay Chouan, him letting her drive his father's pickup, and then Louisa panicking behind the wheel when she saw Franklin running toward them, glancing through the windshield and seeing her with a Cambodian boy. With Chay. How she must have swerved suddenly, and then tried to swerve back. The wheel spinning. A shriek, sudden and high. Chay grabbing for the wheel, but Louisa too strong in her panic. Screaming, and then the thud of hitting Franklin. The terrible dull and strong sound of the thud. The squealing of the brakes on top of the screaming.

And Chay, knowing the disaster, deciding to protect her. Sending her away. "Go home! Go home now!" Rushing off to find help. The police. Chay trying to find the police!

And Louisa on the road, walking and trying to settle herself. Coming back home late. The long nights of waiting, the long days of the pretrial hearing. More alone than any of them.

Except Chay, who had lost everything for love of Henry's sister.

Henry began to weep. He wept for Franklin, for Chay, for Louisa. He wept for himself, for the Trouble that had come upon them.

He wept for how wrong he had been about it all.

And his parents wept beside him—his father, freed from the

house. His mother, beside his father. Louisa, weeping, holding him so hard that he could not breathe without hurting, but not wanting her to stop holding him. And who knows how long they would have stayed that way—so tight and holy that even the efficient nurses and orderlies who came to their door did not come in—until there was a *plink, plink, plink* against the window of the hospital room, and Henry's father went to see what it was, and it was Sanborn, throwing gravel up and trying to hold Black Dog, who had figured out that Henry was somewhere in this building and was doing everything she could to get inside.

She went berserk when Henry came haltingly to the window. She yelped and jumped and twirled in circles and pirouetted on her hind feet and barked the whole time. Henry laughed—even though it was hurting badly now—and he leaned out the window—which also hurt—and hollered down to his dog, until a nurse saw them and harried Henry back to bed. She tightened the sheets around him as though she was putting him in an envelope, and said that if he was feeling well enough to get out of bed, then he should feel well enough to eat something, which he promised to do, and which he did—even though the eggs weren't cooked in butter, obviously, and they weren't sunny-side up, and they had no salt, and the toast was the healthy stuff.

Afterward, the doctor came in and took off the bandages on Henry's side. "You're a lucky boy," he said, and Henry and his parents looked at each other. "Do you know how many of the fourteen pellets entered your lungs?"

"None?" said Henry.

"That's right, none. If even one of them had found its way in, you would have been here a lot longer. As it is, I'll put a dressing on this again, and we'll keep you for just one more night. Then you can go home and brag about how you survived getting shot."

"Thanks," said Henry.

And after the doctor had left with Henry's parents, Louisa closed the door to her brother's room and sat down on his bed and took his hand. He held hers tightly. They talked. He smiled at her. "Great," he said. And then, very quietly, "Oz."

"Oz," she whispered. When their parents came back, Louisa took a deep breath, looked at Henry for a moment again, and said to them, "I have something to tell you."

Black Dog went berserk again when Henry walked slowly out of the hospital the next day. Sanborn could hardly hold her. And when they all got into the car and Sanborn let her go, she was all over him, so that he had to protect his side against the onslaught of her snout, and front paws, and back paws, and tail, and everything in between.

"So," said his father, "how does it feel?"

"Good as gold," said Henry.

"We'll be at the hotel in ten minutes," he said.

"The rooms are lovely. They're near a lake. You can see the lake from the window. It's beautiful," said his mother.

His parents were trying too hard. They had been trying too hard since Louisa told them about the accident.

But the hotel *was* close, and the rooms were lovely, and the lake did look inviting—even though the doctor had warned Henry against infections that might come from swimming. Still, it wasn't inviting enough to keep him awake, and when he lay down experimentally to try the bed in the room that he and Sanborn were sharing—and in which Black Dog was hiding out—he fell asleep almost immediately, waking later that night only when his parents came to check on him, with Louisa between them.

"I'm fine," he said, before they asked.

His father nodded. "We thought you might like to stay up here with Louisa and Sanborn."

Henry's mother looked a little unsure. "You'd be all right?"

"We'll be all right."

His father rubbed the side of his face. "We're going down to meet with Mr. Churchill tomorrow morning. To see about . . . To see what our options might be."

Henry's father looked at Louisa, then at Henry's mother.

"Whatever they are," he said, "we'll . . . well, you were right, Henry. You can't build your house far away from Trouble."

Henry nodded.

His father smiled again. It was so good to see him smile.

"So you think the three of you will be all right with Black Dog?"

The next morning Henry's parents drove off in the BMW to Blythbury-by-the-Sea.

Louisa and Sanborn went to get Henry's continental breakfast—which was a whole lot better than the continental breakfast at some rustic lakeside resorts.

When they came into his room, Henry was standing and dressed.

Sanborn put the breakfast on the dresser. "What are you doing?"

"If I was in trouble, I'd go to Katahdin. That's what Chay said. He said he would wait there, and something would happen. Or someone would come."

"Someone like who?" said Sanborn.

"Someone like us." He looked at Louisa. "We're going to Katahdin. We're going to find Chay, and we're going to bring him back down."

"Henry, the only thing that's holding you together is a few stitches," said Sanborn.

"I'd say that twenty-two is more than a few. And the wonder of it, Sanborn, is that I'll still be able to climb faster than you."

"But Dad told me that I shouldn't drive anywhere," said Louisa. "He told me that fifteen times."

"Did they take both cars home?"

"No."

"Did Mom leave the keys to the Fiat?" said Henry.

Louisa smiled.

An hour and a half later, Louisa was driving the Fiat slowly and carefully through Millinocket, past the museum of Thaddeus Baxter, and on to the turnoff toward Katahdin. Henry sat in the back with Black Dog, and his side ached, but not as much as it had by the lakeside they were passing now. Ahead, Katahdin. The hugeness of the mountain appalled him. And when they came to her foot, where Katahdin adjusted her stately robes, Henry looked upward and scanned the ascent while holding his side. "Jehoshaphat," he said—but only to himself.

They checked in at the ranger station, and they read all the signs about hypothermia and the chronicles of foolish and unprepared hikers who hadn't paid attention to the weather or who had gone without enough water or proper training or sufficient clothing and so had died dismal deaths. "Jehoshaphat," said Henry again, a little louder.

But despite the chronicles, Sanborn and Louisa shouldered the two packs—Henry didn't even try to point out to his sister the rule that said that she was a girl and girls should never, ever carry a pack if an accompanying boy is there to carry it for her—and they started out to find Chay and bring him back down the mountain.

A little way past the station, they could see the Keep Ridge to the south. Above it, to the north, the Hamlin Ridge rose up and cut the blue sky in an impossibly sharp and clear line. The ridges were jagged, and rocky, and naked, and open, and exposed to every wind that might think about playing with the mountain. And it didn't look close to what might be thought of as a steady climb—rock leaped up to rock, boulder to boulder, rise to rise, cut edge to cut edge, until everything fell off at a place high and far away.

Henry wondered if Sanborn could do it. He put his hand against his own side. He wondered if *he* could do it. He let Black Dog loose, and she sprinted ahead. No one wondered if she could do it. And no one wondered if Louisa could do it. She was already taking the lead.

Sanborn looked back at Henry. "This is crazy," he said.

"Yup," said Henry. And they began, pushing through the scrub brush, their feet on the hard and level granite that bore up the mountain. The sun glinted off the mica, and if it hadn't been for the generations of lichens and bright springy moss that had found their way onto the path, it would have been rock all the way. But once they were on it, Henry felt Katahdin's welcome, as if the mountain was easing their way a little. They stopped briefly at the patches of blueberries—a little early for these, but a few mostly blue—and, after a mile or so, they stopped again as the trail tipped abruptly upward.

"This is it," said Henry.

He took one step forward, and so came onto Katahdin herself.

He had come as far north as he could. But even though he had come so far from Blythbury-by-the-Sea, and so far from Merton, all he could think about was Louisa.

He climbed Katahdin, thinking of her. He found a sheltered cleft in the rock, thinking of her. He covered himself that first night with pine boughs, listening to the murmurous haunting of the flies, thinking of her.

But she would be fine. They would all be fine. Henry was in the hospital, and his parents would be around him. Louisa, too. She would be fine. His dog would be fine. Even Sanborn.

If he didn't have anything else—and he didn't—he had that.

He sat against the side of Katahdin, and waited, hopelessly, for what would come.

24

ABOUT A QUARTER MILE into the ascent, Henry's ribs began to ache. He walked so that he didn't show it.

About a half mile into the ascent, Henry's ribs began to throb with every step. He tried to put his feet carefully and softly on the path.

About three-quarters of a mile into the ascent, Henry's ribs were shooting pains that reached up into his shoulders and down to his ankles. He started to take quick breaks to look at remarkable tree barks so that he wouldn't show anyone the aching.

By the time they reached the base of the Keep Ridge and really began to ascend, the deep throb in his side was making him nauseated, which is hard not to show, and which Sanborn would probably have noticed if he wasn't so grateful for any short relief that Henry's remarkable tree bark breaks gave him.

They went on. Slowly.

Loose rocks. Huge boulders. Pulling themselves up by iron staples pounded into the living stone. Louisa in the lead and looking back at them. She wasn't even breathing quickly. Or sweating. Henry turning away from the path for a moment to yield to the dry heaving that was not helping his throbbing ribs.

They came out of a grove of aspen and white birch at the base of the ridge, and then headed up again into a landscape as strange as the moon. Boulders had rolled onto the trail, huge boulders that must have shaken Creation when they came a-tumblin' down. And it did not seem as if the a-tumblin' had been so long ago. Their sides were as rough as sandpaper, and did what sandpaper does to hands. The trail wound through them, and over them, and sometimes over the crevices they had made. For Henry, every boulder meant side-holding agony, and even Black Dog had some trouble getting over them. Once she turned to Henry with her four feet splayed out on three boulders and looked at him accusingly.

Which made him laugh. Which made his ribs ache even more. Which sent him into dry heaves again. Which were not helped when Sanborn pulled out a mayonnaise-and-sardine sandwich he had packed in the front pocket of his backpack. "Want half?" he said.

Henry turned away and looked out from the mountain. Even at only this height, it seemed that the entire state of Maine was spread before him.

Across from where they stood, another ridge ascended as sharply as the one they were on. Past that, the forest had laid itself down as a soft furze over the hard granite, and then some careless giant had broken a mirror into a thousand pieces and tossed it away, leaving the shards to shine brightly in the sunlight. The slightest haze hung over it all—just the slightest—easing and softening the edges of everything.

Henry, holding his side, could have stood there for a long time. They all could have stood there for a long time, and not just because of the pain in Henry's side or the wheeze in Sanborn's breathing. Beauty is like that, and Henry thought, Franklin should have seen this. And then he thought, He didn't think I ever would.

Henry turned and looked up at the next ascent. He sighed. Ahead, the brittle rock of the mountain looked unfinished, as if the same giant had hewn it roughly and then, discouraged by the way the rocks splintered, given it up as a lost job.

More throbbing.

Henry offered to take the pack from Sanborn, who for just a second seemed about to hand it over. But then Sanborn said he was fine, which was probably a lie, but Henry didn't feel like arguing. So he asked Louisa for her pack, and she said she was fine, which was not a lie.

"Are you okay?" she asked.

Henry looked out over the green furze. A puff of wind blew at him from over the ridge to the west, but he felt Katahdin solid under his feet. "Let's go," he said.

They climbed on—Black Dog, Louisa, then Sanborn, then Henry—and not too much later, they reached the top of the Keep Ridge, where the trail leveled off after one more huge boulder, and then set its sights directly toward—Henry consulted his contour map—the South Peak.

After this, the trail didn't even pretend to be level. It hardly pretended to be a trail—just a line of splintered and broken rocks, with none of their edges worn away.

Sanborn and Louisa hitched their packs up a bit higher on their shoulders, and then all three took the first slow upward steps toward the peak, stretching every ligament and tendon and muscle and whatever else holds kneecaps in place.

And just as quickly, the puff of wind blew again, and again, and turned out not to be just a puff but the beginning of a whole front—a drizzly front that dulled all the slivers of mirrors, that hid the green furze, that wet the rocks around them into dark shininess, that clambered over the peaks of Katahdin and shrouded them, and that came down so quickly that Henry could see it breaking toward them like a frothy wave. Then for a moment, it was all around them, and they were alone in the last stand of sunshine, caught in a tiny circle of light.

And then it covered them as well.

Immediately, they were all chilled. Henry shivered in the mist—and found that even shivering could send pain up his wounded side. The mist was so thick, he could weave patterns into it with his hand. He belched experimentally—this hurt—to see what pattern would flare out.

"Stop kidding around," said Sanborn. "This is serious. We have to go back."

Henry swished away the mist and looked at him. "You want to point the way?"

They looked behind them. The whole world had become gray and drippy. They could see, maybe, twenty feet beyond, but then the trail dissolved and became part of the mist.

Everything took on a new color. The lichens and mosses glowed and pulsed with a brighter, slicker green. White mushrooms appeared, bending their round tops like bald old men. And there were suddenly berries where there had been none before, bright red and bright blue, all with a careless water drop oblonging their form.

Sanborn and Henry sat and shivered, and Henry held Black Dog closely so she wouldn't get lost in the opaque air, and so she wouldn't chase after the tiny garter snake wrinkling underneath a rock mound, and so she could keep him warm. Sanborn suggested a fire, but no one moved. Where would they find wood dry enough? The mist, dripping from the air around them, made a dreary and dull sound, as if it was washing away all hope of finding Chay. And it was so cold.

Louisa paced. "We are walking in the clouds," she said, mostly to herself.

And Henry thought, We were heading toward Trouble, and here we are. He was surprised that he didn't at all regret coming. He was surprised how strongly he knew that he was where he was supposed to be. And he was surprised that it had nothing to do with his brother anymore.

It was because he was needed.

Ad usum.

All the while they were sitting enshrouded, the wind that had blown the front over the mountaintop had kept on, dragging the top of the mist into lean shreds and now letting the sun drop in tall columns of light that moved slowly across the granite floors. Above the cloud shreds, the sky blued slightly, and then more than slightly, and then the mist was suddenly thrown away like a magician's cape, quickly and with a "Ta-da!" The lights came up and Henry almost clapped, the trick was so fine and unexpected.

Black Dog barked. Above them, all the way to the top of the mountain, the air was scrub-clean, and smelled of the spice of blueberries and hemlock and bay and balsam. Below them, a hawk yawed away on the wind and so down and around the western slope.

Louisa, Sanborn, Henry, and even Black Dog smiled. Then they began to climb again.

They went more slowly now, because the mist had be-dewed everything and its coolness had urged Henry's ribs to new pain. Now and then another quick shroud of cloud would come over the peak ahead of them, trying to catch up with the front that had left it behind. But one by one, the shrouds of clouds blew past and were gone, and soon Henry could not even hear the dripping that had been all around them, as the low-lying leaves finished emptying what they had caught, shook themselves, and set about the business of drying in the sunlight.

The ridge trail still kept rising sharply, and all the rocks—which still looked as if a giant had thrown them around after finishing with the mirror—seemed looser, so that it wasn't hard for Henry to imagine the whole side of the ridge shifting and shrugging him off the mountain.

Above a particularly loose and wet crag, the trail leveled off to give itself a breather, and they sat in the new sunshine—the shadows by the boulders were still cold with the earlier mist—and they ate lunch, which, since Sanborn had packed it, had sardines in olive oil, beef stew (cold, and eaten from two cans they passed around), peanut-butter sandwiches (Marshmallow Fluff optional), carrot sticks, honey cakes, and oranges.

"You know," said Henry, "no one in the entire world likes sardines by themselves except you."

"Good," said Sanborn. "More for me." He dropped a fishy head into his mouth. "Sardines," he said solemnly, "are the food of the gods."

"Sardines," said Henry, "are little fishes that still have their eyes. They look at you when you eat them."

"You are a jerk, Henry. You just ignore the eyes. You just ignore them like, say, my father ignores everything."

Silence. The mountain watching.

"Like the way it would have been if it had been me with fourteen shotgun pellets in my ribs. Send some money and hire a big-name doctor. Then go back to margaritas before the next business meeting."

"You don't know that," said Louisa.

Sanborn lowered his head. Then he took out his wallet and pulled out his father's credit card. He began to fold it, back and forth, back and forth, until finally it gave at one side, and he tore it in two. He dropped the halves into the empty cans of beef stew.

"I know it," he said.

Henry thought about his father. His father who had finally come out of the house, even if there was Trouble outside. *Because* there was Trouble outside. His father with the lightly graying hair he tried to hide, his arms and hands not as powerful as Henry remembered them once being. But he had come outside to find him. And Henry was filled with such love that the ache in his heart covered the ache in his ribs.

Then he looked at Sanborn, and saw that he was watching him think about his father.

They finished lunch in silence.

The wind that had pushed the mist down the mountain was busy drying it out below them, so that by the time they had finished repacking what was left of lunch—which was not much, except for a few sardines—they could look down the mountain and see only foggy tatters that clutched the darker clumps of trees and were doing what they could to stave off oblivion. Above them, the sky really was a glass pane, and it really did seem that if they could reach the peak, they could stretch up and squeak their fingers on its clean and level expanse.

So they hurried to reach it, though Louisa kept looking back at Henry when they covered a steeper length, until finally Henry said, "I'm not going to die today, Louisa." And she smiled and leaned into the climb and Henry smiled, too, and he tried to keep down his . . . Happiness. He suddenly realized what it was. Happiness. He climbed with an ache and with Happiness all mixed together.

Happiness that could not be choked by the steeper climb.

Happiness even without Franklin.

Happiness to be up on Katahdin.

Happiness that gushed into a gasp when they all three finally took the last short, knee-knocking steps onto the peak and looked out.

The top ridges of Katahdin undulated around them, and the wind, with nothing to block it, tore at them so that they stood with bent knees. For as far as they could see, the state of Maine showed off every shade of green that the retina of the human eye could perceive, until it all faded into a blue that dissolved somewhere into the sky.

But below them! Below them, straight down the sides of the mountain, cascading rock fell into the shadows, and then into pines—Was that a streak of snow and ice, still hanging on into summer?—and then finally into tiny Chimney Pond, as if this was all an enormous backdrop for the blue stage that was the lake.

Henry moved toward the edge, so close that Louisa reached for him but did not stop him. He put his hands to his mouth and cupped them, the way the sides of the mountain cupped the water below. And he called out, as loudly as he could:

"Katahdin.

"Katahdin.

"Katahdin."

No echoes came back to him; the space was too vast. He called again.

"Katahdin.

"Katahdin.

"Katahdin."

Black Dog barked, and then she tilted her head and perked up her ears and barked again. Maybe she could hear an echo. And then she barked again and turned to grin up at them.

The happiness filled Henry. Happiness that had been such a stranger. But here, on Katahdin, he felt it gathering all around him. It was as if a drought had been pierced, and the drizzle that had passed over them had faded and left behind sweet flowers, and sweet air, and a sweet western breeze that drifted happily around them, wakening the birds that suddenly began to sing with merry melodies.

Then a cry came out of the basin, tripping up the walls and jumping over the ravines.

"Henry."

Henry looked back at Louisa and Sanborn.

"Henry.

"Henry."

And then, almost a third of the way down to the bottom of the basin, they saw someone come out from among a grouping of hemlocks. And wave. And begin to climb up toward them.

Louisa dropped her pack and started down—quickly. Sanborn shrugged his off, too, and waited for Henry. And Henry—Henry looked south, behind him, to where he knew the Knife Edge lay. He smiled, then turned away. He held his hand to his side almost the whole way down toward Chay, and he didn't regret a single step, even though they would have to climb back up later to retrieve the packs.

Henry went as fast as he could, and Sanborn tried not to

help him too much. Still, neither Henry nor Sanborn was there when Black Dog and Louisa found Chay. But they did hear Black Dog's joyous barking, and it was the barking that led Henry and Sanborn to them. And when they found them, Henry could see that the Happiness that covered the mountain had found his sister, too.

And Chay.

They asked Chay how he was, and Chay said fine. Chay asked how Henry was, and Henry said fine. Sanborn asked how it felt to spend a night in jail, and Chay said they treated him fine. And then Henry said that Sanborn was a jerk for asking how it felt to spend a night in jail, and Sanborn took a swipe at Henry, and then Henry and Chay tackled Sanborn, who grappled with Chay's head in a cruel lock as he pummeled Henry's belly until he hit his stitches by mistake and Henry yowled in a voice that no human being should use, and they all fell apart in laughter, even though Henry was crying as he was laughing.

And jumping all around them, Black Dog barked and barked and barked.

Afterward, they climbed back to the peak to find the packs. Sanborn opened one and made three peanut-butter-and-honey sandwiches—all for Chay, which he ate without stopping to breathe except that he gave part of the last sandwich to Black Dog, who was watching him with her mouth open and ears perked and head cocked. Then they all sat and let the cold and wind tear against them, Louisa and Chay leaning against each other, until they all started to feel a little chilled and Katahdin began to lay down long shadows.

They started back down. It was not an easy climb.

The cooling and still-damp air had hardened Henry's side,

which was beyond aching now. Every downward jarring step sent an exploration of pain from his ribs somewhere out into his body. His knees were shaking with the rocky descent, and he began to take longer and longer breaks, during which he collapsed upon the rough-hewn stones, dribbled some water into his mouth, and sat with his head down, feeling his whole body move to the rhythm of the throbbing pain. Black Dog sat beside him with her ears limp. Probably, Henry figured, she was hoping they would make camp.

Which was exactly what he was hoping.

Which Louisa said they finally had to do, since Henry looked as if another step would kill him.

Which, when she realized what she had said, made her blanch and pretty much stopped all but the most necessary talk for the next few minutes.

It was dusk when they came upon a small circle beside a ledge that was more or less open, more or less level, more or less grassy (with only a few granite spurs sticking up), and more or less surrounded by new white pines. Sanborn and Chay took the tarp from Henry's backpack and spread it over the ground—taking care to avoid most of the granite spurs. They had left the sleeping bags back in the hotel, but the night was not too cold and they spread out the sweatshirts that Sanborn had packed. They scavenged for wood, and while Louisa and Chay got the fire started, Sanborn brought out the rest of his miraculous stores, drawing them up from the depths of his pack: more bread with peanut butter and honey, bags of cashews, bags of raisins, bags of dried peaches (which can be eaten only on campouts since they are inedible in any civilized place), a packet of soup mix (which didn't help, since they needed water to cook it), and a packet of beef jerky that Sanborn insisted was really good until Henry pointed out that Sanborn also thought that little fishes with their eyes still in were really good, too. And that made Sanborn remember the leftover sardines, which he looked for and pulled out to add.

They ate it all, except for the sardines, which Henry gave to Black Dog over Sanborn's objections, and except for the dried peaches and raisins, which they decided to save for the morning when they would climb down off the mountain.

Louisa and Chay packed everything up by the glow, the beautiful soft glow of the fire, and Henry settled down among the pile of sweatshirts that they would soon have to put on, since it was getting much colder now. Henry looked straight out into the dark sky, feeling the solid rock of the stone ledge beneath him. Far below them, the lights of Millinocket were all on. He thought he could make out the line of lights on the main street where they had been in the parade. He wondered if the Millinocket Junior High School Marching Band was still looking for them.

He watched Sanborn tie the packs up into the pine branches, and he watched Chay and Louisa rearrange the fire together. Other than their murmurs—they were talking about Mike's Eats—the world was quiet and still.

And Henry was quiet and still, too. He breathed deeply, sucking the piney scent down into his lungs. Black Dog lay down beside him and put her head on his stomach when he stretched out, with one hand behind his head, and lay back.

Tomorrow they would climb down off Katahdin, and there would be Trouble enough, he knew.

They'd have to go to the police about the accident, and no matter what Mr. Churchill came up with, there would be Trouble for Louisa and Chay. There would be new stories in the

Blythbury-by-the-Sea Chronicle. And what would Louisa do on the first day she got back to school in the fall? *Would* she go back to school in the fall?

And there was Chay, whose father who wasn't really his father didn't want anything to do with him. Who had set the police on him! Henry wondered what would happen if they stopped at Mike's Eats on the way back home. "Anytime," Mike had said.

And there was Sanborn, whose father gave him a credit card instead of the most important thing.

Henry thought of Captain Smith, standing in his mansion on the ledges above the waves and watching the beached *Seaflower* burn to its frame.

And Franklin.

Earth to earth. Ashes to ashes. Dust to dust.

Black Dog whined a little in her sleep, and Henry stroked her behind her drooped ears. Her fur was so sleek and smooth now. Henry ran his hands over her shoulder blades and down the ridge of her back, to her haunches, all healthy and strong.

Black Dog, whom he had plucked from a drowning sea, beaten and starved. He stroked her again, and then, with a start, he figured out something that he had not figured out before: how it was that Black Dog had fallen into the drowning sea. He looked at Chay, then down at Black Dog again, and thought, What a jerk I am.

And so Henry knew something else, too.

The world is Trouble . . . and Grace. That is all there is.

He turned—slowly and gingerly—and looked up Katahdin again. Above their ledge, the mountain lay bare. Except for the snapping branches of the fire that Louisa and Chay had called up, everything was still. It seemed that they were as far from anything as they could ever get.

And Henry smiled. It was time to get home. No matter what happens, there is always the business of the world to attend to.

Ad usum.

Then, suddenly, Black Dog perked up her ears, and a moment later, Henry saw a bright blossom of light sparkle the dark sky out beyond them. Then came another, silver and gold, and another, just silver, and another, red and blue, and another and another, green circles of light brightening the sky, their *boom, boom, boom* coming up to Henry long after the explosions that lit up the sides of Katahdin. So the people of Millinocket spent the last night of their Independence Day celebrations setting off the most glorious fireworks display of all.

For a long time they flashed out, making the sky a gala, Katahdin herself an audience for this lavish extravagance. Umbrellas of light unfolded, and their sparkling and hissing embers cascaded into sharp explosions.

Henry looked at Chay and Louisa, and at Sanborn. The lights glittered within their eyes.

Black Dog rose beside him, and Henry held her close.

Tomorrow they would be down off the mountain.

Below him, the stars burst upward, back into the sky.